UNLEASHED DESIRE

Her eyes fluttered closed in anticipation, and she felt his warm, wine-tinted breath feather over her lips. Her heart was pumping double-time, and her nerves were strung tight, but not in a bad way. She was more than ready to find out what it was like to kiss Aunt Sophie's big, bad nephew.

"Nice," she whispered involuntarily.

A whining growl sounded, and LeAnne's eyes flew open, as she'd never quite heard a man make such a noise in the throes of potential passion. But then she saw Jake's eyes widen too, staring at her as if she'd done it.

"Not me," she choked out.

"Me either," he said.

They both glanced down to the ground, and sure enough Muffin was baring his teeth in patent disapproval.

Jake responded with a manly growl. "Back off, buddy. . . ."

AGAINST HIS WILL

TRISH JENSEN

LOVE SPELL BOOKS NEW YORK CITY

LOVE SPELL BOOK®

May 2000

Published by

Dorchester Publishing Co., Inc.
276 Fifth Avenue
New York, NY 10001

ISBN 0-505-52377-9

To Philip Lawrence Graves Kruchten. And to Peter Joseph Graves Kruchten. Gorgeous, funny, smart go-getters. Aren't you glad you take after your Aunt Trish?

And to Ross Bennett. What can I say? You held my hand every day. You talked me through this book. You saved my life. Thank you.

Prologue

"Let me get this straight," Jake Donnelly said in a growl to the man sitting across the huge cherry desk from him. "You're telling me my Aunt Sophie left all her worldly possessions to a . . . a *mutt*?"

The lawyer held up a finger as a point of order. "Technically, Muffin is not a mutt. He's an AKC-registered English bulldog."

"Muffin," Jake muttered, trying to determine whether he was feeling more shocked or furious. "A bulldog named Muffin."

And then it blindsided him. Again. Shock and fury had nothing on the grief. Aunt Sophie was gone. He'd been so wrapped up in work the last year, he hadn't even known she'd been ill. The times he'd managed to find a few minutes to call her, she'd been her usual cheerful, eccentric self.

And now that he thought about it, she'd mentioned her precious new canine companion plenty over the last few years. Figuring the dog was her way of filling the void after Uncle George's death six years ago, Jake hadn't paid much attention. Now all of her words came back in painful snatches. Why hadn't he listened more carefully? Obviously she'd been desperately lonely, but too proud to ask Jake to take a few days to visit her. He hadn't seen her since Uncle George's funeral, too busy climbing his way up the ranks at the Bureau. And now he'd never get the chance to see her, talk to her, tell her how much he'd loved her ornery little hide.

Going through her papers had been heartbreaking. Getting her bank accounts in order had brought back so many memories, he'd almost broken down and cried. Except Jake Donnelly hadn't shed a single tear since he was five years old, when it finally dawned on him that his tears brought his son-of-a-bitch father immense satisfaction.

"Technically his name is Kendee's King of Stanton," the lawyer corrected him again. "Muffin was Sophia's pet name for him."

Mr. Rapinov glanced over to a corner of his office, and Jake followed his gaze. Sure enough, a big lump of furry wrinkles snored softly, oblivious to the fact that he'd just been made a millionaire by Jake's daffy aunt.

Jake shook his head. "There has to be a mistake."

"I'm afraid not. Your aunt's wishes were quite clear. Other than bequests to all of her employees and a few favorite charities, her estate is being held in trust to ensure that Muffin is well cared for, for the duration of his natural life. This includes the money, the Rhode Island estate, et cetera. The will is quite airtight."

"I don't care about her Rhode Island monstrosity, or her money," Jake said. "Let Muffin buy all the doggy snacks he wants. All *I* want—and Aunt Sophie knew damn well how much I wanted it—is her cabin on the lake in Pennsylvania."

Mr. Rapinov *tsk*ed sympathetically. "I'm afraid that is included in the trust."

"This sucks," Jake said, glaring at the dog. Then realizing the dog really wasn't to blame, he reverted to glaring at lawyer Rip-'em-off. After all, he'd helped draw up this insane will.

The attorney shifted uncomfortably in his seat and loosened his tie. "All is not lost, however. There *is* good news in here," he said, tapping his Mont Blanc on the will.

"What in hell could that possibly be?"

11

"Your aunt has named you Muffin's guardian."

Jake stared at him for a long minute, waiting for the good news. When the lawyer said no more, it occurred to him that Rip-'em-off considered *that* the good news. "I get Muffin?" he repeated, just to be sure he'd heard correctly.

"Indeed! So in effect, you will have access to pieces of the trust."

It took Jake a few moments to absorb the shock. "There's just one problem. I don't want Muffin."

The heir in question lifted his head and looked directly at Jake with a woebegone expression that would have earned him an Oscar if captured on film. His head was as big as a basketball, but forehead to jowls, one wrinkle of skin folded over another. He was mostly fawn colored, but he had some white markings on his meaty stumps of legs and a black blaze on his forehead. All in all, a face only a mother could love. Or an Aunt Sophie.

"You don't?" the lawyer said, his Adam's apple bobbing.

Jake was so busy refusing to feel sorry for the sad-looking canine, he forgot for a moment what the lawyer meant. It came to him when the dog let loose with a gas attack. *Oh, great, a sad-looking mutt with no couth.* "No, I don't."

12

He held up supplicating hands. "Look, I work for the government—"

"Yes, I know. The FBI," the lawyer said with a condescending sniff.

Jake thought his disdain a little misplaced, considering his own occupation. "Right. In my job I have to pick up and travel on a moment's notice. Somehow I don't think my boss is going to appreciate my carting a dog around with me. And they don't provide pooch sitters, either." He took a deep breath. "I don't qualify to care for a Pet Rock, much less a living animal." He paused as he stared at Muffin. "That animal *is* living, right?"

"He's in mourning."

"That makes two of us." That was no exaggeration. He was in mourning, all right—in mourning for his aunt, in mourning for that cabin on the lake in Pennsylvania, the only place on earth he'd found pleasure in his youth.

The attorney cleared his throat. "Well, Mr. Donnelly, it's a shame that you won't take the dog. You realize this means you relinquish any right to inherit Sophia's millions upon his death."

"I told you, I could care less about the mo—"

"And the Pennsylvania property."

That stopped him in his tracks. "If I take the dog, I'll eventually inherit the cabin?"

"That's correct. Upon Muffin's death."

13

Jake again glanced at the animal. Personally, he felt he could almost make a case for the dog's lack of life at this moment. "How old is Muffin?"

"He'll be five on June fifth."

Jake did the math. That made him about thirty-five in dog years, right? That wasn't even middle-aged. That mutt wasn't going to the great fire hydrant in the sky anytime soon.

"Of course," Rip-'em-off said, interrupting his calculations, "a few other minor stipulations must be met as well."

Oh, boy. Knowing Aunt Sophie, that could mean anything. "A few other minor stipulations?"

Rip-'em-off shrugged. "Very minor."

Jake wavered. No, it was impossible. No matter how much he wanted that old cabin, he didn't need a sorry excuse for a dog hanging around his neck for who knew how long. He'd find another way to get his hands on that property. "Sorry, no can do."

The attorney sighed. "Fine, if that's how you feel. It's lucky your Aunt Sophia made a contingency in case you refused, although I must say she'd be terribly disappointed in you right now, Mr. Donnelly. She so hoped you'd love Muffin as she did."

"Well, I can't," Jake said, but guilt seeped into his gut regardless. The McAfees had been the only good thing that had ever happened to him. No matter how eccentric, Aunt Sophie and Uncle George had been the only loving, caring adults in his life. "I think Aunt Sophie would want the most loving home for Muffin. That's not with me."

"Fine," said the lawyer. "Then by default Muffin will go to Dr. LeAnne Crosby."

Alarm bells started clanging inside his head. "LeAnne Crosby? Why does that name sound familiar?"

"Dr. Crosby is the owner of Happy Hounds Health Spa."

The memory of dozens of checks for thousands of dollars flashed through Jake's mind. "A health spa? Isn't she one of Aunt Sophie's physicians?"

For some reason, the lawyer found that amusing. "I'm afraid not. As a matter of fact, she's a psychologist."

"My aunt was seeing a psychologist?"

"Not exactly," the man said, his thin lips still stretched in an irritating smirk. "Dr. Crosby is an animal psychologist."

Jake felt his jaw drop about a mile. His narrowed gaze returned to the mutt. "Are you telling me . . . my aunt was paying out that kind of money to a dog shrink?"

"Well, most of the outlay was for the dog spa Dr. Crosby runs. Sophia truly enjoyed her stays there every summer. Surely she mentioned the place to you?"

Jake racked his brain, furious with himself for not paying more attention to his aunt's batty stories. "Is this the resort in Virginia?"

"Indeed."

"It's a freaking *dog* spa?"

"Indeed."

"And Dr. Crosby is a freaking *dog* shrink?"

"Yes, she's a highly respected animal psychologist."

"Bullshit," Jake muttered. He knew a shyster when confronted with one. After all, in his work for the FBI he profiled scam artists just like her—soulless folks who made fortunes preying on vulnerable senior citizens. And although Sophie had been smart as a whip, she'd also had a heart the size of Texas, and any good con artist with a credible story could probably swindle her. Why hadn't he protected her? It was his job, and yet it could well be that he'd failed the one person he'd loved most in the world.

A dog shrink. That was a new one. And a clever one. After all, some people would do anything for their pets. Especially older, lonely people. "Let me get this straight. If I don't take Muffin, LeAnne Quacksby gets him."

"Crosby, correct."

"And upon Muffin's death, she inherits the money?"

"Correct again."

16

"And my aunt's property in Pennsylvania?"

"Right. To be turned into an animal refuge."

"Over my dead body." Jake surged to his feet. "Come on, Muffin; we're going home."

Chapter One

"Minor stipulations, my ass," Jake muttered one month later, as he turned onto the dirt road with the sign pointing the way to Happy Hounds Health Spa. "Two weeks of my vacation wasted at a freaking dog farm."

He slowed down and glanced at the far back-seat of the station wagon Aunt Sophie had left him to transport the mutt—a thirty-four-year-old single male driving a station wagon, for God's sake—to the lump of dog flesh lying there. "Hop to, mutt. We're almost there. Try to pretend that you live and breathe, will ya? I don't want this quack diagnosing abuse or something and trying to take you away."

Muffin's answer was a derisive snort.

In fact, in the last month Muffin's answer

was always a derisive snort. The most life he'd exhibited was the time Jake came home early to find Muffin happily munching on his favorite Garth Brooks CD. For the first time in his life Jake had considered violence against an animal. But of course another of Aunt Sophie's "minor stipulations" had bounced annoyingly through his head. For Jake to eventually inherit the Pennsylvania property, Muffin had to live a long, healthy, happy life. No freak accidents for Aunt Sophie's precious mutt, no, sir.

It had galled him at first that Aunt Sophie had set such terms, as if she were worried that Jake would even *consider* pooch-anasia, just to get his hands on her money. But after a month of living with the infuriating animal, he rather understood her concern. Especially when she was adding the stipulation that he waste fourteen days taking Muffin on a dog vacation.

There was only one upside he could see to this whole stupid trip: that was getting an up-close-and-personal look at one LeAnne Crosby and her dog operation. He'd done some unofficial checking on the animal shrink in the last month, and he'd pretty much come up empty. On the surface the woman seemed to be on the level: no complaints on file of her swindling customers, no past record. She was so squeaky-clean he smelled a rat. And if he discovered during this trip that she was ripping off innocent victims, he planned on exposing her—tail, beady eyes, and all.

Jake rolled down the window as he neared a stone gate, manned by a guard. Amazing. Was LeAnne Crosby afraid of gate-crashers?

For the first time Jake took a good look at the scenery. He had to admit the Virginia country-side was green and lush, with gently rolling hills as far as the eye could see. And according to the brochure, two hundred acres of it belonged to the good doctor.

Two hundred acres of prime real estate. At a conservative estimate of five grand an acre, Ms. Crosby—and Happy Hounds—was sitting on a million bucks' worth of primo turf.

There were huge terra-cotta pots of colorful flowers flanking either side of the gatehouse. *Nice touch*. Maybe the gatehouse was there to keep the dogs from wandering out and peeing in them. Lord knew Muffin had wreaked havoc on the pachysandra in his backyard.

He came to a stop, and a mammoth black man with a friendly smile and a single gleaming gold tooth touched fingers to the brim of his Stetson in greeting. "Welcome to Happy Hounds!"

"Thanks," Jake murmured.

The man pulled out a clipboard. "And you're registered to join us today?"

"Yes." *Unfortunately.* "The name's Jake Donnelly."

The man checked his chart; then his face split in a wide grin. "Well, I'll be!" He removed his Stetson, revealing a pate as shiny and bald as a cue ball, then leaned into the window and craned his neck toward the back of the car. "Muffin, you ol' hound! Good to have you back!"

Jake rolled his eyes, but they froze in midroll when he heard a happy *yip* come from the back of the car. The dog could *yip?* He twisted around to find the dog not only on his feet, but with his front paws on the seat, his ears perked and cocked back happily, and what looked like a joyous expression on his normally hangdog face.

Jake scowled at him. A month of feeding him and dragging him outside for walks and building a fence in his backyard to give the dog play space and the most he got for his trouble was a snort! Not once had he gotten a single yip.

"My name's Buzz," the guard said, slapping his hat back on his head, then pumping Jake's arm hard enough to dislocate a shoulder. "You or Muffin need a thing, you just call on ol' Buzz. I'm pretty much a jack-of-all-trades around here." Buzz had Jake sign in, then handed him a card key to bungalow 7B, a map of the grounds, a list of basic rules, and a schedule of events.

Jake dumped all the material on the passenger seat with barely a glance, except the card key, which he shoved in his breast pocket.

"Y'all enjoy your stay, ya hear?" Buzz finished. He spouted directions to the main building, which he called the Hound Dog Hotel. "LeAnne'll be awaiting y'all up there. She's real excited to see Muffin again."

"I'll bet," Jake grumbled. With a perfunctory wave he put the car back in gear and headed up the road per Buzz's directions. "That was real cute back there, Muffin. Real cute. Just don't forget who feeds your wrinkly butt."

Muffin snorted.

"And don't forget our couth lessons. No passing gas in public, no sniffing crotches or butts. Got it?"

Muffin snorted.

Jake had a hard time not admiring the dog spa. The grounds were beautifully landscaped. It looked like a country club, for crying out loud. To the west there were dozens of mulched trails leading into a lush forest. Straight ahead was what looked suspiciously like a golf course. All over the place there were white-fenced corrals filled with various numbers and types of dogs, owners, and young men and women wearing identical hunter green polo shirts and khaki shorts. *Camp counselors?*

Dotting the landscape to the east were Spanish-style condos, or bungalows, as they called them here.

His mind rolled over like a slot machine as he calculated the cost of this place. By the time he hit the stop sign he was up to four million.

He had to pause at the stop sign to allow a

golf cart to pass by. Driving it was a man in his fifties who waved and smiled broadly at their car. On the passenger side sat a gold cocker spaniel with a golf visor on his head.

Gawd almighty! "I don't think we're in Kansas anymore, Toto."

They climbed a rise and Jake almost gaped at what lay on the other side. Beside a large building, also built in the Spanish style, sprawled a huge swimming pool shaped like . . . a dog biscuit? Farther back there were six tennis courts. Behind the courts was a sparkling lake, with canoes and small rowboats dotting the surface.

Jake mentally added another two mil to his estimate.

People and animals lounged or exercised everywhere he looked—all shapes and sizes of both. And he had to grudgingly admit that all of them appeared quite content.

It was a sunny, surprisingly humidity-free early June day, but Jake was still grateful for the canopy to park under in front of the Hound Dog. In the month he'd had Muffin he'd learned one thing about the breed . . . bulldogs didn't take kindly to too much sun or heat.

Actually, he'd learned another thing, too: they didn't take kindly to physical exertion either. The most aerobic activity Muffin had engaged in was chewing his food. Even then he did it lying down.

Jake jammed the car in park and climbed

24

out, stretching his spine. In midextension his eyes landed on a woman standing at the entrance to the Hound Dog Hotel, her hands buried deep in a white lab coat.

Jake swallowed an "ooomph" from the invisible fist that plowed into his solar plexus. If this was LeAnne Crosby, LeAnne Crosby was a looker. Thick auburn hair fell in soft waves to her collarbone. It was parted on the side, and tucked behind both ears, emphasizing a heart-shaped face and high, pronounced cheekbones. She had large, doe brown eyes, and a smile that could jump-start a corpse's heart.

A killer smile, Jake thought grimly. One that could seduce a stone into producing blood. Jake had seen that kind of smile on the faces of some of the most notorious frauds in the country.

The wind picked up for a moment, and flung a hank of hair across the woman's face, bisecting her mouth. She reached up and peeled it away, tucking it back behind her ear while pursing her lips.

Jake had been so intent on studying what the smile did to her entire face, he hadn't focused on the lips.

Until now.

Nice lips. Generous lips. Full, female lips.

Possibly lying, fraudulent lips.

"Welcome," those lips said, curving into a bewitching smile designed, Jake felt certain, to knock the socks off her victims. "I'm LeAnne Crosby." She stepped forward, pulling her hand from her lab coat and thrusting it toward him.

Bewitched and mentally trying to drag his socks back on, it took Jake a moment to shake her hand. "Jake Donnelly."

"I've heard a lot about you, Mr. Donnelly."

"Likewise, Ms. Crosby." *However, none of the reports on you mentioned that you're a socks-knocker-offer.*

"Actually, it's Dr. Crosby," she said softly. "But we're very informal around here. Please call me LeAnne."

"Oh, you're a vet?" he asked, deliberately misunderstanding.

A shrewd light came into her eyes, but she didn't miss a beat. "No, I'm a psychologist. But we have three wonderful veterinarians on staff, so you don't need to worry." She leaned sideways, peering into the car. "Now, where's my favorite bulldog?"

Jake had forgotten Muffin. In fact, Jake had forgotten where he was. Annoyed with himself and her, he stalked to the back of the station wagon . . . to find Muffin prancing impatiently.

Prancing?

Jake opened the back door and was nearly knocked on his butt when Muffin bulldozed his way out in a flying leap of wrinkles and muscle. Jake stared in awe as Muffin landed gracefully and barked joyously at the doctor's cry of greeting.

Awe turned to annoyance when Muffin nearly galloped to the woman, who'd hunkered down with outstretched arms.

The dog could *run?*

Ears perked with excitement, Muffin reared up on his pudgy hind legs and planted his front paws on the woman's chest. As she laughed—a rather nice and throaty laugh for a potential rip-off artist dog shrink—Muffin proceeded to make dog wash of her face.

She didn't seem to mind. In fact, she was almost encouraging him with cooing noises and head scratches that had him wagging his stub of a tail so furiously his butt looked like it was doing the cha-cha.

While they engaged in their little love-fest reunion, Jake took the time to study the woman more closely. Her skin was smooth, with a light tan, an appealing apricot color. Her lashes were thick, framing those velvety soft eyes.

That smile, below prominent cheekbones, was a knockout. He had to remember to ignore it, or else he'd be handing her that cabin on a silver platter.

"Oh, yes, I've missed you terribly, too, sweetheart! I'm so happy to see you!" she said as the dog calmed down a bit.

Jake cleared his throat, suddenly embarrassed and disgusted at this blatant public display of affection. Affection in any form made him uncomfortable; it was as foreign to him as Mandarin Chinese.

Except with Aunt Sophie, he recalled with a pang. He remembered the first summer he'd gone to stay with her. The first time she'd enveloped him in that sweet-smelling hug, he'd gone stiff with shock. It had taken him all summer to become accustomed to her reaching out to sweep back his hair from his forehead, or squeeze his shoulder. Even when he landed himself in trouble, the sum total of her physical recrimination would be a poke in the ribs.

Dr. Crosby gave Muffin a final scratch, then straightened to her full height, which he guessed to be about four inches above five feet. "I hope you'll enjoy your stay."

Like hell. "Obviously Muffin's happy to be here," he said diplomatically. It wouldn't do to insult the woman right off the bat. He had plenty of time—two interminable weeks—to discover whether there was anything nefarious about this place and its owner.

She smiled down at the dog, affection softening her striking features. "Muffin's one of my very favorite guests."

I'll bet, he thought. His Aunt Sophie had dumped a fortune staying at this place. "Mmm," he answered noncommittally.

"Oh," she said, and the smile faded as she glanced back up at him and her eyes lost their sparkle. "I was so sorry to hear about Sophie. I'm truly going to miss her."

28

She sure looked sincere. If she was acting, she had "stricken" down pat.

Jake bent and snapped the leash on to Muffin's collar. "Yeah, me, too."

"I'm sure Muffin's been grieving."

Oh, jeez, two minutes into the introductions, and the spiel begins. Straightening, he took a moment to decide whether to call her on it now, or play along. He supposed he'd play until he got the goods on her. If there were any goods to get. "Well, he's tried to be a trooper."

As if Muffin could understand English, he glanced up at Jake with an expression one could loosely interpret as "Up yours."

Luckily, the woman was too busy gazing at Jake sympathetically to catch that look, or very quickly the jig would be up. For the sake of that Pennsylvania property, he planned on being the most attentive dog owner in history.

For the sake of that property, he wasn't going to let on—at least for now—that he considered this woman a first-class quack.

He thinks I'm a quack, LeAnne thought, a little amused, a little annoyed. It wasn't the first time she'd had this reaction from skeptics, so it didn't really bother her. A couple of days at Happy Hounds usually won over even the biggest cynics.

Besides, she didn't give a dog's paw what this guy thought of her. As far as she was concerned, he'd been horrendously neglectful of his aunt, who had obviously adored and missed him the last few years. *The selfish rat.*

Sophie McAfee had been one of LeAnne's first, and most supportive, clients four years ago. Until last year, she'd spent the entire season at the spa—the season being the months of May through September. Last year she'd had to cut her stay short, due to health problems. But never had LeAnne dreamed that it would be the last time she'd see the feisty woman. Sophie's death had stunned and saddened her terribly.

That she'd been named in Sophie's will had just plain stunned her. And by the sour gleam that shone in this man's electric blue gaze, she'd bet the farm—so to speak—that it had more than stunned him.

Over the years, Sophie had talked quite a bit about her nephew, Jake. She'd even once suggested that she fix Jake and LeAnne up on a blind date. LeAnne had smilingly declined. At that time it had been two years since Stephen's death, but it had been far too soon for her to think about other men. In fact, it was now six years since Stephen's death, and it was still too soon. The psychological wounds she'd received from her marriage hadn't healed yet. She didn't know if they ever would.

Sophie had known all about the details of LeAnne's marriage, about the lack of trust that had become so obsessive on Stephen's part that he'd managed to destroy any love she'd had for him. Even so, Sophie had been adamant that LeAnne get over it, start over. And she'd never stopped hoping that LeAnne would move on with Sophie's nephew, whom she'd characterized as "the most handsome cuss this side of the Mississippi."

Sophie hadn't been far off.

His eyes were so deep a blue they shone almost black. His dark brown hair was cut short, very short. His features were classically handsome and complemented each other perfectly. All in all, a very handsome cuss indeed.

Who was gazing at her as if she were a first-class quack.

And she was gazing at him as if he were a chocolate éclair.

LeAnne gave herself a mental smack and returned her attention to Muffin—who was gazing at Jake Donnelly as if he were Satan incarnate.

Hmmm, no love lost there. Which made her wonder what Sophie had been thinking. The big lug looked as uncomfortable and out of his element as a jewel thief at a police convention.

She almost felt sorry for this man, who'd obviously been bamboozled by his scheming aunt. Then again, if he'd visited more often, maybe his aunt wouldn't have concocted such a bizarre plan. The real loser here was Muffin, who didn't deserve to be saddled with an owner who didn't want him. The next two weeks were going to be a challenge, but one she planned on winning. By the time Jake Donnelly left Happy Hounds, he'd be hopelessly in love with . . . his dog. *That's right, his dog.*

That was the plan, and she silently swore she'd stick to it.

"Buzz will help you get settled," she told him when she spotted Buzz approaching with the luggage cart.

Donnelly's brows lowered quizzically. "I thought that was Buzz back at Checkpoint Charlie."

"It was," Buzz said, his broad smile friendly as usual.

Buzz was one of those people LeAnne wished she had ten of. He was willing to pitch in and help with any job necessary, and his sheer size made him an unofficial security guard, even though he was probably the gentlest man LeAnne had ever met. "Buzz gets around."

"You just leave your luggage to me," Buzz said.

Donnelly gazed back in the direction of the front gate with a frown; then, apparently giving up on discovering how Buzz had gotten from there to here, he shrugged and handed Buzz his keys.

LeAnne offered her professional smile, even though her pulse was a little accelerated for some reason. This man was a challenge. Normally LeAnne enjoyed a challenge—the canine variety. She wasn't at all certain she wanted one in human form. Especially this human form. This big, male, full-of-attitude human form. But for Sophie's sake, and for Muffin's, she was going to do her darnedest. "How does tomorrow at nine sound?"

"How does it sound for what?" he asked, in a voice just gravelly enough to raise her core temperature a notch.

She met his blue gaze and resisted the urge to fan herself. "Oh, I'm sorry, I forgot you're not familiar with our routine." Plunging her oddly itchy hands into her lab coat pockets, she focused on Muffin. "Tomorrow we'll do a routine checkup, and then we'll lay out a schedule for our walks, for Muffin's massages—"

"Massages?" he interrupted. "For the dog? You've got to be kidding me!"

She chanced a glance up, and decided that he wore incredulity well. "Not in the least. While he's here, Muffin gets first-class treatment. He gets twice-daily walks, once with you and one of our trainers, once on your own; he gets massages three times a week, followed by some grooming. Not only is it good for him, but it frees you up for a few hours to golf or swim or do whatever you like." She forced herself not to ask what he'd like to do.

"I see," he said in a tone that said he didn't.

"At the evaluation tomorrow we'll decide whether we need private sessions."

"What kind of sessions?" he asked, his eyes narrowing.

"Therapy sessions," she answered, waiting for the inevitable explosion of disbelief.

"I see," he said, so solemnly she knew he was biting back a snort.

"And you're welcome to schedule training sessions if you want to teach Muffin some advanced commands. He's already learned the basics."

"He has?" the hunk said, practically glaring at Muffin.

"Sure." LeAnne scratched Muffin behind the ear, then said, "Sit."

Muffin plunked his hind end on the concrete.

"Shake," she said, and Muffin dutifully gave her his paw. "Lie down." Muffin plopped down. She looked up. "See?" She rubbed the dog's belly, then straightened. "Up."

Muffin rolled to his feet.

"Sit," Jake Donnelly said in a belligerent voice she'd have to train him to tone down.

Muffin stood as still as a statue, then looked away with a long-suffering sigh. *Yep, they're going to need therapy sessions, all right.*

"See, he doesn't listen to me," the man muttered. "And here I thought he was just dumb as a brick."

Lots of therapy sessions. She took exception on Muffin's behalf. "I've never met a dumb dog, Mr. Donnelly. Only dumb owners."

He appeared to take exception on his own behalf. "Are you calling me dense?"

"Of course not," she lied. She really didn't understand people who didn't understand animals.

Any pretense he might have attempted when they'd first met that he adored Sophie's dog dropped right there and then. He glowered down at the mutt with an I-can't-believe-you-got-me-into-this look. "What if Muffin and I just go on our merry way?"

For just a second, the thought was appealing. She didn't need a surly, reluctant owner on her hands for two entire weeks. Even if he *did* look good enough to eat. But she wasn't about to let Sophie down. Or Muffin. Muffin hadn't asked to be pawned off on a man who didn't understand or even like him. "What if you go on your merry way, and leave Muffin to me?"

His jaw dropped open for a moment, and then his eyes narrowed with suspicion. "Oh, yeah, you'd like that, wouldn't you? You take Muffin and my aunt's property to boot."

That thought hadn't even occurred to her, and she found it highly insulting. *What a turkey!* She wrinkled her nose in distaste. "Mr. Donnelly, you know what you can do with that property?" she began, then took a deep breath and prayed for patience. "Look, Muffin is a wonderful dog, and doesn't deserve not to be loved by his owner. Give us a chance to teach you how to handle him so that you both get pleasure out of the relationship."

He opened his mouth, then closed it again, obviously swallowing whatever retort he was about to make.

"Let's make the best of it, all right?" She was not above using guilt. When she saw him begin to form another protest or retort or insult, she used it. "It's what Sophie wanted."

The tight lines around his mouth eased somewhat at the mention of his aunt, which told her one positive thing in a sea of negatives: he'd cared about Sophie. She considered that a very important piece of information, and wasn't above using it, either.

"Fine," he said grudgingly.

She should feel victorious, but she couldn't quite pull it off, considering she was looking forward to the next fourteen days about as much as she looked forward to Pap smears. "Fine," she echoed. "See you tomorrow at nine."

"Right," he said, then began following behind Buzz. Except Muffin refused to budge. "Come on, dog!" Muffin dug in further. "Please?"

LeAnne fought a smile. Boy, oh, boy, she had her work cut out for her. "Buzz, he's probably telling you he wants his teddy-bear blanket. Don't leave it behind."

Jake Donnelly visibly swallowed. "His teddy-bear blanket?"

LeAnne narrowed her eyes. "Don't tell me

you weren't given his teddy-bear blanket when you took him?"

The man waved. "Yeah, sure. But, you know, it was ratty, flea-infested, *stupid* for a male dog."

Muffin sniffed loudly.

So as not to cause any more tension between beast and dog, LeAnne lowered her voice. "Please tell me you didn't throw out his special blanket."

"Not exactly."

She raised an eyebrow. "What did you do with it, exactly?"

Donnelly lowered his voice also. "Well . . . I sort of . . . burned it."

"Burned it," LeAnne repeated. Up until now, *hopeless* had not been a word in her vocabulary. At the moment, she was considering adding it. "Not in front of Muffin, I hope."

"What do you take me for?" he asked indignantly. "Of course not! But it took a while to wrestle it away from him."

Yep, she was adding it. And fairly close to using it. "Did it ever occur to you that the reason he was fighting you for it was that it was special to him?"

"He's a dog!"

"With feelings!"

Muffin let loose a see-what-I-have-to-put-up-with whimper.

LeAnne sighed. "Our gift shop stocks blankets. Why don't you buy him another one and hope he bonds with it?"

"Bonds . . . with a blanket."

Crossing her arms, she said, "What, you never had a special blanket or toy as a child?"

His teeth clicked shut and his jaw spasmed. "No."

LeAnne didn't know how she knew, but she knew: he was lying. But she didn't call him on it, because the flash that had sparked in his eyes told her he wouldn't appreciate it.

"Besides, he's almost five, thirty-five in dog years. He should've outgrown something like that by now."

LeAnne just shook her head and turned from the turkey. "Go on, Muffin. I'll see you in the morning."

Muffin wouldn't move.

Buzz glanced back and she shot him a pointed look. He nodded slightly. "Let's go, Muffin, my man! I've got a Milk-Bone with your name on it in your room."

Muffin yipped at Buzz and happily trotted up to walk beside him. As he passed Jake Donnelly, LeAnne could almost swear he stuck his tongue out at him.

Lots and lots of therapy sessions.

Chapter Two

"Nice digs," Jake murmured as soon as Buzz dropped his luggage and quietly left. Muffin had plopped down in the middle of the spacious bungalow, and was gnawing on one of the largest dog bones Jake had ever seen.

The place was decorated in green, peach, and cream, and the comforter on the king-size bed was a tasteful floral print. The drapes hanging at the sliding glass door matched the comforter. The two upholstered chairs and a love seat were done in green and cream stripes.

Dr. Crosby had good taste, and sure seemed to see to the comfort of her guests. There was a small alcove kitchen stocked with three kinds of coffee and about ten types of tea, and the fridge contained a plethora of small juice cans of all flavors. There was even a small microwave in case the guest chose to nuke his own food. Although why anyone would want to do that when there were reportedly four excellent restaurants at the main hotel was beyond him. All four of the restaurants offered room service, too. If he didn't watch it, he was going to gain fifty pounds in two weeks.

The bathroom was large, too, with an oversize Jacuzzi tub and two marble sinks. The towels were huge and thick and fluffy, and so was a complimentary bathrobe.

The only way the accommodations could be any more perfect would be if he could find something to complain about.

There was a big stuffed dog bed at the foot of the people bed that looked so comfortable Jake had the feeling Muffin would never accept plain floor accommodations ever again.

Beside the cherry table in the corner was a phone jack for a laptop computer. Another large armoire revealed a television, a VCR, and a CD player. And there were two phones in the room, one beside the bed, one on the table by the glass door that led out to a small porch and a fenced-in backyard beyond.

Yes, indeed, Dr. Crosby had seen to the comfort and convenience of her guests. If she was fleecing them, she was fleecing them in style.

Jake unzipped his luggage and instantly was knocked back by the pungent odor of flea shampoo. "Damn!" he muttered as he stared at his clothes, which were wet and stained from a bottle that had come uncapped.

He dug through, but there wasn't a single piece of clothing unscathed by the damn stuff. Only his Glock and shoulder holster were saved, being tucked into the pocket inside the top flap of the suitcase.

His first inclination was to blame Muffin for yet another insult to his person and belongings. But he had a hard time reconciling that desire with the knowledge that it had been he, not Muffin, who'd packed the bag.

Stalking to the phone by the bed, he glared at Muffin, who was happily gnawing the bone. He checked the list of Happy Hound numbers, then punched in the one for the laundry.

Two minutes later there was a knock on the door, and he had to admit he couldn't complain about staff tardiness, either. When he opened it, Buzz was standing there, his big, friendly smile firmly in place.

Jake stared at him for a moment. "You do laundry, too?"

"Jack-of-all-trades!" Buzz said cheerfully. When Jake handed over the suitcase, he added, "Woo-ee! Potent stuff!"

"Tell me about it."

"We'll get this back to you in a few hours, Mr. Donnelly."

"Just Jake."

Buzz grinned and left.

Muffin was still gnawing on the bone when

41

Jake closed the door. He grabbed a can of apricot juice from the refrigerator, then ambled to the bed and sat down, bouncing a couple of times. Figured. The bed was perfect.

He grabbed the phone again and punched in the number of his office.

"Colson," his partner barked.

"Hey," Jake responded. "What's shaking?"

Mark chuckled. "Ah, the big man has arrived at the little doggy resort."

"Kiss my ass," Jake said pleasantly. "And keep your mouth shut. No one, and I mean *no one*, learns where I am. Got it?"

"What's it worth to you?"

Jake slugged down some juice while he decided which threat to use. After all, this was important. "What's it worth to you that I don't accidentally spill to Barbara what you did at Tito's bachelor party?"

"Oh, man, that's low."

"These are desperate times, pal."

"You weren't exactly hiding your eyes, either."

Jake couldn't legitimately argue with him. That stripper had been one lush lady. Speaking of lush ladies, LeAnne Crosby's lips suddenly swam before his eyes. He shook his head to destroy the image, but that just managed to bring her entire visage into focus. To counteract that, he shifted his gaze to a snoring Muffin, who'd fallen asleep with half the dog bone

42

still hanging out of his mouth. Muffin was the best antiaphrodisiac Jake had ever known.

Back in control—and wondering how he'd lost it just like that over a pair of lips—Jake moved on to subject number two. "Do we have a court date yet for the Winston case?"

"Yep," Mark answered. "July tenth."

"Wow, short date. Good. That ought to make keeping our star witness safe a little easier."

"She's in good hands. Mine."

Jake might have made a joke about that, considering that Elisa Johnson was a gorgeous woman. Not as gorgeous as LeAnne Crosby, of course, but definitely worthy of notice.

But when it came to this case, he knew Mark was absolutely serious. They'd been working it for two straight years, culminating in finally garnering enough evidence to arrest and bring Jacob and Millicent Winston to trial for fraud and money laundering. It was too important to both of them to make light of it. Elisa Johnson was a brave young woman, she was in grave danger, and she deserved their utmost respect. And protection. There was no one in the world he trusted more to keep her safe than his partner.

Lord knew Mark had pulled Jake's ass out of the fire more than once. They'd gone to the academy together, graduated from Quantico together, and had been partners from day one. Jake considered himself the luckiest agent in the Bureau. Of course, he'd admit that to Mark on the day hell turned into a snow cone.

"Earth to Jake."

Jake shook his head, realizing he'd suffered a brain glitch. "Huh?"

"I said, so how's this jewel look up close and personal?"

Jewel was his and Mark's code word for a con man or woman. It was one thing for Jake to characterize LeAnne Crosby as a shyster, but suddenly he felt a little defensive on her behalf. Which was really, really dumb. Just because she was good-looking didn't preclude her from being shady. Just because she had soft, innocent brown eyes didn't mean she didn't have a larcenous heart.

"Up close and personal she looks like someone you'd want to get to know real close and very personal."

"Oooh, a babe, hmm?"

"Definitely a babe."

"Gonna get up close and real personal?"

Because that sounded extremely enticing, Jake scoffed. "Not a chance." *No matter how hard she tries to tempt me with that smile.*

"How's the location look?"

Jake glanced around the spacious, swanky suite. "Looks too good to be true."

"A pooch palace, hmm?"

"It's actually fairly amazing. We're talking a multimillion-dollar operation here, pal."

"Where'd she get the seed money?"

Good question. From his initial investigation into her dealings, Jake had learned that she hailed from a middle-class neighborhood in Kenosha, Wisconsin. Unless she had hit the lottery, he doubted she'd inherited the money. "Hmm, not sure," he murmured. "How about you checking on that for me?" Although the thought of digging deeper into her private affairs was starting to feel just a tad distasteful. Which was a really bad sign, considering it was what he did for a living.

"What's wrong with *your* laptop?" Mark complained.

"Hey, I'm on vacation!" *And besides, my judgment is currently impaired.*

Okay, he admitted it: one look at the luscious doctor and his brain had short-circuited. She was a temptation, and he didn't need any temptations. Especially when he was trying to get the goods on her. "Just do me a favor and look into it. I left a copy of her file in my left-hand drawer."

Mark drew a breath—to wind up for another protest, probably—but Jake cut him off when there was a knock on the door. "I'll check in in a few days. Gotta run."

"Wait a damn—"

Click.

The knock had awakened Muffin and interested him enough to actually raise his head.

"You make a hell of a watchdog, Muffin," Jake said with a grunt as he passed the mutt.

Muffin snorted.

Jake opened the door, and all the blood drained from his head and pooled lower. LeAnne Crosby stood on his threshold, looking breathtaking in ratty denim shorts and a pink, oversize T-shirt with the faded picture of two cartoon guinea pigs on it. The guinea pigs looked wildly happy. As well they should, considering which parts of her anatomy they were covering.

No doubt about it; she was trying to tempt him.

"How in hell did you lose her again?" an angry voice growled into the phone.

Jimmy Delaney tugged at his collar as sweat trickled down his chest and back, plastering polyester to his skin. "Someone must have tipped them off, boss. We were *this* close."

"*This* close," the boss said with a sneer. "*This* close doesn't mean shit, you bonehead."

"We're on it," he said with a lot more confidence than he felt. In his line of work, it didn't pay to appear unsure. "Our source says he thinks they're heading to Delaware."

"Then get your friggin' ass to Delaware." He heard the man take a deep, audible draw on a cigarette. "The court date's coming up fast. We have to shut that woman up. Permanent-like."

"All but done."

"That's the problem, nitwit. You've done everything *but* get it done."

"This time, for sure."

"And I won't complain if you take out them two asshole Fibbies while you're at it. Might even be a bonus in it for you."

"I might be able to get the one. The other's gone missing."

"Gone missing? Where?"

"No one knows."

"Well, find him, too. I know for a fact my boss would be very pleased if there were two less Feds in this world."

"I'm on it."

"Bunny," the man said in a low, ominous voice, "I'd hate to be you if you fail."

Jimmy hardly heard the threat because he was so angry at the man's invoking his nickname. How was he supposed to get any respect in this business when he had a nickname like Bunny? Why couldn't he be Knife, or Snake, or Viper?

"I won't fail," he said, then silently added *asshole*. The man might be his boss, but that didn't mean Jimmy had to like him. After all, he'd been the one to slap that stinking nickname on him. "She's as good as six feet under."

LeAnne fought not to blush with embarrassment. From the dazed expression on Jake Donnelly's face, she supposed he'd expected better attire on the director of Happy Hounds.

Well, tough cookies. She hadn't dropped by in a professional capacity, anyway. She'd come on a mission of mercy. For Muffin.

Resisting the urge to tug her shorts lower to cover more leg, she held out her hand. "I . . . I just thought . . . Muffin might like . . . this."

It took him a moment to drag his gaze from her chest to her offering. LeAnne glanced down at her T-shirt to see if maybe she'd spilled food on herself or something. Nothing there but the guinea pigs.

She looked back up, but he seemed fascinated by the shirt. To fill the awkward silence, she pointed at the left guinea pig, then the right. "Scooter and Bob."

The man nearly choked as his eyes jerked up. "Huh?"

"The guinea pigs. Scooter and Bob."

He glanced down again, but just for a nanosecond. "Oh," he said, then looked like he was biting the inside of his cheek.

Oh, Lord, he thinks I was naming my breasts! She rushed to correct that impression. "Mrs. Perrelli comes every year with her cockapoo"— *Oh, God, LeAnne!*—and . . . and her son, Jamie, and Jamie always brings his two guinea pigs and Jamie's a really good artist and he designed this T-shirt and gave it to me for my birthday and . . ." *And you are sounding like a raving lunatic,* she mentally chastised, sputtering to a halt. "And this is for Muffin," she finished, holding out the blanket again.

"What's that?" he asked as his baby blues cleared, then narrowed.

Her embarrassment vanished at his dumb question. Stifling a sigh of irritation, she shook out the blanket and held it up. "A blanket," she said slowly, in case he had trouble with the English language.

"What are those things on it?" he asked, suspicion coating his words.

Funny, Sophie had never mentioned that her nephew had a single-digit IQ. "Those are called hearts. Why am I not surprised you don't recognize them?"

He opened his mouth, but just then Muffin romped to the door with a muffled woof of welcome, his whole body wiggling happily, a large, half-eaten bone clenched between his teeth.

LeAnne couldn't help smiling. She loved all animals, but for some reason Muffin had always held an extra-special place in her heart. She hunched down to pet him. "Hello, big boy! Look like Buzz is already spoiling you. Are you settling in okay?"

"Careful, he gets real mean when he has a bone and anyone goes near it," the man said.

"Is that right?" LeAnne asked, just as Muffin shot the big oaf a look of disdain, then dropped the bone at LeAnne's feet.

She tried not to laugh as she glanced up in time to catch Jake propping his hands on his hips and growling his exasperation. "This animal is out to get me."

"He probably feels the same about you."

"I have done nothing but take care of him since I brought him home!" he retorted, indignation making his eyes turn an even darker blue.

"Exactly," LeAnne handed the bone back to Muffin and straightened. "Where's the love? The respect?"

He pointed at Muffin. "Ask him!"

But Muffin was already waddling back into the bungalow.

"Look, how about we put this blanket on his bed, and see if he takes to it?" she suggested.

Donnelly glared at it. "Wasn't there anything a little more manly?"

"Would you prefer the baby bunnies or the pink bows?"

His expression said no. A big fat no.

"There's nothing unmanly about hearts, you know," she said. "Especially for Muffin. He's a lover, not a fighter."

"A . . . lover?" he sputtered.

"Sure. In fact, he has a major crush on a shih tzu named Dolly."

The man stared at her in patent disbelief, then broke out in astonished laughter. And his laughter was sexy as sin. As were his eyes, crinkling beautifully. LeAnne looked away before she forced herself on him.

Finding this lug attractive was not a good idea. In fact it was a terrible idea. Ranked right up there with driving blindfolded.

"A shih tzu, huh? Can you imagine? If he weren't neutered, he and Dolly could produce little bull-shihtz, pardon my language."

It was LeAnne's turn to stare. "You had Muffin neutered?" she almost screeched.

"Uh, no . . . Didn't Aunt Sophie have Muffin neutered?"

"No! He is a show-quality animal, Mr. Donnelly. She fully planned to have him sire a few litters in his lifetime. She wanted his bloodline to continued!"

"Don't you ever listen to Bob Barker? 'Always have your pet spayed or neutered.'"

"Well, normally I'd agree with that sentiment completely," LeAnne conceded. "But in Muffin's case, Sophie definitely wanted to continue the line."

Jake snorted rudely. "Like that's gonna happen. How soon can I schedule the operation?"

They both turned toward Muffin, but he'd vanished, abandoning about two inches of bone.

"Where'd he go?" the man wondered aloud. Truly, *dense* was just not a strong enough word for this guy.

"May I come in?" LeAnne said, trying to keep her utter exasperation under control. How in the world did the man swim in the same gene pool as Sophie?

He hesitated, then stepped back and waved her in. LeAnne walked into the room and draped the blanket over Muffin's pillow before dropping to her knees and lifting the comforter off the bed. Sure enough, Muffin had taken refuge. His head rested on his paws, and his eyes were wild with the need to bolt.

Jake Donnelly might be good-looking, but he had the sensitivity of a rock. "Come on out, sweet thing. Nothing's going to happen to you, I promise."

"Don't count on it," Jake said ominously from behind her, his voice grittier than usual for some reason. "That dog is not giving me puppies."

Muffin, who'd started to inch forward, quickly scooted back.

LeAnne exploded. "What kind of moronic, mean, heartless jerk are you?" She twisted to face him, ready to continue ranting but her words died halfway up her throat when she saw where his attention was directed: straight at her butt, which was poked in the air. In her hurry to get to Muffin she hadn't considered the compromising position she'd dropped into.

Embarrassment swallowed all the fire inside her as she scrambled to lower her bottom to the floor. Knowing her face was probably red as a fire engine, she kept her back to him while leaning sideways and lifting the comforter again. Muffin had backed up almost to the wall. "Don't you worry, sweetheart. This turkey's not cutting anything of yours while you're in my care."

Muffin didn't look convinced.

Feeling she'd conquered most of her blush, she turned and faced him again. "Assure him in a calm, gentle voice that you are *not* going to N-E-U-T-E-R him anytime soon."

Jake had managed to pull his gaze from her posterior, but he still looked a little stunned. She immediately wondered if these shorts made her butt look big.

Which was irrelevant because she didn't *care* if her butt looked big to him. Well, not much, at any rate. She wouldn't want her butt looking big to anyone.

Jake swallowed hard, realizing he'd just had the greatest view of the sweetest female bottom he'd ever had the pleasure to see. He tried to assimilate the last sentence she'd uttered but it was lot of work when his mind was coated with lust.

He reached up to loosen his collar, but realized he was wearing a polo shirt, open at the throat. The constriction probably came from having just swallowed his tongue. He cleared his throat. "Huh?"

She looked at him as if he were a moron, and now that he thought about it, hadn't she just called him one? "I *said* get down here and reassure Muffin that you are not going to N-E-U-T-E-R him."

"But I don't want him to P-R-O-C-R-E-A-T-E."

53

"Fine. But if you don't want him spending the entire two weeks under this bed, I suggest you get down here and make nice."

Jake shook off the lust and conjured a scowl at making nice to a dog who was hell-bent on making his life miserable. Personally, he couldn't care less if Muffin holed up under the bed for the entire vacation. In fact, it was almost an appealing thought. But the glare in her eyes was rather ferocious for a beautiful animal freak. "Fine. But I reserve the right to have the O-P-E-R-A-T-I-O-N in the future," he said, and couldn't believe he was spelling out words for a fleabag.

He dropped to his knees on her left, then leaned to the right to look under the bed. Which managed to put him eye-to-eye with the good doctor, as well as in perfume-sniffing proximity. And her perfume was wonderful. Light, with just a hint of springtime and flowers about it.

Trying to ignore her scent and forget that her lips were less than six inches from his, he said, "Come on out, Muffin. Nothing's going to happen to your . . . doghood."

Muffin was scowling at him. Jake chanced a glance at LeAnne—which was a really pretty name, now that he thought about it—to see if she was scowling, too. But she wasn't. She was smiling encouragingly at Muffin, and Jake found himself wishing she'd smile encouragingly like that at him. Only not to get him out from beneath a bed, but on top of one.

Jake mentally kicked himself. He had to remember she was probably trying to tempt him on purpose, just to distract him from her shady business practices. Although if this place was a scam, it was a really nice one.

He reached over and grabbed the gummed-up remnants of the bone, managing, accidentally on purpose, to brush against her arm. Sparks didn't fly, but his pulse accelerated dramatically, which just proved that he was losing the "no temptation" battle. And it made him mad enough to decide to blame her. After all, what was she thinking, showing up in shorts and a suggestive, baggy T-shirt and wearing really great-smelling perfume?

Gritting his teeth against the small flame of desire that had erupted in his belly, he held the bone under the bed for Muffin to see. "Why don't you come on out and get the rest of your bone?"

Muffin snorted.

"Bribery will get you nowhere when his masculinity is on the line," LeAnne commented. "Males of all species are alike that way."

She managed to make that sound like a *bad* thing. Jake would take offense if her perfume weren't turning his gray matter into pudding.

"Reassure him again," she commanded.

"No neutering," Jake repeated. "Scout's

honor," he added, holding up two fingers and hoping that was the right amount, because he'd never been a Boy Scout in his life. He figured it was a rather clever loophole.

"You've never been a Boy Scout in your life," LeAnne murmured, keeping a fake smile plastered on her face as she looked at Muffin.

"Says who?"

"Says your L-Y-I-N-G fingers. I have three older brothers, all of whom were Scouts."

"Oh," he said, dropping his hand.

"You know how pathetic it is to L-I-E to your dog?"

"Like he can tell the difference."

Muffin snorted.

LeAnne shot him a look that told him he was lucky she didn't have a baseball bat in her hands, because sure as hell it'd be connecting with his skull right about now. "Bring me his leash."

Jake frowned. "What, you want to drag him out of there?"

She rolled her eyes, and Jake could feel her estimation of him dropping faster than an anchor. Not that it had far to fall, considering that her first impression probably hadn't been all that exalted to begin with.

For some reason that fact irritated him. Normally he didn't give a good damn what anyone thought of him—which was just as well, since in his line of work he tended to accumulate enemies—but it irritated him anyway.

"No, I am not dragging him out of there. We're going to offer to take him for a W-A-L-K."

"You might as well offer to give him a B-A-T-H while you're at it. That animal *hates* going on walks."

"Just please bring me his leash."

Jake shrugged and stood up, but not before inhaling deeply one more time to get a final whiff of her scent. Definitely a tempting scent.

He dug through his duffel bag, where he'd dumped the leash, and pulled it out. He handed it to her, even if he knew her idea was hopeless. He figured Muffin would actually prefer to be neutered; at least he could do that lying down.

"Stand back," she ordered.

"Why?" he asked, trying to define exactly the color of her eyes. Sort of the color of fine, aged cognac. And just as intoxicating.

"If you're not part of the solution, you're part of the problem."

Her mouth was a different matter. Especially when she was using it to speak to him. But considering he knew she was making a big mistake about this walk thing, he decided to humor her. He stepped aside.

She leaned down again. "Come on, sweetheart; you're going to be fine. I won't let the big, bad oaf do anything to you, I promise."

"Hey!"

"I have an idea," she said brightly, rattling

the leash. "How about if we take a walk? We might even run into Dolly!"

Muffin shot out from under the bed like the Lone Ranger's silver bullet. Before Jake's disbelieving eyes, Muffin raced directly to the door and started prancing in circles while yipping excitedly.

LeAnne stood up with a smile. In her defense, it wasn't a smug smile, just a delighted one. An enchanting one. A damn tempting one.

"Looks like we're going for a walk," she said as she strolled by him to the door.

"I didn't know shrinks were allowed to use bribery," Jake muttered, following.

"Not exactly bribery." LeAnne snapped the leash on Muffin's collar. "Just a working knowledge of the male mind. Ready for a walk?"

Chapter Three

"So what do you do for the FBI?" LeAnne asked as they followed a meandering mulch path through the western woods.

Jake had been busy glaring at a happily trotting Muffin, who was suddenly displaying the energy and enthusiasm of a retriever puppy. But at her question, he stumbled. "How did you know I work for the Bureau?" he asked suspiciously.

She laughed. "Mister, I know what kind of pajamas you wore as a child."

That startled him for a moment longer than it should have. "Oh. Aunt Sophie."

She nodded, that killer smile firmly in place. "Scooby Doo, Winnie-the-Pooh—"

"I wore those under protest!"

"But your favorite was Bullwinkle."

"Hey, Bullwinkle had class. He was busy kicking some Cold War commie butt." He squeezed his eyes shut. "God, this is embarrassing. What else did she tell you?"

"Well, let's see. There was the time you got pulled over for drunk driving—"

"That was a mistake!"

"On a *bicycle!*"

"I was just hotdogging!"

"Or how about the time you got caught necking with the Baptist minister's daughter?"

"Oh, Lord."

"In the basement of the church."

"It seemed like a good place at the time."

"Or the time—"

He groaned. "Enough! I get the picture."

"You were, by far, Sophie's favorite subject."

Something shifted in his chest: part loss; part abiding love for the woman who'd taken him in every summer, saving him from long, sultry days of hatred; part guilt for not being there for her in the end.

Whatever was going on in his chest must have seeped up into his face, because LeAnne was studying him intently, her smile having faded.

He schooled his features. "Yeah, well, that must have been a real bore."

She shook her head, her silky hair drifting back and forth. "Oh, not at all. The way she described you made James Bond look like a snore." She paused, still searching his face. "She was very proud of you, Jake."

He already knew that, deep in his heart, but hearing this woman say it made it so much more meaningful for some reason. Especially when she said it using his name. He really liked the way it rolled off her tongue. Which immediately made him think of other things he'd like to see in contact with her tongue. Like any and every inch of his anatomy.

To counter that thought he said, "No fair. You know all kinds of details about me, and I don't know any about you."

"Sleeping Beauty."

"Huh?"

"My favorite pj's were Sleeping Beauty."

How appropriate. A vision popped into his head that had no right to be there: coming upon LeAnne, sleeping in a meadow—naked, in his version—and kissing her awake.

By the time he banished that thought from his head—it didn't leave willingly—Muffin had yanked on his leash and pulled LeAnne ahead of him. She continued walking, leaving him standing there, speechless. With a perfect view of the backs of her legs and that sweet butt swaying in a way only a sexy woman could pull off. He tossed a quick thank-you to her creator for doing such a bang-up job.

He gave himself an extra second or two to

admire and imprint the vision on his brain, then caught up with her. They walked in peaceful silence for a few more minutes, coming to a clearing and a fairly large pond. There was a dock, and on the other side of the pond was a rope swing hanging from a large sugar maple, perfect for flinging yourself into the cool water. It reminded him so much of his aunt's place in Pennsylvania that nostalgia nearly laid him low.

Damn, he'd loved summers. He'd loved the freedom of choosing any adventure he cared to, whether it was fishing or hiking or building a tree fort.

More than that, he'd loved his uncle's teaching him to track animals, quietly follow them, learn to identify the different species, and photograph them in their natural element.

As a red-winged blackbird clucked at them from a limb high up in a pin oak, Jake was swamped with memories. Standing out here in the early evening air, he could almost smell the vinegarish scent of chemicals, as if he were standing in his uncle's darkroom. But then the memory of how his photography came to an abrupt end also intruded, and he decided that was definitely enough nostalgia for one day.

He dragged his mind back to the present—and his breath hitched audibly as he caught the fading sunlight doing amazing things to LeAnne's hair. What he'd considered auburn before, he now realized was an incredible array of colors, from spun gold to wine red to gleaming mahogany.

She didn't seem to notice the hitch in his breathing. She held out her hand to him, the one with the leash in it.

He looked at it as if it were a poisonous snake. "Uh, do you think that's a good idea?"

Smiling, she said, "Yes. We're going to teach you and Muffin to trust each other."

Ha! He trusted Muffin about as much as he'd trust a tax return signed by Al Capone. And from the look on Muffin's face, he had the feeling Muffin shared the sentiment.

LeAnne said "Stay" to Muffin, then "Come here" to Jake. Both were ordered in a tone that brooked no argument, so both of them complied. Besides, being close to LeAnne was becoming more appealing by the second.

Reluctantly he took the leash from her hand. "What do you want me to do?"

"Let's start with basic commands. Ask him to S-I-T."

"Sit!" Jake barked.

Muffin stared at him blankly, as if he'd just spoken in Arabic.

LeAnne rolled her eyes. "I told you to *ask* him, not order him."

"I'm the master. He's the dog. He's *supposed* to obey orders."

"He's not going to obey animosity. Try to ask nicely."

Jake raised his eyes heavenward. "Muffin,"

63

he said in sickly sweet tone. "Would you do me the honor of plunking your butt down on the ground?"

Muffin snorted.

LeAnne hunkered down to get Muffin's attention. "Please, baby, a little cooperation here." She looked up, squinting against the setting sun. "Now ask nicely."

"Sit?"

Muffin glanced away, but then slowly, and ever so reluctantly, he sat.

This was a major victory, but Jake figured Muffin wouldn't appreciate his celebrating. Going with the flow, he leaned down and held out his hand. "Shake!" he commanded, then for good measure added, "Please?"

Muffin wouldn't look at him, but he obeyed.

Something yanked Jake's heart at the gesture. He couldn't figure out how such a small thing could affect him that way. Especially over a dog whose sole goal in life was to make Jake's life hell. But there it was. He glanced up and grinned with genuine pleasure. "*Now* we're getting somewhere!"

The pleased smile on LeAnne's face faded as her gaze dipped to his lips. Jake stood slowly, so as not to mess with her focus. The air suddenly sizzled around them. Awareness unlike anything he'd ever experienced spiked through every nerve ending Jake possessed.

Desperately, he wanted to reach out and

touch her soft-looking skin. His lips itched to cover hers.

And he might have tried to kiss her, too, if Muffin hadn't broken the spell with an indignant *yip, yip, yip, yip, yip* that Jake translated as "Don't even think about it."

LeAnne must have interpreted it the same way, because she took a jerky step back and yanked her gaze from his mouth.

Her hands fluttered as she glanced everywhere but in his direction. "Well," she said in a squeak, then cleared her throat. "Well, let's try some more advanced stuff."

Oh, he'd like to try some advances, all right. And he knew just which ones, too. But then he remembered she was temptation incarnate, and making advances on her wasn't good for his long-term goals. So he should actually be grateful to Muffin. Which made the fact that he'd like to muzzle the beast fathomless.

"Like what?" he asked, and in contrast to LeAnne's squeak, his voice sounded full of gravel.

"Hmmm," she said, still staring toward the pond. "How about we walk a bit and teach Muffin to heel?"

Just then a woman who looked remarkably like Carol Channing entered the clearing, walking a small brown-and-white mop. All hell broke loose. Muffin jumped about a foot in the air—another feat Jake had had no idea Muffin could pull off—then started running circles around Jake's ankles while making noises not of this earth, but which Jake figured constituted some kind of canine come-on.

Within a few seconds Muffin ran out of leash, because the entire thing was now hopelessly tangled around Jake's ankles. But that didn't deter Muffin, no, sir. He just kept trying to surge toward the little hairball, and with Muffin's strength, it was all Jake could do not to topple over. "Chill, dog!" he demanded, which—in the throes of puppy love—Muffin ignored entirely.

The object of Muffin's affection was doing a darn fine job of acting aloof, but her step got a little bouncier, which Jake figured was the equivalent of a human female adding a little more swing to her hips. It definitely said, "Catch me if you can, big boy."

"Hello, Mrs. Merriweather," LeAnne greeted warmly. "Hello, Dolly."

"Hello, Dolly?" Jake repeated stupidly. *A Carol Channing look-alike and she says, "Hello, Dolly?"*

Jake glanced at LeAnne while also trying to remain upright. "Does Mrs. Merriweather appreciate the irony?"

LeAnne shook her head. "Not a clue."

Okay, so this was the famous shih tzu, Dolly. Muffin had strange taste in females. Then again, Muffin seemed to have a crush on

LeAnne, too, which said there was hope for him yet.

Jake, on the other hand, was in dire straits. If he didn't get this leash untangled, he was going to fall flat on his nose. And he just knew Muffin wasn't about to cooperate. Thinking fast—if not well—Jake quickly unsnapped the leash from Muffin's collar, keeping a tight hold on the collar, lest Muffin lovingly attack the woman's beribboned dog and begin the process of producing little bull-shihtz.

He started to unravel the leash, but then Muffin surged forward again and he lost his balance—and his hold on Muffin's collar. He fell hard on his side and a twig dug into his rib. Before he could even get out an "oomph!" Muffin was off like a heat-seeking missile.

Surprisingly, LeAnne stood serene, a fond smile on her face, making no move to stop the dog. Jake looked over to find that once freed, Muffin regained some semblance of dignity. He came to a halt in front of Dolly, and they touched noses, kind of Eskimo-style. And Carol Channing didn't look upset, either, which said a crisis probably wasn't impending.

Jake sat up, biting back the slew of epithets that were threatening to spill from his lips. He had just finished untangling the leash when out of nowhere a Frisbee sailed over their heads, straight into the center of the pond.

He understood Muffin's intent one split second before the dog took off again like a runaway train. The damn dog wanted to show off for his woman.

"Muffin, get your ass back here!" he yelled, which apparently wasn't in the dog's repertoire of acceptable commands, because Muffin didn't even slow down.

As he scrambled to his feet, Jake watched in horror as Muffin sailed headlong into the water. Oh, great, just what he needed—Muffin sinking like a stone and Jake's inheritance of that cabin sinking with him.

Jake didn't stop to think. He chased the damn mutt and dove in after him. He gasped as he hit the water, which because of the unusually cool weather was maybe a degree or two above ice-cube temperature.

When he surfaced, two things hit him right away: One, it was almost worth letting the damn mutt drown, because he was more trouble than *any* piece of property was worth. And two, he wasn't losing that property anytime soon, because Muffin could swim like a champ.

"Why d-didn't you t-tell me M-Mark Spitz-tzu here c-could swim?" Jake said, standing just inside the door to his bungalow, dripping and shivering.

LeAnne turned off the air-conditioning, then went and pulled several towels from the rack in the bathroom and returned to the front hall. "I tried. You were too busy playing superhero and weren't paying attention."

He actually looked adorable standing there soaking wet, water droplets meandering down his strong cheeks and lingering on his chin. His hair was spiked wildly, which was also rather cute. He looked like Alfalfa on a bad-hair day.

Only LeAnne never remembered Alfalfa having such a wonderfully broad chest, clearly outlined by the cotton polo shirt plastered to it, defining every muscle the man possessed. And boy, oh, boy, he possessed a lot of them.

A wet ring was forming on the carpet at his feet, so LeAnne laid down a towel and said, "Stand on this."

Dutifully he stepped forward, still shivering. Pointing toward Muffin's bed, where Muffin had calmly headed when they entered the bungalow, he said, "Why isn't that m-mutt fr-freezing, too?"

"He's not wearing soaking clothes. Speaking of which, neither should you."

"Oooh, Dr. C-Crosby! You've known me one day and already you're t-trying to g-get me naked."

LeAnne bit her tongue. She had to remember that this man was miserably cold. She also had to remember that there wasn't a bit of truth to his words. Well, maybe a bit, but not a lot. After all, who wouldn't want to see a handsome man in all his naked glory? Strictly human nature.

And the way his khaki pants were sticking to his lower half like skin was rather revealing, too. He had powerful thighs. Not only that, but weren't men drenched in cold water supposed to *shrink* in places? If that was him shrunken, she'd hate to see the man aroused. Well, technically she wouldn't exactly *hate* it.

Irritated at her own train of thought, she shoved the other two towels at him and said, "Get out of those clothes. Take a hot shower."

He looked as if he wanted to protest for a moment, but then with a final full-body shudder, he stepped past her and into the bathroom. "Wanna share? I'll let you scrub my back."

"Tempting," she said, hoping she sounded more sarcastic than she felt. "Truly tempting. But I think I'll pass."

"Darn," he said, before closing the door in her face.

LeAnne was left standing there, wondering what the man would do if she *did* slip in and join him. Most likely call the police and have her arrested.

She thought about leaving, but figured she still owed him. Why she owed him, she didn't know. After all, she'd *tried* to stop him from diving into that pond, but he'd been in a panic. Which was a pretty good sign for the future of his and Muffin's relationship, even if he'd been more worried about the will than the dog. That type of blind heroism deserved a reward.

With that in mind she turned, moved to the bed, and picked up the phone.

* * *

The hot shower helped warm Jake's skin, but he still felt a chill inside, and the cause irritated him. He'd actually been terrified for the damn mutt, and that was almost unforgivable. He refused to care about the wrinkly little beast, especially since that wrinkly little beast was doing everything in his power to make him look like a fool. And he didn't like looking like a fool in front of the good doctor.

Although he had to admit that it had felt *really* good when Muffin had obeyed his commands. He hadn't thought he'd be so proud to feel that paw laid in his outstretched hand. He'd like to write it off as finally taking control of the ornery creature, but he had to concede that it had been more than that. Exactly what, he couldn't say. It was new. It was foreign. But it sure felt good.

Jake turned off the faucet and stepped out of the shower. He scrubbed his head and body with the soft cotton towel, then wrapped it around his hips. Since his brush was still in his duffel bag, he finger-combed his hair, then walked out into the bungalow.

And stopped dead.

He'd assumed LeAnne would have left by now. He sure as heck hadn't expected to find her sitting on the floor beside Muffin's bed, giving Muffin what looked like a massage. He was mesmerized by the way her fingers moved over the animal, and all he could do was stare and feel really, really jealous of a dog.

71

She glanced up with a smile, but it died a quick death and her eyes nearly popped out of her head. Thank goodness he'd covered his lower half, or she'd *really* grab an eyeful.

The thought of that actually made his groin tingle, and not unpleasantly. He shot the woman—who was swallowing convulsively—a lopsided grin. "Oops!"

"I . . . I . . ."

"Apparently forgot that I don't keep my clothes in the bathroom."

"I . . . I'm sorry! I'll leave. I . . . was just waiting for . . . for room service."

That stopped him. "Room service? I didn't order room service."

She was intently studying a spot on the wall over his left shoulder. "No . . . I did. For you. Something to warm you. To make up for . . ." Her voice trailed off, as she apparently had run out of her store of fragmented sentences.

She looked incredibly tempting with bright red spots of embarrassment staining her cheeks and throat. And those guinea pigs had to be taking the greatest ride of their lives, the way her breasts were rising and falling, as if she'd been holding her breath for a week, and now badly needed to fill her lungs.

Realizing that if she peeked lower, she'd catch some major proof of just how tempting he found her, he moved to the dresser to pull out a change of clothing. Then it occurred to him he didn't *have* a change of clothing. And he didn't think she'd appreciate his wearing merely a gun and a leather holster.

"Oh, boy," he muttered. "I'd get decent real fast, except I don't have any clothes."

"No clothes?" she said in a squeak.

"Travel accident. All my clothes are at the spa laundry."

Her hand went to her heart, as if trying to contain it inside her chest. He wouldn't mind replacing her hand with his, but he was afraid his towel would suddenly take on the dimensions of a tent.

"You . . . uh . . . are injured," she murmured.

"Huh?"

Without tearing her gaze from the wall, she pointed vaguely at him. "You . . . have a cut on your . . . umm . . . ribs."

He glanced down and for the first time noticed that the twig he'd fallen on had indeed broken skin. He'd known it hurt, but he hadn't realized it had drawn blood. Now suddenly it hurt a little more, but of course he wasn't about to admit it. "It's just a scratch."

"You should disinfect it. I'll be sure to have"—she waved—"someone deliver"—she gulped—"something for it."

"Nah, no big deal." Besides, disinfecting it sounded more painful than the actual scratch. He wasn't into pain as a rule.

"I . . . guess I should go," she said, inching

toward the door while determinedly avoiding his person. "Just . . . just tell whoever delivers the brandy to . . . charge it to me."

"Brandy?" Jake said, reaching out to stop her. "You ordered brandy for us?"

She stared down at his fingers, wrapped around her upper arm. "Umm, no, just for you. I . . . don't care for brandy."

Jake almost didn't hear her, because he was so busy enjoying the petal softness of her skin.

"Stay anyway," he coaxed. "You know what they say about drinking alone. I'd worry myself."

"I told you," she said, disengaging herself from his grasp, "I don't like brandy."

"What do you like?" he asked, and had an insane desire to hear her say, "you."

"Well, I like wine."

Not exactly "you," but he could work with that. "Let me put on a robe and you call room service back and order wine, too." She didn't look all that excited by the proposition, so he added, not the least bit ashamed at playing the guilt card, "It's the least you can do for not stopping me from taking a header into that pond."

"I *did* try to stop you, dummy!"

"Not hard enough. Please stay." He didn't want to analyze why it was important to him, so he didn't.

She hesitated a beat, then nodded. "All right."

Before she could change her mind, he whirled to the bathroom. "Be right back."

As he dropped the towel and grabbed the robe from the door hook, he kept an ear tuned to LeAnne's soft voice, but couldn't make out what she was saying. Damn, her voice was as pretty as she was.

It didn't surprise Jake that he was attracted to the good doctor. A guy would have to have no pulse to be immune to her. But it sure did aggravate him, because she was playing havoc with his head.

Picking up his pond scum–soaked clothes and the towel, he left the bathroom and found LeAnne doing that massage thing again. Muffin had an ecstatic look on his homely face. Ecstasy didn't do much to a bulldog face. Although he realized he was beginning to see the appeal of butt-ugly to a bulldog owner. You got used to it, kind of like homicide cops got used to dead bodies.

LeAnne looked up, and when she saw his robed self, a relieved smile lit up her face. Relief definitely looked good on her, except that it was somewhat irritating. He would have preferred disappointment.

"The refreshments are on the way," LeAnne said, giving Muffin a final stroke and gliding gracefully to her feet.

Muffin glanced up, disappointed. Then he summoned the energy to turn his head and glare at Jake.

Jake held out his hands, innocent. "Hey, it's not *my* fault she stopped petting you!"

Muffin snorted.

"You know," Jake complained to LeAnne, dropping the towel on the carpet, then the wet clothes on top of it, "I'm getting a little tired of him blaming me for all his supposed misery. I'm *not* the bad guy, here!"

"If you'd R-E-S-P-E-C-T him a little more, he'd come around."

"Thank you, Aretha."

LeAnne grinned and Jake's brain blinked off. Right now he didn't think he could spell the word *cat*.

This woman was worse than dangerous. She was lethal. Not wanting to die anytime soon, Jake dragged his gaze from that smile and focused on something less tempting. Muffin.

"How . . ." he began, then cleared his throat. "How do you propose I go about showing him you-know-what?"

"How about sitting down on the floor with me and petting him? My guess is he's been starved for human touch."

Getting down on the floor with LeAnne sounded like an excellent suggestion. So did petting. But nowhere in that scenario did he envision Muffin.

He searched for a valid excuse not to do it, but was saved from that overly taxing brain activity by a knock at the door. "I'll get it!" he said a little too quickly. Then he realized how dumb that sounded since it was his and Muffin's bungalow, and as far as he knew, Muffin hadn't learned to answer the door yet.

Naturally, it was Buzz. But he wasn't wearing his laundry hat this time. This time he was Mr. Room Service.

Jake stepped back. "Are you sure there aren't five of you?"

Buzz offered his wide, dazzling smile. "I like to keep busy." He carried a large tray laden with goodies into the suite and set it on the table in the corner. LeAnne hadn't just ordered booze. There was a large bowl of iced shrimp cocktail, an antipasto platter, and several types of gourmet crackers and party bread.

An unopened pint of Courvoisier and a brandy snifter sat beside a bottle of Napa Valley cabernet sauvignon and a wine goblet.

And beside all that was an ominous-looking bottle labeled Betadine, and a box of bandages.

Muffin had worked up the energy to jump to his feet and trot over to Buzz, his stumpy tail wagging and his ears cocked back with excitement. After arranging everything just so on the table, Buzz bent and rubbed his big paw of a hand over Muffin's wrinkled head. It was a testament to the size of the man that his hand could span Muffin's entire forehead.

"You worried I wouldn't bring something for you, my man?" Buzz said, then pulled a dog bone from his pocket. "Ol' Buzz never forgets his friends."

Muffin gave Buzz a look that said, "If you were a female shih tzu, I'd marry you." He accepted the bone and headed back to his bed and heart blanket.

"Thank you, Buzz," LeAnne said. She grabbed the chit and pen on the tray and quickly added a tip, then signed her name before Jake could protest.

And why should he protest, anyway? He considered himself an enlightened man of the new millennium. Nothing wrong with a woman treating him to fine liquor and finger food. Especially a beautiful woman.

Except that Buzz was suddenly assessing the situation—Jake could tell by the worried light that entered the man's brown eyes as he took in the entire picture. Cozy suite. Liquor. Finger food. Big bad man in bathrobe.

To alleviate Buzz's fears—and to make certain he didn't find himself at the wrong end of those meaty fists—Jake moved to the pile of clothes and picked them up. "Could I ask you to add this to all my other clothes at the laundry?" he asked. "I . . . sort of had an accident."

Buzz took them, and his eyebrows hiked. "Didja fall into the pool?"

"Something like that." He held out his arms. "At the moment, I don't have a thing to wear."

Buzz didn't appear all that appeased by the explanation, but he nodded. "I'll get your clothes back the second they're out of the dryer."

I'll bet. Jake figured Buzz's next order of business was to go harass the dryer into working harder.

Before he took his leave, Buzz addressed LeAnne. "You need anything, *anything,* you just give me a ring, you hear?"

LeAnne smiled. "We're fine."

"I'll be just a page away," Buzz added. "I'm just going to head on up to the hotel and share a cold one with a few of my old buddies from the state pen." He said this, of course, with his wicked gleam directed straight at Jake. With a last pointed glare that said LeAnne had better *stay* fine, Buzz took his leave.

Besides Muffin, busily gnawing on another bone, that left Jake and LeAnne alone once again, staring at each other across the span of the room, a king-size bed between them.

He didn't know how LeAnne felt about this fact, because her eyes gave nothing away. But he was acutely aware of how his body felt about it. His traitorous body, which was anticipating something that should never happen.

"Buzz is an ex-con?" he asked, one eyebrow raised.

LeAnne waved. "He's exaggerating. He spent *one* night in a county jail."

"Uh-huh. For what?"

"It was just a little misunderstanding."

"What kind of little misunderstanding?"

79

"He didn't like the guy his sister was dating, so he just wanted to warn him off."

Jake folded his arms over his chest. "And just how did he go about warning him off?" He figured forewarned was forearmed.

"Well, the police called it simple assault, but really, it was harmless."

"What?"

"He dumped fire ants down the man's pants."

Jake waited for the punch line. None came. "Ouch," he said, and the sudden tingle in his groin had nothing to do with the beautiful woman alone with him.

LeAnne pulled a bandage from the box, picked up the Betadine, then seemed to assess the situation. If she forced him to open his robe, it just might reveal a whole lot more than she needed to see. She took his arm and dragged him to the bathroom. "Go in there and apply some of this to the cut."

He frowned. "Is it gonna sting?"

"If it does, I'll be the second one to know."

How comforting. "I don't think so."

"I do."

"I'm a great natural healer."

She rolled her eyes. "Don't be a baby!"

He took exception to that. "I'm *not* being a baby. I just like to let my body do the healing."

"Look, you *baby*, you got hurt on *my* premises. What if it gets horribly infected and you get sick and die on me? I'd feel real guilty."

"I absolve you of all guilt."

She shoved him into the bathroom. "Put it on, *now*."

Jake swore under his breath, but dutifully he closed the door. He waited a couple of heartbeats, then opened his robe and applied the bandage without disinfectant.

"Did you put it on?" she called through the door.

He grunted noncommittally, hoping she'd take that for assent.

"What color did it turn your skin?" she asked, her voice filled with suspicion.

He swore and peered into the bottle. "Brown."

"Wrong answer. It turns the skin yellow. Put some on."

"I'm color-blind."

"I doubt it. But you sure are a lousy liar. Put it on."

Man, she was a pain in the butt! Swearing some more, he pulled the bandage half-off, then tentatively touched the applicator to the top edge of the cut. "Ouch! Shit!"

"Apparently it stings. Good boy. Now cover the entire cut."

He gritted his teeth against the sting and a slew of retorts he wanted to fling at her, but did as she asked, waved his hand frantically in front of the wound, then reapplied the bandage.

After closing his robe he threw open the door

81

and glared at her. "Revenge will be sweet," he threatened.

She grinned. "I'm shaking in my sneakers." She pointed at the tray. "Drink?"

"Oh, yeah," Jake answered. "Make it a double."

Chapter Four

The night was balmy, abundant with stars, and a brilliant half-moon hung low in the sky. The air smelled faintly of roses, although there didn't seem to be any in sight.

Jake and LeAnne were sitting in lawn chairs on his small back porch, while Muffin snoozed near LeAnne's feet.

On his third snifter of cognac, Jake was feeling relaxed and back in power over the temptation LeAnne presented. Probably because he was doing a fairly good job of ignoring her gorgeous bare legs and luscious lips.

He couldn't avoid her soft, sultry voice, but the conversation so far had been rather easy and impersonal, so that didn't present too much of a problem.

"How did you get into this line of work?" he asked her, and found he was truly curious.

LeAnne topped off her wine and took a sip before answering. "It's kind of a long story."

"I've got no plans."

"Well, when I was ten, we had a golden retriever named Bruiser. The name was a joke, because Bruiser had to be the biggest coward of a dog I've ever met. He was even scared of chipmunks." She laughed softly, and the sound worked its way down Jake's torso. "My brother and Bruiser were out hiking one day, when they accidentally came upon a black bear mama and her cubs."

"Uh-oh." From Jake's nature walks with his uncle, he knew just how dangerous that situation could be. His uncle had taught him to track deer, elk, raccoons, the works. But whenever they came upon bear tracks, his uncle would immediately make them change course.

"No kidding," LeAnne said, and her voice turned sad. "Bruiser could have easily run away from that furious bear, and if he'd been alone, he probably would have done exactly that. But he knew that Drew couldn't outrun the bear. So he placed himself between the bear and Drew, and he barked furiously. Drew ran home to get our father. By the time they got back, the bear was gone, and Bruiser was critically injured."

"Oh, no. Please tell me Bruiser survived."

She looked over at him then, and smiled. "Why, Mr. Donnelly, I'm shocked. You, the big, bad FBI spy and adamant canine detractor, rooting for the dog?"

"Hey! I don't dislike dogs!"

Even in his sleep, Muffin snorted.

Jake scowled at him. "Well, not *all* dogs. And I'm not a spy." He squelched the niggling guilt over investigating her. "So, did Bruiser make it?"

LeAnne nodded. "Yes. He was in surgery for several hours and it took some three months before he was back to normal, but he made it, and lived to the ripe old age of fifteen."

Jake was a little confounded by the relief he felt at that news. After all, what did he care? Worse, he found himself hoping Muffin lasted that long, too, although from all he'd read on the breed, the typical life span didn't extend much beyond ten years. He was in real trouble if he was starting to worry about Muffin's health already. He shook his head. He didn't want to think about that. "So how did that affect your career choice?"

"While we waited for word on Bruiser, I made a pact with God. I told Him that if He let Bruiser live, I'd devote my life to animals."

"Why not become a vet?"

"I faint at the sight of blood," she said, a rueful grin on her face. "Besides, I was fascinated that Bruiser ignored all of his strong self-preservation instincts in the face of danger to his owner. I wanted to study what made animals tick up here," she said, tapping her temple.

Jake found himself stupidly touched by the story—so much so that animal psychology had begun to sound like a legitimate profession. Which made no sense, because he didn't even believe in people psychology. He figured you were a good or bad person who made either good choices or bad choices, and that pretty much defined your life.

His father: bad person, bad choices. His mother: good person, bad choices. Aunt Sophie: good person, good choices. Jake glanced down at his aunt's dog. Well, *mostly* good choices.

The problem here was that he'd come to Happy Hounds *expecting* to find a bad person. And, unfortunately, his instincts were telling him she had *good* written all over that pretty face and body of hers. "Do you really think you can delve into the minds of animals?"

"Absolutely."

"I have to tell you, it sounds awfully wacko to me."

"You're not the first skeptic I've run across, Agent Donnelly."

Jake thought this was as good a time as any to ask where she got the money for Happy Hounds, but he couldn't think of a tactful way to bring the subject up. *What the hell?* He'd give it a shot. "Did you build this place from scratch?"

"Most of it. Some of it was already here, like the golf and tennis courts."

His eyebrows arrowed downward. "This was once a country club?"

She chuckled, then sipped some more wine. After which, she licked her lips. Slowly. "I guess you could say that. This was once the site of a minimum-security prison."

Whoa! "How did you know that's what they're called?" he asked, trying to keep the suspicion out of his voice.

"What what are called?"

"Minimum-security prisons. How did you know they call them country clubs?"

"Oh, they do? I *didn't* know that. But any prison that offers golf and tennis to its invited guests isn't exactly Alcatraz."

Sounded plausible. But this was still another point of interest to pass on to Mark to check out. Like why the prison was no longer in existence. And how LeAnne got her hands on the property. And whether she got the land for a song, considering its history.

"May I use your bathroom?" she said, jerking him out of his musing.

"By all means," Jake said, standing. He held out his hand to help her to her feet, and she hesitated a moment before accepting his assistance.

Her palm was so small and soft, it caused a squishy feeling deep in Jake's chest, for reasons unknown.

Without consciously thinking about it, Jake pulled her harder than was clearly necessary, bringing her flush against his body. The wine in her hand sloshed a little, but she didn't seem to notice. She was too busy staring up at him with huge, startled eyes.

And he was acutely aware that he was naked as a jaybird beneath the thick terry robe. Not thick enough that he couldn't feel her breasts pressed to his ribs, however. Or her hips against his upper thighs. Or—

Jake stepped back before he bared all his secrets, so to speak.

The relief that washed over her features annoyed him unreasonably. He wasn't a braggart by nature, but he *did* acknowledge and appreciate that women tended to like him. A lot. And want to get close to him. Real close.

But this lady had looked as if she thought she was facing a boa or something, and was preparing for its death grip to encircle her pretty little throat.

"I . . . uh . . ." she stammered, while wine still dripped from her hand.

Some demon took over Jake's good sense. He took the goblet from her hand, then grasped her wrist and brought it right up to his mouth. "Uh-oh, you spilled," he said softly. Before she could yank herself from his grasp, he swiped his tongue along her knuckles.

She gasped softly, but didn't pull back—just stared at him as if he were a mental patient. And at the moment he was likely a very good candidate, because the taste of wine on her hand was delicious, but he had the feeling it would taste a whole hell of a lot better on her lips.

LeAnne had the feeling she should be protesting—screaming like a banshee and kicking this man in the shins, at the very least. But as she watched smoke settle into his blue, burning eyes, she couldn't even manage a squeak of indignation.

He was dangerous. Big and sarcastic and potentially lethal. But he exuded a brutally savage sex appeal that she found very enticing. Which made not a lick of sense. He wasn't her type. She liked quiet, bookish men. Nonthreatening, thoughtful, sensitive. *Boring!* her mind whispered, even though she tried to quash the thought.

When he lifted his head, his gaze slid from her hand to her lips to the wineglass and back to her lips. And she knew his intention before he made a move.

In horrid fascination she watched as he dipped his thumb into her glass and wet it with wine. Then he smiled and lifted his hand to her mouth, his damp thumb rubbing first across her bottom lip, then the top. "Bet you taste like heaven, darlin'," he whispered.

Definitely, she should be protesting. But somehow her vocal cords had frozen—completely in contrast to the rest of her. A warm, fuzzy feeling was seeping into every molecule of her body.

"Is it a good year?" he inquired in a silky voice.

"What?" she said in a croak.

"The wine. Is it a good year?"

Taste for yourself were the first words that popped into her head, so she pressed her lips together to keep them from escaping. That just managed to make her damp lips tingle, so without thinking about it, she poked her tongue out and swiped it across them.

Bad move. His eyes followed her tongue with a burning hunger that threatened to singe her. She couldn't remember the last time a man had looked at her with such feverish intensity, if one ever had. Stephen certainly had never displayed such passion, except those times he was angry and accusing her of one ludicrous affair or another.

His thumb again dipped into the burgundy liquid; then instead of bringing it to her lips, he brought it to his own. With a sensuality that felt like a bomb going off in her lower belly, his tongue tipped out and slid along the pad of his thumb. "Mmm, I'd say a *very* good year."

LeAnne was mesmerized, totally bamboozled. Her lips parted and her breathing started sounding a little choppy in her ears. She was helpless to do anything but stare as for the third time the man dipped his digit in her goblet, resurfacing with a glistening droplet of liquid.

"Your turn," he said in a growl, then laid the pad directly on her lower lip. Without thinking about it, she slid her lips over his thumb, surrounding it and sucking it into her mouth knuckle-deep.

"Ah." He moaned, his eyes hooding a bit, a muscle in his jaw spasming.

Emboldened, LeAnne swirled the tip of her tongue in circles, then applied some suction.

"Damn," he whispered, bending and setting the goblet on the table. He pulled his thumb from her mouth, and for some reason she felt the loss.

He was going to kiss her. No doubt about it. And she was going to let him. No doubt about that, either. She wanted those hard lips moving over hers, molding, shaping, pillaging. She didn't think she'd ever wanted to be pillaged before.

Her eyes fluttered closed in anticipation, and she felt his warm, wine-tinged breath feather over her lips. Her heart was pumping double-time, and her nerves were strung tight, but not in a bad way. She was more than ready to find out what it was like to kiss Aunt Sophie's big, bad nephew.

She could smell him. His scent was a combination of fresh soap and man. No aftershave, but that wasn't surprising, considering he hadn't shaved again after taking the swim in the pond, if the stubble on his face was any indication.

"Nice," she whispered involuntarily.

A whining growl sounded, and LeAnne's eyes flew open, as she'd never quite heard a man make such a noise in the throes of potential passion. But then she saw Jake's eyes widen, too, staring at her as if she'd done it.

"Not me," she choked out.

"Me either," he said.

They both glanced down to the ground, and sure enough Muffin was baring his teeth in patent disapproval.

Jake responded with a manly growl. "Back off, buddy. You didn't see me giving you grief about nosing it up with Dolly, did you?"

Muffin snorted.

"How would *you* feel if I got in the way whenever you run across her moppy little butt the rest of this trip?"

Muffin's fierce scowl collapsed, and he picked himself up and trotted out into the yard, apparently deciding that giving them privacy was the more prudent move on his part.

Jake's jaw dropped a little. "What do you know, blackmail works."

She *tsk*ed at him. "But it's not a real sound way to build a relationship."

Jake shrugged irritably, but then his gaze fastened on her lips again.

The encounter with Muffin had given LeAnne just enough time to have second thoughts. Unfortunately, her second thoughts were just like her first thoughts. She really, really wanted to know how it felt to be kissed by this man.

But she had another pressing problem at the moment, having to do with her bladder. She didn't think she wanted it distracting her, lessening her probable enjoyment of the kiss.

"Umm, I could really use that bathroom now," she said.

He frowned. "Oh, yeah. Sorry about that. Somehow it slipped my mind."

"Mine, too," she admitted with a smile, just so he wouldn't make the mistake of thinking she was coming up with an excuse to extricate herself from the situation. Which was really a confounding thought. This was not like her at all. She hadn't felt this giddiness and anticipation since Danny Rae Josephson had trapped her under the football bleachers in eleventh grade.

She wondered if she was just deprived, or if she had developed a fondness for kissing any man just because he was good-looking. Otherwise, her attraction to him made no sense whatsoever. She didn't even think she *liked* the guy.

Jake slipped the sliding glass door open, then raised his arm high against the edge, giving her a tunnel to travel under into his room. She smiled her thanks, then sailed right in.

Disappointment was a sour thing in Jake's gut at the moment, but only because he wanted to kiss her *now*. Still, her acquiescence, her seeming willingness to let him taste her, was a heady intoxicant. She had lips sculpted in heaven, and soulful doe brown eyes that quietly whispered "yes."

He whistled, then picked up his cognac and sipped. This two-week vacation was looking up in a big way. With any luck, he and the good doctor would have a couple of weeks to enjoy one another's company before he headed on back to his normal life.

He glanced out to the yard and saw Muffin eyeing him balefully. Jake sighed. "Come here, Muffin." When Muffin just sat there, he added, "Please?"

Muffin hesitated a moment, then shuffled over to him. Jake was so damn thrilled by the concession, he stepped into the suite and grabbed several crackers from the leftover snack plates.

Back out on the deck, he hunkered down and gave Muffin one. While Muffin chewed, he said, "Look, I appreciate your being protective of Dr. Crosby and all. I really do. Don't blame you a bit. But hey, there's just us guys here. You gotta admit she's one beautiful lady."

Muffin did not snort at him.

Jake nodded. "Yep, she sure is, just like your Dolly there. And I'm just as attracted to her as you are to Dolly. So could you just give us some space to get to know each other?"

Muffin sighed, then glanced away.

Jake said, "I'll treat her right, I promise. I won't do anything she doesn't want me to do."

Muffin yipped.

Jake couldn't believe how much such a little thing meant to him. And especially from the infuriating mutt. But he couldn't stop the grin that exploded on his face, and impulsively he scratched Muffin behind the ear. The dog's eyes went wide, but after a stiff moment, he leaned his basketball-size head into Jake's hand. And another brick fell off the wall around Jake's heart.

Which made his voice a little gruff when he said, "You just let luscious LeAnne and me enjoy time together in peace, and I'll make sure you get the same with Dolly. Understand?"

Muffin yipped.

Jake fed him a cracker. "Hey, maybe we can even compare notes later. You know, guy talk."

Muffin woofed.

Jake handed over another cracker. "Maybe between the two of us we can figure out how chicks' minds work." He stood up, all tied up in knots of strange and foreign emotions. "I got a couple more," he said, showing Muffin the two crackers left in his hand. "Wanna sit?"

Muffin sat. Jake grinned and fed him.

Trish Jensen

"And let's shake hands and seal a man pact."
Muffin offered his paw.

Jake handed Muffin the last cracker, feeling
high as a kite, when he turned to pick up his
snifter . . . and encountered "luscious LeAnne"
standing in the doorway, her eyebrows raised,
her arms crossed.

"Uh-oh," he mumbled.

Chapter Five

"Chicks?" LeAnne tried to sound irritated, even as she fought not to burst out laughing. She hadn't overheard the entire conversation, but enough to get the gist. Muffin and Jake were engaged in meaningful negotiations. A very promising step forward.

"Did I say chicks?" Jake said, going for the innocent look.

LeAnne glanced down at Muffin, who was also trying his best to appear angelic. Both males failed miserably.

"I could swear I didn't use the word *chicks*," Jake added. "I'm much more enlightened than that."

"Really?" LeAnne said. "Enlightened males make 'man pacts'?"

97

"You know, it's not nice to eavesdrop."

LeAnne grinned. "This from an FBI spy."

"I am *not* a spy."

She knew that. But it was fun to rib him just the same. He looked so adorable yet sexy at the same time, standing barefoot in that robe. LeAnne hadn't realized the potential sensuality of men's feet before. Either she was losing her mind, or Jake Donnelly had extremely sexy feet.

His lips were gorgeous, too. And she'd really like to resume where they'd left off, but she was somewhat at a loss how to do it. Not only that, but knowing that Muffin was willing to give them privacy now so they could get on with the kissing was almost embarrassing.

Realizing the mood had somehow been broken, she shoved her hands into her shorts pockets. "Well, I suppose it's time to head out."

"But you didn't finish your wine!" Jake said, practically lunging for her wineglass on the table. He turned and she saw a desperate light in his eyes that was really cute, too.

"If I drink any more wine, you're going to have to carry me back to my bungalow."

"I'm not averse to that."

LeAnne laughed. "I'm heavier than I look."

He swept his gaze up and down her skeptically, then offered, "Why don't we put it to a test?"

Oh, yeah, she'd had just enough wine to

make the prospect of jumping into his arms a very appealing idea. Which was amazing to LeAnne. Where had this wild side come from? She'd never considered having a loveless affair in her life. And here she was, more than considering it. She was actually *craving* it.

But that kind of decision was best not made with a head fuzzed by two plus glasses of wine. She opened her mouth to tell him exactly that, but was prevented by a knock at his door.

Jake frowned. "Buzz has some god-awful timing."

"Depending on your point of view," LeAnne countered.

Muffin trotted right past them on chubby little legs. Then Jake waved LeAnne through the sliding glass door, and followed. He strode fairly swiftly to the door, probably worried that Buzz would break in with guns blazing if he didn't open up in a timely manner.

It was true that Buzz was overly protective of not only LeAnne, but *all* of the female employees at Happy Hounds. Though he was one of the gentlest men LeAnne had ever known, he also knew how to subtly intimidate any forward guests or male employees.

Last year a guest named Bernard Simpson had developed an unhealthy crush on one of LeAnne's dog trainers—unhealthy mostly because they doubted Mrs. Bernard Simpson—who was visiting her sister in Poughkeepsie—would approve.

Buzz had made it a point to be in the vicinity whenever Bernard Simpson took his two Dalmatians to training classes. Then one day he followed Simpson into the woods when the man was walking his dogs alone. They got to chatting, and Buzz "accidentally" let it slip that the trainer's boyfriend was a famous professional wrestler with the name Death Wish, who had a nasty habit of breaking opponents' bones.

Bernard Simpson lost interest. Fast.

So it didn't surprise LeAnne when Buzz barreled his way into the suite the moment the door opened and gave everything—the bed, the tray of food and drink, and LeAnne—the eagle eye.

Apparently satisfied, he dumped a basket of laundry on the bed and flashed his glittery smile at Jake. "All done," he boomed. "You can get dressed now."

Okay, so sometimes Buzz wasn't all that subtle.

Jake rolled his eyes as he rooted through his neatly folded clothes. He pulled out a pair of underwear—colored Jockeys, LeAnne noted with more interest than was probably proper—a blue shirt that would likely do amazing things to the man's eyes, and khaki chinos. "I'll just go change," he said.

"Want me to walk you back to your bungalow?" Buzz asked LeAnne quickly.

"No, that's all right," Jake said just as fast. "I'll just dress in the bathroom."

No matter how interested LeAnne was in seeing what those chinos did to Jake Donnelly's backside, she shook her head. "It's getting late. Besides, I have something I need to discuss with Buzz anyway."

Jake actually looked disappointed, much to LeAnne's amusement.

"Are you finished with this?" Buzz asked, waving at the tray.

"Yeah, sure," Jake mumbled.

"Leave the cognac," LeAnne said.

"Do I need to worry about that guy?" Buzz asked as they made their way up the walk toward LeAnne's bungalow.

No, but I think I might need to. "No, I don't think so. He seems nice enough."

"He didn't try to get fresh or nothing, did he?"

Hmmm, how to answer that? "He didn't do anything I didn't want him to."

Buzz's step faltered a bit. "Well, now, okay, but he gets out of line, he answers to ol' Buzz."

LeAnne decided to change the topic, fast. "You *do* remember that Muffin's birthday is Thursday, right?"

"Sure thing."

"Got everything arranged?"

"Ten-four. Does the man know?"

"No. I'm not sure he'd show up."

* * *

Jake lay sprawled out on the bed, engaging in the time-honored male ritual of channel surfing. Nothing could grab his attention. His thoughts, all of them, were focused on one very beautiful quack.

He considered himself fairly savvy when it came to the opposite sex. So he was pretty certain that his attraction to LeAnne wasn't just running one way. The problem was, how intelligent would it be to pursue it? And would his attraction cloud his judgment about whether this place and its owner were legit?

Rationalizing that he'd done his duty by calling Mark and telling him to gather information on the background of this prison-turned-resort, Jake settled on a baseball game, but even though he'd loved baseball all his life, the game couldn't distract him.

Hearing a rustling sound to his left, he glanced over. Muffin was standing with his front paws on top of the bed, his heart blanket dangling from his mouth.

"You have got to be kidding me. You think I'm going to invite a fleabag like you up onto this bed?"

Muffin's woof was a little muffled by the blanket.

Jake scowled at him. "Give me one good reason why I'd want to do that."

Muffin's stub of a tail started jiggling.

Rolling his eyes, Jake said in a growl, "Fine. But you're not sleeping up here all night. Just till the baseball game's over, got it?"

Muffin yipped.

Jake patted the bed. "Fine, get up here already. But don't get too comfortable."

Muffin jumped up, not all that gracefully, but he managed to make it, blanket in tow. Delicately he dropped his blanket, then stood there expectantly.

Jake scowled at him again, but spread out the blanket. When Muffin was satisfied, he turned three times before plopping his wrinkly butt down. He made a big production of getting comfortable, to Jake's way of thinking. He sat there staring at Jake, more expectation written on his homely features.

"What?"

Muffin emitted a low whine.

"Jeez," Jake said, then switched the remote to the other hand and began scratching behind Muffin's ears.

The dog immediately got into it, leaning this way and that to direct the scratching exactly where he wanted it.

By the ecstatic look on his face, Jake figured LeAnne had been right: Muffin had been starved for physical contact. A twinge of guilt bit into Jake for having deprived the dog for so long. Aunt Sophie had probably petted the mutt constantly.

"I'm sorry about that," he said aloud. "You

just have to understand that I'm not used to this dog-owning business."

Muffin growled.

"I don't mean owning!" he quickly amended. "Umm, cohabiting. I'm not used to cohabiting." He dropped the remote and reached over to the side table for his can of apple juice. As he sipped, a horrible thought occurred to him: if he and Muffin reached a truce, they'd have no reason for a dog shrink.

That was not good.

"Listen, Muffin, let's make another pact."

Muffin's ears perked up.

"Let's not let on right away that we're . . . you know . . . getting along a little better. Not in front of LeAnne, anyway." When Muffin cocked his head, Jake added, "You know, let's make sure she thinks we still need,"—he paused— "you know, counseling or help or whatever she gives." When Muffin looked skeptical, he added, "That way we get to go on more walks with her. We get to run into Dolly more often. Get my drift?"

Muffin immediately agreed.

Jake nodded. "So we're going to have to act sort of like we still don't like each other very much. You know I won't mean it, though, right?"

Muffin barked, which strangely felt so satisfying, he added a bone, so to speak. "And if we pull this off, I'll make sure to try to find out when Dolly's getting her manicures and massages and stuff, and try to time it so you get them then, too."

Muffin yipped.

"But one more stipulation. When we're out with LeAnne, you make sure not to give me any shit about . . . touching her or . . . anything."

Muffin sat stoically.

"Look, it's not like I'm forcing myself on her. If she says no, that's the end of it."

Muffin looked skeptical.

"Hey, you might not realize this, since we've only been cohabiting for a few weeks, but I don't have to force myself on the ladies, if you get my drift."

Muffin snorted.

"It's true!" Jake defended himself, then shook his head. Was he really trying to convince a dog that he was some sort of Casanova? "Besides, I didn't exactly see Dolly climbing all over you out there."

Muffin looked so crestfallen, Jake felt guilty. "Well, leave it to a mop to play hard to get. What's the attraction, anyway? You can't even tell what kind of figure she has under all that hair."

Jake had had no idea that a dog was capable of getting that moony, dreamy, lovesick look in its eyes, but Muffin was definitely moony. "Good Lord, I sure as hell hope I never look that pathetic."

* * *

The next morning, after dropping Muffin off for his grooming and massage sessions, Jake headed to the hotel to get some breakfast. He'd been in the lobby of the hotel yesterday when he'd gone on a tour of the place, but he hadn't stopped to appreciate its aesthetic appeal.

A water fountain gurgled soothingly, surrounded by lush green vegetation and colorful flowers he couldn't begin to identify, except for the occasional daisy and marigold here and there.

Beside the fountain was a statue of a man, his German shepherd faithfully standing by his side. The floor was green-and-cream marble, with Oriental runners strewn over it. On the walls were large framed paintings of probably every species of canine known to man.

Considering the place was called the Hound Dog, Jake would have expected to see an Elvis impersonator manning the concierge desk. But when he glanced over at it, he wasn't all that surprised to see Buzz there, speaking with an elderly gentleman. At the same time Buzz was petting the man's dog, which looked like some kind of cross between a poodle and an alien.

Jake considered going over to Buzz to see if he knew LeAnne's whereabouts, but decided that probably wasn't a smart idea, considering the man's suspiciousness of the night before.

He studied a sign with arrows announcing the locations of the four restaurants. He had a choice of the Chihuahua, which he assumed would lean toward Mexican, the Bouvier de Flandres, apparently French, the Italian Greyhound, which spoke for itself, and the Pekingese, which he'd guess was Chinese. The sign also indicated a coffee shop called the Chow Chow, and Jake decided that might be a good place to start.

He strolled by several guests, all towing dogs along in their wakes. He had no idea there were so many funny-looking breeds of canine in the world, and thought that in comparison, Muffin was rather an okay-looking mutt.

In fact, Muffin was actually coming to look normal, he decided, when he saw a dog the size of a guinea pig peeking out of a woman's beach bag.

It was in Jake's nature and training to observe people and form opinions on their states of mind. He didn't see one unhappy camper in the place. In fact, he was hard-pressed to find someone not smiling as they passed, or not chatting animatedly with their companions.

Definitely, if these people were being swindled, they were real happy about it.

He had to pass all the restaurants on the way to the Chow Chow. Only the Bouvier de

Flandres was open for breakfast. It was nearly full of customers, most of whom appeared to be pigging out on some sinful-looking crepes. LeAnne wasn't there, but Jake made a note to dine there for breakfast, early and often.

The decor he spied in the Pekingese told him he'd been right on. Chinese. He looked forward to that, too.

He passed clothing shops and souvenir shops and a small drugstore. The outside of this hotel was deceiving. The place was *huge*. Again, he had to wonder where LeAnne had gotten the capital to build this facility.

The Chow Chow was located right next to a swimwear shop, which might be the only logistical mistake in the hotel. Who wanted to pass skinny mannequins in skimpy bikinis right before heading in to eat?

He wasn't an expert, but Jake found the coffee shop charming. Instead of a bunch of tables all set out in an open room, it contained wooden booths of various sizes, affording people privacy. Here, as everywhere, greenery abounded, and the view overlooked part of the golf course and the lake. LeAnne had made the most of this land of hers, and animals didn't seem to be the only thing she loved. She was a plant lover, too.

A sign at the entrance read, "Please check all four-legged customers at the door." He figured since dogs were welcome everywhere else, some sort of health code was probably involved.

The place smelled absolutely mouthwatering. Although Jake had a healthy respect for any and all food, breakfast was his favorite meal. Probably because Aunt Sophie insisted on his starting the day with a healthy meal, and, boy, could she cook.

A pretty young blond waitress greeted him. "Table for one, sir?"

He offered his most engaging smile. "Well, now, that depends. Is Dr. Crosby having breakfast, by any chance?"

"Yes, but—"

Before she could voice an objection to disturbing LeAnne, he said, "Please just ask her if she'd mind company. I have . . . umm, a problem with my pet I'd like to discuss with her."

"Who should I tell her wants to see her?"

"Jake Donnelly."

"One moment, Mr. Donnelly."

LeAnne watched Darla approaching her secluded back booth; there was a frown on the girl's face. LeAnne set down the file she was reviewing on a troubled chocolate lab named Ranger.

"There's a man here who'd like to join you for breakfast."

LeAnne sighed and gestured to the five plates in front of her. "You know I like to eat breakfast in peace."

"Well, the man said he had a problem with his dog he'd like to discuss." She leaned down and whispered, "And he's a hunk." She held her hand over her head. "About six-three. Dark hair . . ."

LeAnne's heart tripped up. "Blue eyes?"

Darla nodded rapidly. "That's him. Jake Donnelly, he said."

LeAnne started stacking all the plates, mourning the waste of all that food. But she sure didn't want Jake to see how much she ate in the mornings. Everything but the fruit plate had to go. "Quick, take these away," she said. "Then give me a minute before you bring him back."

Darla grinned and saluted, then grabbed the stack and strolled away. Quickly LeAnne finger-combed her hair, pinched her cheeks, and bit her lips to bring more color to them.

Not that it mattered. Well, not much. Well, okay, it mattered. She'd had a tough time falling asleep last night as thoughts of too-blue eyes boring into hers kept her tossing.

She smacked the side of her head. What was it about that man? Sophie had painted a picture of a sweet, troubled boy who'd grown up to be a sweet, responsible man. LeAnne had known him for all of a day, but had been in his company long enough to recognize that *sweet*

110

was not an adjective she'd associate with him in any way, shape, or form. In fact, up until she'd overheard him trying to negotiate with Muffin last night, she'd wondered whether the guy even had a heart.

One thing he had in abundance, she decided as she watched him approach, was sex appeal. Tons of it. Megatons of it, she amended as she admired his masculine stride and muscular legs. He was wearing black running shorts and a white T-shirt that read, IF AT FIRST YOU DON'T SUCCEED, DESTROY ALL EVIDENCE YOU EVER TRIED.

He stopped at her table and smiled down at her, and LeAnne tried not to stare or be dazzled. "Good morning, Agent Donnelly."

He raised an eyebrow. "My, my, back to formality, Dr. Crosby?"

That was probably best. Distance and formality. No more intimate little chats beneath the stars while sipping fine wine. But she didn't even like her employees to address her formally, and it wasn't really fair to him to use a different standard, just because he unnerved her somewhat. It's LeAnne, Jake," she said, conjuring a smile. "Have a seat."

As soon as he slid into the booth, Buzz materialized by the table to take his order. For some reason, that seemed to flummox the man, because he just stared up at Buzz as if he'd sprouted antennae.

"Would you care for some breakfast?" LeAnne urged gently.

Jake finally pulled his gaze back to her. "Admit it. You've had him cloned."

LeAnne laughed and Buzz's chuckle rumbled. "I wish," she said, and meant it.

Jake's amazement gave way as his eyes focused on her mouth, but then he shook his head quickly and picked up a menu. Without studying it too closely, he just started rattling off menu items. "I'll have two eggs over easy, a short stack of blueberry pancakes, bacon, home fries, and toast. Whole wheat. I'm on a diet."

LeAnne's jaw dropped open. And here she'd tossed away all that marvelous food in order not to appear like the breakfast glutton she was.

Even Buzz appeared impressed, and he was as big as a bear and ate like one. "And to drink?"

"Coffee, big glass of milk, big glass of orange juice, and ice water, please."

Straight-faced, Buzz said, "Would you like that to be skim milk, seeing as you're on a diet and all?"

"Skim milk is for sissies."

Buzz nodded, then glanced down at the table in front of LeAnne and frowned. He knew darn well she loved a big breakfast. "You gonna starve to death on that," he said. "Let me get you something to stick to your ribs."

LeAnne pretended to ponder it. "Well, okay. How about some French toast and some scrambled eggs."

Buzz looked ready to protest, as LeAnne usually ordered about double that, so she interrupted him before he began. "And more coffee please."

After Buzz left, LeAnne glanced over to see Jake smiling his approval. Why that gave her a warm feeling in the pit of her stomach, she didn't know. Probably because her parents had always teased her about her breakfast-eating habits.

She cleared her throat. "Darla tells me you're having some problems with Muffin?"

He appeared confused for a moment, but then his expression cleared. "Oh. Yeah, I am."

"What seems to be the trouble?"

"Well, for one, he's a stubborn little brat. Last night he demanded to get up on the bed, and then when I wanted him down he wouldn't budge. You know what it's like to sleep with a bulldog who holds his legs straight out? I almost fell out of the bed, he was taking up so much space."

A mental picture formed that made LeAnne smile big inside, but the man looked so put out, she didn't think he'd appreciate her laughter. He didn't know it, but that admission spoke volumes, most of it good for both man and dog. "Well, it might not have been a good idea to give in to his wanting to get on the bed. Once you allow a behavior, it's harder and more traumatic to undo it, than never to have allowed it to begin with."

"Yesterday you were telling me to R-E-S-P-E-C-T him," he reminded her indignantly.

"Respect and letting him get away with murder are not the same thing, Jake."

"Now she tells me," he muttered. "And you know what's worse? He snores."

"Oh, and you don't?" she asked, then immediately regretted it. Because another mental image formed of this man all rumpled and vulnerable in sleep. And it was a very appealing mental image.

"No, I do not," he retorted.

Darla arrived with their drinks. Jake smiled his thanks as she deposited them, and she blushed like a schoolgirl, which wasn't too surprising considering she *was* a schoolgirl.

"What?" he said with a wink. "Buzz slacking off on the job?"

"He's back in the kitchen cooking your orders," Darla said blithely, then moved to refresh LeAnne's coffee, oblivious to Jake's jaw dropping.

LeAnne grinned as she mixed a little more cream into her coffee. Everyone who worked there was used to the amazing, floating Buzz by now, but she knew how incredible the man could appear to a newcomer.

"So," LeAnne said, drawing out the word, "what do you want to do about your relationship with Muffin?"

"Well, I think we need some of that therapy cr . . . stuff."

114

"You do, do you?"

"Yes," he said, eyes wide with a sincerity that was as believable as Bill Clinton's grand jury testimony.

LeAnne sipped her coffee before commenting, "I thought you considered my profession a bunch of bunk."

"Well, maybe at first," he conceded. "But there's no denying that Muffin really likes you, and I was figuring that if we had some of those lessons, or whatever you call them, and he sees that you like him *and* me, he'll start warming up to me."

Definitely stated in layman's terms, but he had something of a point. "Well, I can't force Muffin to fall in love with you, but we can certainly work on getting him to enjoy spending time with you."

Buzz had decided to serve them his feast himself. He set two plates in front of LeAnne, one stacked with two thick pieces of French toast, the other with scrambled eggs . . . and bacon and home fries. *Bless his sweet soul.*

He'd also been very generous with Jake, who looked at the food and smacked his lips. "Buzz, you're a man after my own heart."

"I use my own *special* ingredients," Buzz said.

Jake looked up from his breakfast, his eyes narrowed. Buzz just smiled down at him, all innocence. "Y'all enjoy your meal now, you hear?" he added, nodding to LeAnne.

115

She stifled a giggle, because Jake had now picked up his fork and started lifting the different foods, apparently searching for some kind of booby trap or something.

Not being able to stand the thought that he wouldn't eat his breakfast, she assured him, "Relax. Buzz didn't poison your eggs."

"You have to admit that man doesn't like me."

"Buzz likes everyone. He's just very protective."

Adding salt and pepper to his eggs, he said, "So how do we go about setting up these lessons or sessions or whatever you call them? You got a doggy couch?"

"Very funny. That's not how we do things around here."

"How do we do things around here?"

"We want to engage in activities that will be fun for Muffin."

After drowning his pancakes in syrup, he cut off a bite and moaned with pleasure as he chewed. When he swallowed, he said, "The only activity that's fun for Muffin is doing everything in his power to irritate me."

"Let me ask you this," LeAnne said. "How many humans does Muffin come in contact with at your place?"

"Huh?"

"Do you have . . . friends coming in and out? Neighbors? Kids? Umm, dates?"

"Almost never. Except when I have to go out

of town. Then Marly comes over to take care of him."

She wanted to ask who Marly was, but figured it wasn't any of her business. "So, Muffin's day consists of his own company, or yours?"

"I've bought him every toy known to dogkind!"

"And my guess is that when you get home you're tired and cranky and if you bother to walk him you make sure he knows you resent it and you probably toss his food at him and then say, 'Leave me alone, I'm beat,' and then you veg on the couch watching some sports event and ignore him completely."

He blushed. The man actually blushed. "I also like to read, you know."

"Oh, now there's an activity Muffin can sink his paws into."

Jake set down his fork. "Okay, okay, I get your point. So, what, am I supposed to get yet another mutt to keep him company?"

She shook her head. "No, no. What you want to do is play together."

"Oh, jeez."

"Come on, it can be something you both enjoy doing. You'd be surprised how much fun it can be to play with your dog."

"You're going to have to teach me."

"I can certainly try."

"So . . . what should we do first?"

LeAnne pulled her Day-Timer out of her lab

Trish Jensen

coat and opened it. "I have appointments until eleven this morning. How about we meet then?"

"Okay. What are we going to do?"

"Hmm, let's see. Do you play tennis?"

Jake finished off his pancakes. "Tennis? Yeah, I play. Not great, but I play."

"Why don't you call and reserve a court for eleven?"

"But . . . tennis? How is that supposed to be playing with Muffin?"

"Just wait and see."

"Now just remember, we're still having relationship problems," Jake reminded Muffin, then rolled his eyes at the idea of talking psychobabble to a dog.

Muffin had no problem warming to the role, Jake noted, as the dog immediately slowed down and began fighting the leash.

They were walking the path to the tennis courts, and Jake found it embarrassing that the people they passed frowned as they witnessed a poor, reluctant pooch being dragged against his will to some unknown destination. Muffin was enacting an Oscar-winning performance of *Dead Dog Walking.*

"Save it for LeAnne," Jake said in a growl.

Muffin stopped fighting, but he sniffed loudly as he picked up the pace.

LeAnne was already there when they arrived,

and the moment Muffin spotted her he yelped and fought to run to her. Jake released him from his leash and let him, then stood back and enjoyed the view. LeAnne wore a white tennis skirt and a blue-and-white-striped cotton shirt that outlined her body in all the right places. She wasn't a tall woman, but her legs seemed endless, and he couldn't help thinking about them wrapped around his waist.

Fighting off arousal, he strolled over to where LeAnne was hunkered down, happily accepting Muffin's slobbery greeting.

Jake noted that all but two courts were in use, and between the far courts and the lake was a large pen, where two of the employees were baby-sitting a variety of animals, playing what looked like a game of tag with them.

He wasn't quite sure how putting Muffin in with a bunch of other dogs was supposed to be therapeutic, but it was fine by him. He wasn't going to argue about having LeAnne all to himself, so to speak.

"So who runs the tennis courts?" he asked LeAnne. "John McEnruff? Bjorn Bark?"

She straightened, laughing. "You get that from Sophie."

He cocked his head, trying to ignore the thousand-watt dazzle that was her smile. "Get what?"

"Playing on names. She used to do that all the time." LeAnne tucked a hank of that incred-

119

ible hair behind her ear. "She used to call Dolly 'Madogna' because Sophie thought she was a rampant little hussy. There was a toy poodle who *loved* to run an obstacle course. Sophie called the dog Mary Lou Ruffin.' "

A small pang zapped Jake's chest as he realized LeAnne was exactly right. Sitting around the supper table, Aunt Sophie, Uncle George, and he used to make a game of it. He remembered the laughter that at times got so out of control they all ended up with tears streaming down their cheeks.

"There was a dog at a neighboring cabin that never stopped howling," he recalled wistfully. "Aunt Sophie dubbed her 'Barbra Streishound'."

LeAnne laughed. "Yep, pure Sophie. We had a mastiff one year that did the same thing. She called him 'Barky Manilow'."

Jake joined in the laughter, realizing that he enjoyed the fact that Sophie and LeAnne had apparently been close. And that LeAnne had *genuinely* cared about his aunt, whom he had loved like a mother.

Their laughter tapered off slowly, and as it did, sparks of electricity filled the void. At least they did for Jake. And by the small flare that lit up LeAnne's eyes, he had to believe she felt the attraction, too.

She cleared her throat, then pulled a blue sweatband out of her skirt pocket. "You ready to play some tennis?"

"What are we doing with Muffin while we play?" Jake asked.

"Oh, didn't I tell you?" she said, bending and placing the sweatband over Muffin's head. "He's going to be our ball dog."

Chapter Six

Jake was amazed and impressed at how quickly LeAnne taught Muffin to be a mighty fine ball dog. He was amazed and impressed at how quickly Muffin caught on. And he was totally floored by how much Muffin seemed to be enjoying himself engaging in physical activity.

And throughout the volleying that followed, not only did Muffin gently retrieve the ball and trot it on over and hand it to LeAnne, he also never forgot to show Jake an utter lack of respect.

While Muffin delivered balls directly into LeAnne's hands, whenever she directed him to take them to Jake, Muffin made a point of dropping them at least five feet away, then turning his back and trotting back to his place at the sidelines without so much as a by-your-leave. When he took them to LeAnne, he lingered for as long as she'd continue to reward him with scratches and "Good boys!"

At one point LeAnne came over to Jake's side of the net, stood beside him, tossed a ball onto the court, and said, "Fetch, Muffin!"

He did, with glee. When he brought it over—all the way, since she was there—she said, "Give it to Jake."

Muffin hesitated for a moment; then his jaw clamped shut, the hiss of air rushing through his teeth. By the time he finally let go of the ball, it was a gummy, deflated mess.

Jake should have been happy Muffin was doing such a great job, but he realized it was beginning to irritate him. He didn't like looking like a monster dog owner in LeAnne's eyes.

LeAnne's fist hit her hip. "Was that nice?"

Muffin hung his head a little and whimpered softly.

She pulled another ball from her skirt and tossed it toward the net. "Fetch it, Muffin." When he returned with it, she said in a stern voice that would have had even Jake quaking a little, "Now hand it over to Jake. *Nicely!*"

Muffin did so without hesitation. Jake was so absurdly happy about it, he dropped to one knee and started patting Muffin's back. "Excellent! Perfect!" And Muffin forgot himself for a moment and preened. LeAnne, too, dropped down. "Good boy!" she said, and their hands collided on Muffin's back. Which made them both forget the dog for a moment and instead concentrate on the fact that their mouths were mere inches apart.

LeAnne's lips parted on a soundless *Oh.* Jake's parted in anticipation. The sounds of balls cracking against rackets faded. So did everyone around them.

Jake started to lean toward her, but she stopped him with a question. "Who's Marly?" she whispered.

"Huh?"

"Marly. The person who takes care of Muffin when you're out of town."

"Oh. Her. She's my next-door neighbor's kid."

LeAnne's lips lifted in a beguiling smile. "Oh. Good."

He frowned. "Good? Why . . . oh. Thought I might have a girlfriend, did you?"

"Yes."

He considered that an excellent sign . . . that she was wondering about possible encumbrances. "I don't."

"Don't what?"

"Have a girlfriend."

"Oh. Good." Another smile.

Which he returned. "You?"

"I have several girlfriends."

He chuckled. "Have any girlfriends of the male persuasion?"

"Well, I have friends of the male persuasion. No girlfriends of the male persuasion."

"Oh. Good."

A ball came bouncing over to them from one of the other courts, and it served as a reminder that they weren't exactly alone. LeAnne surged to her feet and Jake scrambled right after her. That was when they realized that Muffin had turned his back on them. He was either being discreet or he was thoroughly disgusted.

Jake was beyond caring which. LeAnne Crosby was fair game.

Except LeAnne Crosby had other obligations. As much as Jake wanted to dominate her time, she was busy from immediately after their tennis match to well into the evening. Jake hadn't counted on her accepting dinner invitations and evening activities with other guests.

Which meant he didn't get to see her again Tuesday. Instead, he spent the time following Muffin around, who was on a mission to further his own love life.

At sunset they'd found Dolly and Carol Channing playing Frisbee at the picnic area near the lake. Muffin had done his best to show off for the little hairball, and Dolly had done her best to appear uninsinterested, even as she wiggled her fluffy butt when she retrieved the Frisbee.

Carol Channing, aka Elaine Merriweather, turned out to be your run-of-the-mill eccentric. Divorced, rich, with lots of time on her hands, she had a thing for shih tzus and balloon animals.

She also had a tendency to call everyone "darling."

While Dolly pranced and Muffin puffed out his chest and graciously allowed Dolly to beat him to the Frisbee every single time, Elaine Merriweather *squeak-squeak*ed her way through a balloon monkey, a balloon elephant, and a balloon giraffe.

The problem was, she wasn't real adept at the craft yet, and she popped more balloons than she saved. The dogs didn't seem to mind, but the popping sounded so much like gunfire, it made Jake itch to go retrieve his Glock. And it was a strange feeling. In the big, bad outside world, he never went without his gun. He was trained to consider it a vital appendage. But here he'd lost that sense of necessity. This place bred a feeling of serenity and goodwill—something he hadn't felt since his summers with Aunt Sophie.

The peace and tranquillity, he realized, were testament to LeAnne Crosby's taste and sense of comfort. She knew instinctively what put her guests at ease, what made them calm, comfortable, and happy. She was an amazing woman—one he wanted to get to know in all kinds of un-calm but happy ways.

Down at the lake Buzz was busy helping to launch rowboats for folks and their pets who wanted to catch the sun setting on the water. Fireflies were beginning to wink over the lake and in the woods.

And LeAnne appeared lakeside with a man and his Saint Bernard.

Jake peered at the guy, sizing him up. He looked to be in his early forties. Way too old for her. But, unfortunately, a very fit early forties. And not that he judged such things, but the man sure didn't look butt-ugly, either. Worse than that, he was making LeAnne laugh, and for some reason, the idea that she was bestowing that awesome smile on another guy stabbed right into his gut.

Bang!

Jake jumped about a foot as another balloon blew a gasket. The sound must have carried the fifty or so feet to the lakeside, because both LeAnne and the man whirled to check its source.

Mrs. Merriweather gave them a sheepish smile and held up the ragged remains of the balloon. LeAnne smiled, waved, then turned back to her client and his owner without even glancing Jake's way.

Which irritated the living hell out of him.

After all, they were going to be lovers. Soon. He hoped. Of course, there wasn't a guarantee, but it certainly was Plan A. And when it came to his personal life, he never formulated a Plan B. He figured that was self-defeating. *Know your goals and bulldoze directly for them.*

As he watched LeAnne teaching what looked like hand signals simultaneously to the Saint Bernard's owner and the dog, he tried to slough off this unpleasant feeling in the pit of his stomach. He knew better than to try to identify it. He didn't think he'd like the answer one bit.

To get his mind off the pretty animal shrink, he glanced back over at Dolly and Muffin. They'd abandoned the Frisbee in favor of sharing a particularly enticing scent surrounding a sugar maple. Seemed Muffin was having a lot more luck in his love life than Jake. Jake didn't begrudge him that. Much. But he sure wished Dolly's owner would decide to take her leave, so he could do the same.

He knew better than to be the one to separate Muffin from his paramour. His truce with the mutt was uneasy at best, and he wasn't about to do anything to incur Muffin's wrath all over again.

Involuntarily, Jake's gaze wandered back toward the lake. And LeAnne. He sort of wished she'd dress a little more formally when with her other clients. Those powder blue shorts weren't indecently displaying leg, but when a woman had legs like hers, showing even an inch of skin was provocative. Especially when she kept bending over to pet and reward the dog whenever he performed on command.

Jake considered himself a practical man. But as far back as he could remember, he'd fallen into a fantasy in times of stress. As a child his fantasies centered around thoughts of running away from home and joining the circus. Or forming a really cool rock band. Or becoming president of the United States, and making his first act as leader of the nation deporting his father to Siberia.

As he grew into his teens, his fantasies morphed into ones involving girls. Having Suzy the cheerleader seduce him under the bleachers at the football stadium. Finding himself stranded on a deserted island with his sexy math teacher, and introducing her to the joys of sex, even as she was trying to explain what a cosine was.

But when he'd actually decided his life's goal—to join the FBI and fight bad guys—his fantasies had been replaced by hard work and vision.

Right now, as he watched LeAnne frolicking on the beach, his fantasy world came crashing back in on him. He saw himself walking down to the beach, grabbing her, and laying her down. Removing those skimpy shorts and that top and touching every inch of her. Taking her right there by the water. Feeling her muscles contract around him while he swallowed her moans of ecstasy with a deep and wet and wild kiss.

Jake shook his head. Fantasies were for dreamers, for people not in control of real life. He gritted his teeth and checked his watch. "Getting to be suppertime," he noted, hoping Mrs. Merriweather would agree.

Relief flooded through him when she smiled

and began gathering her balloons. "She's free, you know."

"Excuse me?"

"LeAnne. She's not seeing anyone."

"What makes you think—"

"Oh, don't worry, darling. Your secret is safe with me."

"I don't have—"

She held up a perfectly manicured hand. With those nails, no wonder she kept popping balloons. "No need to deny it. I've been a great observer of human nature all my life. Call it my gift. I've been watching you watching her."

Jake pressed his lips together.

Mrs. Merriweather smiled. "Nothing to be ashamed of, darling. I've been coming here as long as your Aunt Sophie, and I've always thought it such a shame that LeAnne showed no interest in getting involved with a man again after the death of her husband."

Jake's pressed lips went slack as his mouth dropped open. "Her *what?*"

One perfectly plucked eyebrow rose. "You didn't know she's a widow?"

"No."

"Oh, indeed. LeAnne is the former Mrs. Stephen Latimer."

"*The* Stephen Latimer? Electronics guru? Predecessor to Bill Gates?"

"The one and only." She patted Jake's cheek. "So you can see it's been a long time. She needs companionship, and you're just handsome enough to maybe pull it off, darling. As the young people say, go for it!"

She called Dolly over while Jake stood there, mute with shock. Snapping the leash onto Dolly's collar, she delivered her parting shot. "How do you think LeAnne could afford to open such a wonderful place as this?"

"You heard me. Her ex was Stephen Latimer," Jake growled into his PCS cell phone. He didn't feel comfortable talking about this on the Happy Hounds line.

Mark whistled. "Well, at least you know where the seed money came from."

Oh, definitely. Stephen Latimer, full-time electronics genius and mogul, part-time race-car hobbyist, full-time suspect as a traitor to his country and a money launderer to boot. His name popped up in no less than fifty different case files in Jake's office alone, but somehow there had never been enough evidence to pin any kind of crime on him. But Jake and Mark both had great noses, and Stephen Latimer had always smelled just a little dirty to them both.

Jake vaguely recalled that at some point about ten years ago Latimer had married a woman rumored to be half his age. But if Jake's memory served, Latimer was very protective of his child-bride, shielding her from the public and the press with a zeal that seemed oddly out of character for the flamboyant man.

A few decades ago Latimer had developed a process for building digital switching circuits that drastically increased their speed. The implications for computer control systems were staggering. The Department of Defense had pounced on Latimer, classifying the crucial parts of his research and development of the process in the interest of national security.

Latimer hadn't been happy about it, but he'd finally come to terms with the DOD's classification, opting not to sue. And he was making good money from the government contracts, anyway. Then a few years passed, and suddenly Latimer was racking up frequent-flier miles to and from Europe. The government started getting suspicious that he might be illegally exporting and selling his research overseas. It could never be proven, and when Latimer died suddenly in a race-car accident, all interest in his former activities had ceased.

"The question here is how clean that seed money is," Jake speculated aloud.

"You want me to look into it?"

"Quietly. Do *nothing* official until you get back to me."

"Gotcha." Mark paused and Jake could hear him swallowing a sip of what was probably his fiftieth cup of coffee of the day. "We have a slight problem with our package. Our Chicago guests keep trying to unwrap it."

Translation: the organization run by indicted racketeer Jacob Winston was trying their damnedest to track down the star witness for the prosecution, Elisa Johnson. "Why don't you hide the package in another closet? Preferably locked."

"We have. We've moved it twice. But you know how kids are at Christmas."

"Yeah, well, keep them away from it until Christmas morning."

"We're getting closer."

"Closer doesn't mean squat, you idiot!" his boss yelled.

Jimmy flinched. "Our songbird's been right-on every time," he said, trying to keep the whine out of his voice. "But somehow they always find out we're on to them."

"Ever consider your bird's laying his eggs in more than one nest?"

"The Rat wouldn't do that," Jimmy said. The Rat. Now *there* was a nickname to be proud of.

"The Rat *works* for the Feds, dumbass."

Jimmy was getting real tired of being called names. He almost preferred Bunny. "Yeah, well, he ain't happy with them. Thinks they're all a bunch of Nazis. And he's real sure about this. They're on their way to Richmond."

"So why aren't you on your way to Richmond?"

"We are. We're on the road right now."

"Get them this time."

"We will," he said. He wasn't sure of that by a

long shot, but he'd die before saying so. Actually, he'd die *if* he said so. That asshole Fed was a slippery son of a bitch.

"And how about his partner. Find that one yet?"

"Still working on that."

He pulled the phone away from his ear before it popped from the sound of very, very loud swearing.

"Bunny," the man said in a growl after his tirade sputtered to a halt. "Ever see the movie *Fatal Attraction?*"

"Can't say I have."

"Rent it sometime. And make sure to pay special attention to what happens to the rabbit."

Jake had considered taking an evening dip in the pool, but thunder and lightning rolled in and seemed to settle directly above Happy Hounds. Which pretty much ruled out strolling the grounds in search of LeAnne.

A crash of thunder practically shook through the bungalow as Jake reached into his duffel bag for a book. He pulled it out, but then LeAnne's chastisement about giving Muffin quality playtime tugged at his guilty bone, and he set the book on the dresser. Turning, he said, "Hey, Muffin, want to play?" He stopped and glanced around. No Muffin.

A flash of panic swept through him for the barest moment, but then he shrugged it off.

Muffin was a pretty smart dog, but Jake was fairly certain he hadn't mastered opening doors by himself.

"Muffin?" he called. "Where are you?"

Jake walked to the bathroom and looked in. Empty. He returned to the suite and glanced in all the corners. *Nada*. Then a bit of the comforter wiggling at the bottom of the bed caught his eye. He moved to it and dropped to his knees, lifting the skirt. Sure enough, there was Muffin, sitting there shaking for all he was worth.

"What's wrong with you?"

Muffin whined softly.

"What's got your knickers in a twist, dog?"

Thunder cracked overhead, and Muffin covered his eyes with his paws.

"The thunder?" Jake guessed. "Big, bad stud-Muffin's afraid of a little thunder?"

The dog's entire body shook, and Jake found himself feeling bad for the mutt. "Hey, don't worry. We're safe from the thunder and lightning."

Muffin didn't appear convinced, seeing as he continued to shake like Jell-O and kept his eyes covered.

Jumping up, Jake pulled a dog biscuit out of his duffel. If there was one thing Muffin couldn't resist, it was a snack. Again Jake pulled up the skirt of the bed. "Hey, Muffin, look what I have for you."

The dog didn't budge, so Jake waved the biscuit near his nose. "Mmm . . . good."

One paw dropped and Muffin eyed the biscuit but didn't make a move for it, which meant this was serious business. Jake sat back and considered the dilemma. Where had this fear come from? How had he never before noticed that Muffin was deathly afraid of thunder and lightning? There had to have been a thunderstorm or two in D.C. in the last month, but Jake couldn't recall one, or what Muffin had been doing at the time. Which was pretty pathetic. Just how neglectful had he been?

He laid the bone in front of Muffin's face and placed his hand on the dog's back. "Hey, really, thunder's not dangerous when you're inside."

The shaking under his fingertips bothered him immensely. He felt helpless to make Muffin understand he wasn't in harm's way. And he wondered how many times in the last month Muffin had suffered the terror of thunderstorms all on his own, while Jake had been so callous he hadn't even noticed.

Aunt Sophie would have been so disappointed in him. Although she'd never had a dog during his childhood—Uncle George had been allergic—she had always taught him to respect all living creatures. And here he'd been totally, utterly indifferent to one that Sophie had loved.

His eyes got a little gritty as he began stroking Muffin's back. In as soothing a voice as possible, he said, "That's going to change, starting now, I promise. The moment we get back to D.C. I'm going to hire you a baby-sitter, so you won't be alone during a thunderstorm if I'm not there."

Muffin lowered the other paw from his face. His big brown eyes were filled with fear, which broke Jake's heart.

"I don't know what to do to convince you you're safe, Muffin. LeAnne would probably—" He stopped. "Of course, LeAnne." He patted Muffin's head. "I'll be right back, okay? I'm bringing in the big guns on this one." He felt bad about leaving the dog, even for a minute or two, but it couldn't be helped. "Honest, I'll be right here."

He jumped up and strode to the phone by the bed, then called the concierge desk. *What do you know?* Buzz answered. "Buzz, it's Jake Donnelly. I need to get in touch with Le—Dr. Crosby."

"Is this an emergency?" Buzz asked suspiciously. "She's off-duty for the night."

"It really is. It's completely about Muffin. I swear."

"He's sick?"

"Well, not exactly," Jake said. For some reason he was reluctant to humiliate Muffin by sharing his phobia. "But I really have a question for her. Please, let me have her number."

"I can't do that, but I'll page her and let her know you want to talk to her."

Jake figured Buzz was protecting LeAnne from him, but he was a little too worried at the moment to be irritated. He paced beside the phone until it rang, one very long half minute later.

"Donnelly."

"Hello, Jake," she said softly. "Buzz tells me you have a problem."

"Yes. Well, Muffin does. At this very moment he's sitting under the bed shaking with T-E-R-R-O-R."

"Oh, of course, the thunder."

"You mean, this is normal?"

"Are you saying this is the first thunderstorm you've gone through with him?"

"Well, umm . . . yes."

"Some dogs get very upset during thunderstorms."

"What do I do? He's hiding under the bed."

"The best thing you can do is just comfort him until the storm passes."

"Can you prescribe some kind of doggy tranquilizer or something? I'm scared to death he's going to have a heart attack if he doesn't settle down."

"A tranquilizer would be more harmful than the fear, Jake. Believe me, it's not unusual for a dog to hate storms. My guess is at least half the bungalows have dogs shaking in their skin right now."

He wanted to ask her to come over and settle Muffin down, but he knew that was purely selfish on his part. Not to mention potentially dangerous to her. "So there's pretty much nothing I can do but wait it out?"

"There's plenty you can do. Talk to him. Pet him. Just be there. He'll calm down eventually."

"Okay, thanks. Sorry to bother you."

"You're welcome," she said. Her voice held a hint of huskiness when she added, "It's no bother."

Jake hung up and returned to Muffin, who was still shaking alarmingly. "LeAnne says to tell you there's nothing unmanly about hating thunder. So, no problem."

He petted Muffin and talked nonsensically for who knew how long. They discussed baseball stats and the big fish that got away and the chances of the Redskins winning a game next season.

They talked about Dolly and LeAnne and women in general, and Jake was pretty certain Muffin agreed with him that women were unfathomable but absolutely necessary in the scheme of things.

And they talked about Aunt Sophie. That was when Muffin started settling down in earnest.

When he suddenly pounced on the dog biscuit, Jake knew the crisis had passed. Jake scooted backward. "Come on out of there, fleabag. You're making me miss the Orioles game."

Muffin climbed out from under the bed, went straight for his blanket, picked it up in his mouth, and turned expectantly to Jake.

Jake tried to ignore him, clicking on the TV and flipping the channels until he found the ball game. Muffin was nothing if not patient, and when Jake had fluffed the pillows and settled back, the dog was still standing there waiting for an invitation.

"Oh, all right! Seeing as you had a bad scare tonight. But this is *not* going to become a habit. Hear me?"

Muffin's muffled woof was immediately followed by a surge up onto the bed.

"You're a pain in the ass, you know that?" Jake said as he arranged the blanket to Muffin's liking.

"We can't miss this time," Jimmy said.

"How'd you miss in Richmond?"

"We found the neighborhood, but it was swarming with cops."

"And you know for a fact that they've left the area?"

"We know for a fact exactly where they are. We planted a trace in his car."

"Are you sure you got the right car?"

Jimmy was offended but he swallowed his retort. "I'm sure."

"This is your last chance, Bunny. You bungle

it this time, you might as well plan on early retirement."

Jake's plan to get close to LeAnne wasn't going well. She had the nerve to be busy with appointments all day Thursday. She even had an appointment for dinner.

So Jake and Muffin spent the morning rowing on the lake. After lunch they played a round of mutt-putt golf. Jake taught Muffin to paw the golf balls out of the holes and return them to him, and he had to admit he found Muffin's willingness to learn and play endearing. Still, no matter how much better they were getting along, Muffin's company wasn't quite the same as LeAnne's.

It was during their walk that disaster struck. They were meandering down a lazy path that bordered part of the golf course. Jake had removed Muffin's leash to practice the "heel" command. As they passed the three-par thirteenth green, a ball came rolling up the hill onto the green, heading straight for the cup.

Muffin immediately decided that the ball had his name on it, and he broke away from Jake and ran for it. Just as it was about to sink into the cup, Muffin scooped it up and proudly returned it to Jake.

"Uh-oh," Jake muttered.

He glanced up the fairway, and sure enough a man was on the tee, jumping up and down furiously. Muffin had just relieved the guy of a hole-in-one. Problem was, he couldn't really get mad at the mutt, because he'd taught him that trick himself.

He made Muffin hand over the ball, then waited for the irate golfer to zoom his cart up the fairway.

Jake shielded Muffin behind his legs, in case the guy took it in his head to run Muffin over. The man came to a screeching halt, and Jake recognized him as the guy he'd encountered on his first drive inside the gates. Mostly because that gold cocker spaniel sat on the passenger seat, golf visor sitting jauntily atop his head. Unlike last time, the man wasn't smiling.

"Look, I'm real sorry about that," Jake began.

"That could have been a hole-in-one!" the man roared.

"Oh, it was definitely going to be a hole-in-one," Jake said. "Listen, give me your score-card and I'll sign that I was witness to it."

"What kind of evil dog trick is that, stealing a man's golf ball?" the man said, his face flushed red as a tomato. He yanked his scorecard out of his breast pocket and shoved it and a tiny pencil at Jake.

Jake quickly signed and witnessed the feat, mumbling his apologies the entire time. Muffin peeked out around his leg, and Jake used his calf to push Muffin back.

"Beautiful dog you have there," Jake said. He was learning the ropes of dog ownership quickly: compliment the dog, flatter the owner.

It worked to a degree. The man glanced proudly at his pup, then turned back and grabbed the scorecard from Jake, making certain he'd filled it out and witnessed it properly. "You might want to walk that dog somewhere else," he demanded, disguising it as a helpful suggestion. "Or keep him leashed."

"Oh, will do," Jake said, nodding rapidly.

"Well then . . . good," the man replied, and deigned to shake his hand before returning to his cart and zooming off toward the fourteenth tee.

Jake leaned down and snapped on Muffin's leash. "Who do you think you are?" he said in a growl. "Tiger Woofs?"

After supper at the Chihuahua—delicious shrimp fajitas—Jake retrieved Muffin from his play session and walked back to the bungalow, feeling strangely edgy. Suddenly two weeks didn't seem nearly a long enough time to spend with the good doctor.

When they entered the bungalow, Jake's phone light was blinking, so he called the front desk. Amazingly, it wasn't Buzz who answered, but another man.

When he identified himself, the man said, "Yes, you have a message from LeAnne. She'd like you to call her."

Now that was the best news he'd had all day, and he wasted no time punching in the number the man offered him.

"Pool," Buzz answered.

Jake pulled the phone from his ear for a second, then said, "Buzz? It's Jake Donnelly. I was told this was LeAnne's number."

"No, it's the pool phone, but she's here. One second."

LeAnne came to the phone a moment later. "Hello, Jake," she said cheerfully. "I hope you and Muffin had a good day."

Jake was feeling just a bit peeved, even if he was absurdly happy to hear her voice. "Yeah, well, we could have used a session."

"From what I hear, you seemed to be getting along well today."

Uh-oh. "Well, maybe a little better."

"That's great. I was wondering, if you're not busy, do you and Muffin want to come take an evening dip in the pool? It's a beautiful night."

LeAnne in a bathing suit. LeAnne wet-skinned and slick. That was a no-brainer. "Yeah, that could be nice," he said, even as he lunged for the dresser and started digging for his swim trunks.

"Okay, well, I'll be inside the clubhouse," she said. "Come in and get me when you arrive."

"Will do."

He hung up and turned to Muffin. "Jackpot."

Chapter Seven

"Surprise!"

Jake stared in astonishment at the sea of people and dogs inside the pool clubhouse. There were balloons everywhere, multicolored streamers, and a huge sign proclaiming, HAPPY FIFTH BIRTHDAY, MUFFIN!

In the center were Buzz and LeAnne, standing in front of a Milk-Bone–shaped cake. If that was for the dogs, he didn't even want to know what it was made of.

All of the dogs and some of the humans were wearing party hats.

Muffin, apparently, understood the entire event, because he started prancing and generally looking excited.

Jake had forgotten all about Muffin's birthday. Jeez, he was a horrible pet owner. He'd had no idea that one celebrated a dog's date of birth.

And apparently one also bought presents for one's dog as well, considering the number of wrapped gifts that littered a long banquet table.

Jake vaguely recognized most of the people and animals in the room, because they were made up of the group Muffin took advanced training with. All of the other dogs were free of leashes, so Jake snapped Muffin's off. Muffin immediately started working the room. LeAnne strolled over to Jake, and no matter how flabbergasted he was, he still managed to take in her attire.

Yowza! She wore a navy blue Speedo-type one-piece bathing suit, and wrapped around her hips was a colorful filmy scarflike thing that just barely covered her upper thighs. She had sandals on her feet and her toe-nails were painted a pretty coral color.

For the second time in two days a fantasy involving LeAnne implanted itself in his head. One involving her and a boat anchored in a calm blue lagoon. Of them splashing and playing and touching until they couldn't stand it and he stripped off her suit and his, then made love to her right there in the water, her legs wrapped around his waist as he drove into her over and over.

"You can close your mouth now," LeAnne said, laughing and snapping him out of the fantasy.

"Holy cow," was the most intelligent thing he could think of to say. And it wasn't in response to the party. He was exceedingly grateful that the red T-shirt he wore over black swim trunks was oversized and baggy, hiding the proof of how much she affected him merely with made-up fantasies.

"I take it you forgot about Muffin's birthday?"

"Well . . ."

"That's all right. I didn't expect you to remember."

"I can just imagine his attitude when he realizes I didn't buy him a gift."

"Yes, you did," she said, pointing at the table. "Yours is the one wrapped in the clown paper."

"You, Dr. Crosby, are a lifesaver."

She tossed him a brilliant smile that brought his breath to a screeching halt. "My pleasure."

"I take it we're not going for a swim?"

"Sure we can. After Muffin gets his fifteen minutes." She twisted to find Muffin, who was now sporting a cone-shaped birthday hat, and showing it off for Dolly. "Ready to get the show on the road?"

Jake tried not to feel disappointed. He told himself that they'd get some time together later, and for now he should just relax and let Muffin enjoy his day. But it wasn't completely easy when he had the proof right in front of him of how luscious the good doctor looked in a bathing suit. "Ready."

"Let's get some punch," she suggested, pointing at the table filled with food and drink. She leaned closer and Jake got a whiff of that incredible perfume. "The bowl on the left is spiked a little," she said softly, smiling.

They headed straight for the bowl on the left. Jake filled two paper cups and handed one to LeAnne. "What does one do at a dog bash?"

"Mingle," LeAnne said, then grabbed his hand and started dragging him toward a small gathering of humans.

All around them, the dogs played. It was a rather chaotic scene, but he marveled at how well all the animals got along.

LeAnne introduced him to several human guests, pointing out their animals. "This is Bob Levy. He's here with Tabitha, the Newfoundland."

Jake shook the older man's hand, trying not to grin at the white puffs of hair peeking out from under a party hat.

"And this is Eugenia Littleford. Her black lab, Buster, just completed the Seeing Eye program."

"My sister's blind, you see," the woman explained.

"That's . . . terrific. I mean about the exam, not the blindness," he clarified quickly. "Nice to meet you, ma'am."

"You're a good-looking young thing," the

woman said bluntly. "If I were twenty years younger, you wouldn't stand a chance."

Considering she looked about eighty, he somehow doubted it, but he just winked and said, "Personally, I go for mature women."

He was introduced to several other folks before he quietly begged LeAnne for a short reprieve and more of the delicious punch and some snacks.

They were munching on cheese cubes and apple slices when two women he'd noticed around the grounds approached. After all, he couldn't help but notice. They were identical twin redheads, both nearly as tall as he was. Both carried little dogs that were almost indescribable. They were the size of small poodles, and colored like Dalmatians, but they seemed to have no hair on their bodies, except a big tuft of it on top of their heads and at their ankles. He was put in mind of a genetics experiment run amok.

Other than the different style of party hats on the two women's heads, they were dressed identically in some kind of colorful muumuu-type dresses. Both were quite thin, he thought, though the dresses disguised their figures. Except for one fact: their breasts would put Dolly Parton's to shame. Jake was surprised they didn't fall flat on their faces.

LeAnne greeted them, then turned to Jake. "I'd like you to meet Connie and June Folkdell. Connie, June, Jake Donnelly." Then LeAnne reached out and petted Connie's dog. "And these two fellows are Book and Bug."

"So *very* nice to meet you," June said with feeling while her sister nodded eagerly.

"Likewise," Jake replied. "And what type of . . . err, breed are Book and Bug?"

"Oh, these are Chinese cresteds," Connie said, stroking Book's head. "Aren't they adorable?"

"Uh, yes, mm-hmm," Jake said.

"Happy birthday to Muffin," June said, while feeding Bug a cracker.

"Thank you."

"So Muffin's a Gemini!"

"Actually, he's a bulldog," Jake corrected.

The two laughed as if he'd just cracked the funniest joke on earth.

LeAnne must have recognized the befuddlement on his face, because she chimed in, "His astrological sign is Gemini. June and Connie are pet astrologers."

Jake choked, then hid it behind a cough. "Oh. I see," he said. Here was a profession even more wacky than animal shrink.

"Book and Bug are Geminis, too," Connie volleyed while nuzzling her dog. "May thirty-first."

"Congratulations," Jake said, glancing desperately at LeAnne, who appeared to be enjoying herself immensely. Her brown eyes sparkled and her mouth twitched.

"You know what they say about Gemini dogs?" June piped in.

"I'm sure I don't."

"They're usually the life of the party."

"June's right," Connie said. "Other dogs get along with them great because they're so charming, not threatening at all."

Muffin, charming?

"The life of the party, huh?" Jake said, trying to appear fascinated. He slugged down a healthy sip of punch. He glanced around for Muffin and decided he was definitely the center of attention at the moment. If Jake wasn't mistaken, Buzz had the animals playing a doggy version of Duck, Duck, Goose.

"But," June added, cutting right through Jake's amazement, "Geminis can also be volatile, restless, and inconsistent."

"That fits," Jake said.

"What's your sign?" Connie asked, batting her lashes at him. "Let me guess. Aries, right? They're strong and virile and have a way with women."

Jake nearly spit out some punch. "Umm . . . I'm not sure. Leo, maybe?"

"You're not sure!" June squealed.

"I'm afraid not. I've never, er, had the . . . opportunity to study astrology."

"When's your birthday?"

"July thirtieth."

"Definitely a Leo," they said in unison, smil-

153

ing knowingly at each other. "That also makes sense," June added.

Connie took a step closer. "I'm a Pisces," she said, as if that was supposed to mean something to him.

"We both are," June added unnecessarily, also crowding in on him. "Everyone says Pisces women are practically irresistible to men. Especially Leos." Another step closer. "Would you like us to read your chart? Or Muffin's?"

Connie moved so close, her breasts nearly brushed against his T-shirt. "We're staying in the hotel. Room two-twelve. I could also do a Tarot reading on Muffin."

"Mine's room two-fourteen," June said. "And I could do a Tarot reading for you."

"Where's Buzz when you need him?" Jake mumbled in an undertone to LeAnne, who was having *way* too much fun at his expense. He turned back to the twins. "Umm, yeah, maybe sometime. We . . . have a pretty full plate, but maybe we can, umm, squeeze you in."

The only thing being squeezed in right now was Jake, and he was beginning to feel like a piece of fresh meat in a tiger cage. He looked helplessly at LeAnne. "Shouldn't we be cutting the cake or something?"

LeAnne took pity on him, but she sure looked as if she did it reluctantly. "Right. And we ought to open the presents."

The twins shot him identical parting smiles,

and Jake released a breath of relief. He refilled his cup, then looked at LeAnne. "*Dog* astrologers?"

She grinned. "They also run a dog dating service called Puppy Love."

"Oh, Lord."

"They're actually quite successful. They're the ones who introduced Muffin to Dolly."

He began to make a sarcastic remark, but changed his mind. Muffin really *did* seem to love Dolly's company. Right now, Jake could relate. "Thanks for the help back there," he grumbled instead.

"Oh, you mean you were looking to be rescued? You, the tough-as-nails FBI spy?"

"I am *not*—" He bit off the rest of the sentence as Mrs. Merriweather approached with Muffin and Dolly.

Muffin looked ridiculous with his party hat on, but after seeing the display of doghood the twins were carrying, Muffin's jowly happiness was a welcome relief. He was actually beginning to look rather handsome in Jake's eyes, which made Jake wonder if he'd entered the canine twilight zone.

Muffin's eyes were shining brighter than stars, and his body was wiggling like a caught fish. Jake should have been embarrassed by the dog's utter lack of dignity, but couldn't quite bring himself to feel it. Muffin was just too dog-gone happy.

Trish Jensen

LeAnne leaned down and gave him scratches
and all kinds of birthday wishes, which Muffin
soaked in like a desert cactus during a rain-
storm. And then LeAnne lifted her head and
smiled at Jake and the world stopped spinning.
Her eyes, too, were shining and happy, and at
that moment she was the most beautiful creature he'd ever seen in his life.

As if some invisible tether had just formed,
connecting them, she rose slowly, eyes locked
on his, and he felt small jolts throughout his
system. At this moment he wanted her more
than he'd ever wanted anything or anyone in
his life.

Unfortunately, grabbing her and ravishing
her in front of Mrs. Merriweather and about a
dozen of her loyal guests wasn't the brainiest
idea he could have. But no doubt about it, even
if he had to toss pebbles at her window at midnight tonight, he was going to get her alone.

Her smile had faded, a smoky awareness filling her large brown eyes. But then she blinked
twice and looked around with a shaky laugh.
An almost imperceptible shiver traveled up her
body. She quickly crossed her arms over her
chest, but not before Jake caught her breasts
tightening behind the bodice of her suit. Jake
considered that an excellent sign. Her body
was responding, at just his look.

Muffin got Jake's attention by knocking
Jake's shin with his paw. Jake glanced down,

156

and Muffin seemed to nod his head toward Dolly, then shoot Jake a look that he interpreted as "Be nice and don't make a fool out of yourself this time."

Jake leaned down to Dolly. "Don't you look ravishing today?"

Dolly preened.

Muffin grunted his approval.

Jake started considering whether he'd lost his marbles. Because he actually felt proud that Muffin okayed his greeting. And then he felt even better when he straightened and found both LeAnne and Mrs. Merriweather smiling. He felt as if he'd just passed some kind of super-important exam.

Never in his life had he looked to others for approval. Well, maybe Aunt Sophie and Uncle George, but other than them, Jake had never given a rat's behind what people thought of him. That he was now feeling so satisfied that he'd somehow made the grade was unfathomable. Especially when it included Muffin's thoughts on the matter.

Buzz materialized by their side, flashing his smile at the group before saying, "Got a problem, LeAnne."

"What's up?"

"Darla's got a hot date tonight, not that I approve of that boy," he added. "But she's meeting him in town for a late supper, and her car won't start."

Trish Jensen

For the life of him, Jake couldn't figure out why Buzz would bring a mechanical problem to an animal doctor.

LeAnne frowned. "Turning over?"

"Yep, just not firing."

Nodding, she said, "Okay, I'll go have a look. Excuse me, folks. This shouldn't take long. But Darla takes her love life very seriously."

"Buzz can't take care of it?" Jake said, and even to his own ears he sounded a little sulky.

Holding up his hands, Buzz said, "I don't know nothing about cars. That's LeAnne's department."

This, Jake wanted to see. He shot a glance at Mrs. Merriweather, who nodded. "Why don't you go keep LeAnne company? I'll keep an eye on Muffin. And Buzz can keep an eye on the party."

"Oh, you don't have to do that!" LeAnne argued.

"It'll be my pleasure."

The employee parking lot was located behind the Hound Dog, and as they made their way down the well-lit path Jake had a hard time stopping himself from taking LeAnne's hand or draping his arm across her shoulders.

Very strange, indeed. He tried to think back on the last time that urge had hit him, and for the life of him, the senior prom with Sara Jean Davis was the only occasion he could recall.

After the drenching storm the night before, the air smelled cleansed and somewhat flowery. Which made sense, as LeAnne's grounds crew had probably planted about a zillion of them.

"Thank you for the party," he said into the comfortable silence.

"Oh, it's always my pleasure."

"I'm just floored at how well the dogs all get along. You'd think fights would break out."

"Well, the first day or two of class can get a little tense between a few of the more aggressive dogs, but they learn soon enough that playing is more fun than fighting."

"And I was pretty surprised that Muffin recognized Dolly right off. I thought dogs had memories the size of peas or something."

"You never forget your first love," LeAnne said, laughter in her voice.

"Yeah? Who was your first love?"

"Oh, no question, Robert McDowell."

"In high school?"

"Kindergarten."

Jake laughed. "Wow, you started young."

"It didn't last long. Word got out that Robert kissed me on the monkey bars, and when my brothers found out, they made sure Robert lost interest fast."

A wistful pang zapped Jake. He'd always hated being an only child. Of course, in a way, it had been a blessing. He didn't think he'd have been able to stand watching his old man beat on a little brother or sister. "How many brothers and sisters do you have?"

"Three older brothers."

He laughed again. "That had to have wreaked havoc on your love life."

"What love life?" She chuckled softly. "I couldn't wait to get away to college. Unfortunately, I had to go to school on an athletic scholarship, and the only school that offered me one was the University of Wisconsin. Where two of my brothers were still in school."

"Which sport?" Jake asked. He had made it through school on a football scholarship.

"Field hockey."

Oh, jeez. Now all these images of her in one of those field hockey skirts filled his head. Grabbing her after the game, taking her someplace private, and lifting that skirt—

He squelched the thought before he did something indecent.

They hit the parking lot, which was brightly lit. Jake marveled that even the parking area looked classy, cheerful, welcoming. The concrete was a gleaming white, the parking lines a bright royal blue, as were the metal poles of the streetlights.

Darla's blond hair shone under a halogen lamp, and when she saw LeAnne, she came rushing over from a blue Mustang.

She was all dolled up in a denim miniskirt and a white cotton tank top. Her eyes were filled with fear and frustration. "Oh, LeAnne, I'll just die if my car's dead. I'll just *die.*"

"Relax, sweetheart; we'll fix you up. And if worse comes to worst, you can borrow my car."

"You're the best," Darla said on a sigh of relief.

Jake was beginning to agree with her. The three of them approached the Mustang, and Jake listened in amazement as LeAnne grilled Darla about the car's symptoms, as if it were a patient. He would have liked to offer his opinion on the problem, but he knew the insides of a car engine about as well as he knew the insides of a human. Uncle George had never been mechanically inclined, so that wasn't one of the activities they'd engaged in together.

"Try to start it up," LeAnne commanded when they reached the car. Darla hopped in and turned the key. The engine cranked over and over without kicking up.

"It's not the battery," Jake said with authority, because at least *that* much he knew.

LeAnne glanced at him, amusement making her lips twitch. "Absolutely right." She held up a finger at Darla in a "one second" gesture. "Pop the hood. I'll be right back." Then she glanced back at Jake. "Will you open the hood for me while I get a couple of things?"

"Sure," he said, pleased she was asking for help, even if it was pretty pathetic help. While he fumbled with the latch on the hood, it occurred to him that she had probably asked him that on purpose, just to make him feel useful.

And he wasn't being very useful. Because the damn latch wouldn't give. He felt a little panic at the thought that he couldn't even complete this task. He was a highly decorated FBI special agent, who almost always got his man. He could run surveillance, testify like a pro in court, stare down armed criminals, and protect his witnesses zealously and successfully. But as he groped and pushed and pulled at the damn car hood, he realized just how out of his element he was. And so far in LeAnne's eyes he hadn't performed one task admirably.

He'd dived into a pond for no good reason, he'd driven a poor, love-starved dog under a bed in terror, he'd been wiped out at tennis, and now this. All in all, he wouldn't blame LeAnne for thinking he was an idiot.

Finally he caught the latch right, and with a grunt of relief he lifted the hood. But the raised hood blocked light from the lamp, and he had to grope for the metal thing that held it up. Stepping back, he smacked his hands together triumphantly. His hands stilled in midclap when he saw LeAnne approach.

She'd donned mechanic's coveralls and she was carrying a small toolbox. A hand towel was draped over her left shoulder.

He'd never seen a sexier sight in his life.

She stopped beside him and set down her tools.

"I got it open," he boasted stupidly.

"I saw that," she said with an approving smile that wasn't patronizing.

"Why the duds?" he asked. *Thank you, Lord, for the duds.*

"I didn't want to get grease on my swimsuit. Or get burned." She stepped to the side of the car and directed Darla to start it again and keep trying until she had Jake give the signal to stop.

Then she returned and centered herself over the engine, bending over the machinery in a way that filled out the coveralls in a Victoria's Secret sort of way. He was really, really beginning to like coveralls.

A fantasy called to him. One that involved catching her lying on a trolley under a car. Of pulling her out, only to find her nude and covered with patches of grease, which he then leisurely spread all over her body, making her slick and primed to let him inside her. Of taking her right there on that hard bed on wheels.

Damn, she had a great ass, and he wanted his hands all over it. All over her. In her.

Darla cranked up a storm, and Jake dragged his attention from LeAnne's backside to watch what she was doing. Within seconds she signaled him, and he signaled Darla by slashing a finger across his throat.

Silence slammed into the night, and Jake watched as LeAnne unclamped some brown upside-down cuplike thing, using a screwdriver. Popping it loose with the hand towel, she turned it over and peered in with a small flashlight, then shook her head and set the cup aside.

"Tell her it's probably moisture in her distributor," she said.

Jake told her. He listened to Darla's response, then said, "she asked if that's fatal."

LeAnne bent down to her box again, and he almost lost her answer in his fog of utter lust. He figured he was exceedingly sex-deprived when he found a woman wearing grease-stained overalls irresistible.

"Tell her if I'm right, it's about the puniest problem she could have. Must have seeped in there from the storm last night."

"Puny," Jake repeated. "Seeped. Rain."

Darla asked for clarification, but Jake was too busy watching LeAnne work and deciding exactly how he'd love to peel that uniform off her body. How he'd love to make her do mechanical things to his car buck-naked, while he kissed every inch of her and made her forget the difference between a spark plug and a battery.

LeAnne pulled out a bright yellow and blue can of something called WD-40 and sprayed it into the cup. Then she replaced the cup in the car and clamped it down again. "Tell her to try again."

"Try what again?"

"To start the car, Jake."

"Oh." He leaned to his right. "Start her up."

The car chugged a few times, but finally kicked up. Even over the roar of the engine, Jake heard Darla's delighted squeal. LeAnne nodded, then dropped the hood and packed up her tools in her adorable little car doctor kit. She moved aside, dragging Jake with her. "You're good to go," she called over the growl of the old car. "It looks like you have a small crack in your distributor cap. We'll have to replace it before the next big rain, but you're okay for now. Have fun, but be careful."

"You're the absolute best!" Darla yelled back, then peeled out so fast her tires squealed.

LeAnne shifted her toolbox to her other hand, then looked up at him. "Give me a minute to get out of this gig?" she said, waving at her outfit.

"Oh, please, let me help," he said with a wink.

She laughed, then began strolling down the parking lot. "I think I can handle it."

"Actually," he said, catching up and falling into step beside her, "that's sort of what I was hoping to do."

She glanced askance at him. "Are you always this open about trying to seduce women?"

"I feel it's only fair to be honest about it."

"How noble," she said dryly.

"I think so."

He took the arm holding the toolbox and pulled it to him. His fingers covered hers. "Let me carry that for you."

"It's not heavy," she said, her voice low as she stared at his hand covering hers.

"I'm trying to be chivalrous, here."

She let him take the box. "Wow. Noble *and* chivalrous."

"Don't forget seductive."

Her eyes rolled skyward. "I'm sure if I do, you'll happily remind me."

They stopped behind a black Nissan Maxima. Jake was a little surprised that she didn't drive a more luxurious car. After all, she could probably afford a Ferrari. But the more he thought about it, the more he realized this was more her style. She wasn't a flashy woman. When it came to her guests, she spared no expense. But in all of her personal affairs, she remained firmly down-to-earth. What other multimillionaire woman wouldn't think twice about donning coveralls and diving right into a car engine? What other rich woman would wear the simplest of jewelry, a plain—if capable of driving him wild with lust—navy bathing suit? What other very wealthy woman would openly and affectionately admit that her family couldn't afford to send her to college?

"Where did you learn all that mechanical know-how?" he asked.

"My father's the best mechanic in Wisconsin," she boasted. She sounded so happy Jake wanted to hug her. "I used to go to his station after school when my mom was at work. I learned by osmosis."

"What does your mom do?"

"She's head librarian at the Kenosha Public Library."

The affection in her voice told him all he needed to know about her home life. He envied her, but not in a bad way. After all, those folks had shaped this woman, who was climbing his admiration ladder at a faster and faster clip.

LeAnne produced a key and opened the trunk of the car, taking her toolbox from him and tucking it in the corner. But what caught his eye was the neatly folded scarf that had been lovingly caressing her hips earlier. Which meant the only thing hugging her hips at the moment was that so-unsexy-it's-mind-blowingly-sexy bathing suit.

Jake casually took a step back, not to give her space but to allow him a more all-encompassing view. It'd probably be more gallant for him to turn his back and give her privacy, but at the moment he figured gallantry was a highly overrated trait.

It occurred to him that she was chatting on about her brothers or something and he hadn't been paying attention because he was too busy watching the way she unsnapped the front of her coveralls.

She pulled her arms free and the material dropped to her waist. She stopped talking abruptly when she realized his attention wasn't on the conversation.

The parking lot was well enough lit that Jake could see the blush that began on her creamy, bare chest and crept up her neck. And he wanted to follow every climbing inch of it with his fingers and lips.

He forced himself to raise his gaze to her eyes. They were lowered shyly, and she'd stopped pushing the cotton material down her body.

He wasn't turning around. After all, he'd already seen her in the suit. But to make her feel less self-conscious, he averted his gaze just enough that he wasn't staring directly at her, but could still see her in his peripheral vision.

"Thank you," LeAnne said softly.

"Don't thank me too much. I have a very vivid imagination." *And great peripheral vision.*

LeAnne knew her responding laughter was shaky and breathless and silly. She also had to concede that she was just a little disappointed that he'd decided to act the gentleman. There had been something sizzlingly sensual about the prospect of stripping down to her bathing suit with him watching. Even if it *was* the most functional, sexless bathing suit she owned. She'd debated long and hard. This suit was her "business suit." Whenever she took a swim with dogs and their owners she wore this Speedo.

Tonight she'd pulled out her lime green and

black bikini without even thinking. And she had to admit it was because she'd forgotten for a moment that he was a guest and she didn't get involved with guests. She'd been thinking of him only as a man whom she'd wanted to entice.

Luckily, she'd remembered just in time that they weren't actually having a swimming session, but were in reality setting Jake up for Muffin's party. Well, she hadn't actually remembered. Buzz had reminded her with a last-minute call about arrangements.

She shook her head and quickly slipped the coveralls off, not bothering to fold them. She slipped the sarong around her hips and tied it, grinning at his tuneless whistling, his classic profile, not to mention great legs. Sophie might have exaggerated Jake's finer qualities, but not by much. The more LeAnne got to know him, the more she liked about him. "Especially that cute butt," she murmured aloud, then slapped a hand over her mouth in horror.

"Excuse me?" he said, his head swiveling to her.

"Stephanie's a cute mutt," she improvised.

"Huh?"

"Never mind, I was just thinking out loud."

"Oh."

"All done." She dropped her trunk lid.

He awarded her with a thorough thrice-over. Then before she knew it, he stepped forward, trapping her against the trunk of her car.

169

"Damn, lady, you're the sexiest woman I've ever seen."

LeAnne could try to say that her suddenly galloping heart rate was due to alarm, but she didn't see any good reason to lie to herself. She was excited. This man was big and broad and hard and gorgeous.

And he was about to kiss her.

She sucked in a breath just as his head lowered to hers. "Hold on to your hat, Doc."

"Oh, yes," she said, the words coming out on a sigh.

And then his mouth was on hers, hot and seeking. His hands landed on her shoulders, then drifted up her neck and plunged into her hair. All the while his mouth moved over hers in a way she'd never been kissed before.

Thoroughly.

He licked her and nipped her and plunged into her, and LeAnne felt almost pummeled, but in the most wonderful way possible. He leaned into her, and all parts of him touching all parts of her set off fires down the length of her. His bare legs pressed into hers, and the crisp hair brushing her skin felt absolutely wonderful. Lifting his head, he stared at her, his breath coming out raspy. "Damn," he said with a groan, "your mouth should be illegal."

"Shut up and kiss me."

And he did, gloriously ravishing her mouth, her neck, her cheeks. His hands weren't idle by a long shot, either. They roamed over her back and waist and hips, then cupped her bottom and pulled her against him, leaving no doubt he was enjoying himself immensely.

LeAnne had never been *devoured* like this before, had never felt a man so hungry for the taste and feel of her. His hands were so large she felt small, but happily feminine. And though she had no doubt that he'd take her right there if she asked, those hands never came near the parts of her crying out for his touch, his invasion.

Which would be sweet if it weren't so darn frustrating.

Her hands weren't idle, either. She had a burning need to touch every hard inch of him, to explore his body in excruciatingly wonderful detail. The muscles in his back rippled with his movements, his arms a wonder, his chest breathtaking.

Never in her life had she had this insane desire to tear a man's clothes from him, to taste every inch, to bring him to a crashing orgasm with her hands and mouth and body.

With his knee he nudged her legs slightly apart, then brought his thigh up to her pulsing center. She gasped into his mouth and he lifted his head, breaking the kiss. "I want you so much."

She blinked and tried to grab for a shred of sanity, but sanity was in short supply out in that parking lot. "I . . . we need to get back to the party."

"To hell with the party."

"Buzz might come looking for us."

That got his attention. He stepped back and glanced over his shoulder, then looked back at her. "After the party?" he rasped.

Her head cleared a little more, even if her body was still crying for his touch. "Is this a good idea?"

His hand lifted to her face, his knuckle stroking her cheek. "Lady, this is singularly the best idea I've had in my entire life."

"I don't get involved with guests," she said, and even to her own ears her voice sounded glum.

"Well, technically I'm not a guest. Remember, I'm here under protest."

"That's true," she said, cheering up right away, even if that was the lamest loophole anyone had ever devised.

He kissed her hard one more time, and LeAnne felt in that kiss a sealing of a deal of sorts. "Tell me I can come to your place after the party."

"You can come to my place after the party."

His smile just about undid her. It was full of promises that she couldn't wait to have him fulfill. Jeez, she was truly surprised at herself. It wasn't that she'd never been turned on before, but not like this. And not by a man she'd known only a few short days. And not by a man who was destined to walk out of her life at the end of his enforced two-week stay.

She was turning into a hussy right before her very own eyes. Worse, she was happy about it. And so, apparently, was he, if his hot, smoldering smile was any indication.

He held out his hand. "Let's get this party over with."

"You put your right paw in, you take your right paw out, you put your right paw in, then you shake it all about. You do the hokey-pokey and you turn yourself around. That's what it's all about!" *Bark!*

Jake stared in utter amazement as he watched a dozen dogs doing the hokey-pokey at Buzz's direction. And not doing a half-bad job, either.

Buzz started in on the second chorus, but then noticed their return, and he tripped up for a moment as he took in LeAnne's face. Jake didn't have to look at her to know what Buzz saw: kiss-swollen lips and a rosy blush. Buzz's perusal, even as he continued the ditty, was narrow-eyed, and even more so as his gaze slid to Jake. But after a moment he returned his attention to the dogs, in particular a retriever who was having a tough time telling his left from his right paw.

Jake shook his head and glanced at LeAnne, who was smiling at the scene before them, but not looking at all bemused by the sight. "I bet they perform a mean Charleston, hmm?" he said dryly.

"Actually, Muffin prefers the tango," she retorted, grinning. Then she started to walk away.

Jake grabbed her arm and pulled her back for one final reminder. "Lady, tonight I plan to take a trip to heaven."

"Is that right?" she said in a husky voice.

"That's right. And you're coming with me."

LeAnne was doing her best to concentrate on the party's guest of honor, but she couldn't quite do it when she was so utterly aware of his owner. She watched as the twins once again tried to engage Jake in flirtatious conversation, but somehow it wasn't as amusing now as it had been before the episode in the parking lot.

It was utterly ridiculous, not to mention dangerous, to nurture any possessive or jealous feelings. Jake wasn't hers. Not in any way. He wanted her, she had no doubt about that. But purely in the hormonal sense. She had to keep that in mind. What they were about to engage in was a fling. Sexual enjoyment between a man and a woman.

And though she was flattered and excited that a man as boldly sexy as Jake had chosen her as the object of his desire, she was also acutely aware that he could have just about any woman he set his baby blues on.

Stephen had been the same way. He hadn't been as handsome as Jake and he'd definitely been older, but he'd had a charming air about him that drew women like flies.

LeAnne hadn't been worried about it, believing with all her heart that Stephen loved her too much ever to cheat on her. That was, until he began having her followed, and when she'd discovered it, started accusing her of having affairs with everyone from the mailman to her hairdresser to the vice president of his electronics firm.

Since she'd given him absolutely no reason to suspect infidelity on her part, she'd had to come to the painful conclusion that he was engaging in illicit affairs, and to assuage his guilt, began to believe the worst of her, as well.

His sudden lack of trust had all but killed her love for him—shredded it as surely as the contraption in his office that he'd used to destroy documents.

LeAnne shuddered and pushed the thoughts away. Trust was something she and Jake needn't worry about. Because the only sharing they were promising each other was the sharing of pleasure.

Mrs. Merriweather strolled over to LeAnne just as she poured herself another cup of punch. The woman's smile was warm, but knowing, as if they shared a secret. LeAnne greeted her.

"Nice party," Mrs. Merriweather said.

"Yes, it is."

"As soon as Jake peels himself away from Connie and June, I'm going to ask him if Muffin can spend the night at my bungalow."

"Really?" LeAnne said, trying not to grin. "Muffin will probably love that."

"I figured you'd think so. And I'm fairly certain Jake won't object."

LeAnne had to resist the urge to hug the lady. She didn't know how Mrs. Merriweather had concluded that she and Jake would welcome some time alone, but she wasn't going to argue. Not having to worry about Muffin would free them up all that much more. She knew she was probably blushing like a schoolgirl, so she hid behind her cup of punch and looked around.

That was when she saw Buzz leading in an unfamiliar man and woman, an unusual thunderous expression on his normally cheerful face.

The man seemed to be in his mid-thirties, and was handsome in a rugged sort of way. He was wearing jeans and a Planet Hollywood T-shirt.

The woman was beautiful. Tall and willowy, she had grace and poise. She wore tailored off-white slacks and a peach-and-cream silk shirt.

Buzz paused for a second, glancing around. LeAnne followed his gaze, and when it landed on Jake and grew even darker, LeAnne got a funny feeling in the pit of her stomach.

Buzz led the two over to Jake, and when Jake finally glanced at the approaching couple, his jaw dropped and he immediately extricated himself from the twins. He strode toward the strangers, his face suddenly grim.

"What in hell are you doing here?" he said in a growl.

The woman looped her arms around his neck, and he stiffened perceptibly. "Why, darling, is that any way to greet your fiancée?"

Chapter Eight

"I'm going to kill both of you," Jake said, after shoving Mark, Elisa Johnson, and Muffin through the door of his bungalow. He dropped the bag of presents Muffin had received on the ground. "What the hell were you thinking?"

Elisa glanced at him worriedly; Mark looked as if he didn't have a care in the world. "It was the best plan I could come up with."

"It wouldn't have hurt for you to warn me," Jake said with a growl. He couldn't get LeAnne's face out of his mind. She'd looked so stricken, and then so angry, he flinched even now thinking about it.

The party had ended abruptly after that, and of course Muffin blamed *him*. LeAnne had left almost immediately, not even waiting for introductions or explanations. Of course, he couldn't tell her the real explanation, but he might have been able to come up with *something* that would have appeased her. As it was, he sincerely doubted she'd speak to him at all for the rest of his stay.

"No time," Mark said. "I had to get her out of Richmond fast, and I didn't want to risk a phone call."

"This is ridiculous. They've been hot on your heels since we put her on our witness list. How are they dogging your every move?"

For the first time, Mark looked grim. And Jake didn't need a verbal answer. Someone in the department was ratting them out. He mentally listed all the people who were aware of Mark's movements. Three, that he could think of: their boss, Jered Thomas, his secretary, Frank Fordham, and the lead federal prosecutor, Tony Malone. That was it.

He and Mark spoke volumes to each other silently. When this was over, they were going to find the snitch.

Mark bent and scratched Muffin behind the ears. "Anyway, this is perfect. No one knows you're here, you can keep an eye on her, it's win-win. So what's your problem?"

Since he couldn't tell them his problem was that he'd just lost all hope of making love to the owner of this resort, he pressed his lips together and just glared. "Did you have to pass her off as my fiancée?"

"That was the brilliant part of the plan. That way no one here raises an eyebrow when the two of you share a room."

Jake almost choked. "What do you mean, share a room?"

"Face it, pal, you're playing bodyguard for the next several days."

"I'm on vacation!"

Mark got a real guffaw out of that one. In the FBI, there was no such "official" thing. Sure, agents planned vacations and actually got to enjoy them much of the time. But they were basically on call twenty-four/seven/three-sixty-five.

"In case you haven't noticed, there's only one bed in this room."

"Nice couch," Mark commented dryly. "Looks real comfortable."

"Why couldn't *you* have played the part of boyfriend?"

"Because *I'm* the one testifying, or have you forgotten? I've got to get back to D. C. and consult with the prosecution team over the presentation of our evidence."

"I'm sorry to be such a bother," Elisa said quietly.

Jake immediately felt a world of guilt. This brave young woman had placed her life on the line when she agreed to testify to what she knew about Jacob and Millicent Winston's operations. And here all he'd been concerned about was his personal life.

181

"No!" he exclaimed. "No, no, you're not a bother. I . . . I'm glad to have the company." He almost choked on that one. "And Mark's right. This place is about as secure as we're going to get." He looked around. "Umm, where's your luggage?"

As if on cue, there was a knock at the door. And Mark, whom Jake was seriously considering beating to a pulp, said, "That'll be her luggage now."

Please don't let it be Buzz, Jake thought.

But of course, it was. He entered loaded with luggage, flashing his normally friendly smile at Mark and Elisa. Then he turned his attention to Jake, and his smile evaporated. The contempt in his eyes was enough to make Jake flinch. "Where you want me to put *your lady's* things?"

Jake waved at the bed. He had never felt the need to defend his behavior in his life. Right now his sole desire was to get Buzz and LeAnne alone and explain himself.

Which was ridiculous.

His job was the most important thing in his life. And the most satisfying. He *liked* bringing down bad guys, people who had no qualms about taking advantage of those weaker than themselves. In fact, he realized, he was somewhat fanatical about it.

Which, until this moment, he'd considered a *good* thing.

"Will your future brother-in-law be needin'

accommodations for the night?" Buzz inquired of him after dumping two suitcases on the bed.

"Who?" Jake asked, with all the intelligence of a rock.

Mark jumped in fast. "No, no, I won't. As soon as my sister's settled, I'm taking off."

Jake wasn't usually so slow on the uptake. Of course, he'd been flustered from the moment Elisa and Mark had shown up and dropped the bomb.

With one last glare at Jake and nod at the two others, Buzz took his leave. It was a testament to Buzz's anger that he hadn't even acknowledged Muffin, much less slipped him a bone. And naturally Muffin felt the slight and turned accusing eyes on Jake.

Nothing like being made to feel like scum of the earth by a dog, a handyman, and a dog shrink.

While Elisa unpacked her belongings, Jake went to the kitchenette and pulled out three cans of apple juice. He and Mark moved to the sitting area.

Mark started to brief him, and Jake tried to concentrate. But his mind wasn't on the Winston case. His mind wasn't anywhere but on a woman with big brown eyes and a mouth that could tempt a eunuch. He had to find a way to let her know he hadn't betrayed her or his supposed fiancée. That he wasn't a cheating rat.

But without blowing Elisa's cover, he couldn't think of a single story that would wash. Restless and anxious beyond reason, he started to pace. That was when he glanced down the hall toward the front door. And found it open.

He scanned the room and found two things notably absent. Muffin, and Muffin's heart blanket.

Looked like his dog had just run away.

LeAnne couldn't decide whether she was more angry or embarrassed. Even worse, there was a hint of disappointment lounging around in her head as well.

For someone trained to evaluate and understand human and animal psyches, she'd really blown her estimation of Jake. She'd actually fallen for his supposed growing love for his dog, his growing attraction to her.

LeAnne put her heart and soul into scrubbing the already gleaming tub. She absolutely *hated* scrubbing tubs, so she figured it was a fitting punishment for her stupidity. Had Jake's fiancée not shown up when she did, LeAnne's fall from grace would have been utterly, completely humiliating.

She'd just almost fallen happily into bed with a nearly married man.

"You are an *idiot*," she reminded herself. "A first-class *idiot*."

Between her self-recriminations, the scratching of the brush, and the running water,

LeAnne almost didn't hear the noise coming from the front of her bungalow. She dropped the brush and shut off the water, listening, wondering if she'd imagined it.

But no, there it was again. Sounded like scratching and a muffled *woof*.

She stood and pulled the rubber gloves from her hands and checked her watch. It was ten-thirty at night.

The sounds came again, and LeAnne rushed to her front door. She checked the peephole but saw nothing. Keeping the chain in place, she cautiously opened the door.

Her jaw dropped. "Muffin! What are you doing here?"

Muffin whined.

She looked behind him for any sign of Jake, but it appeared Muffin had arrived alone. Quickly she shut the door and unchained it, then reopened it. "Come in."

Although she tried to keep her private living quarters exactly that—private—she wasn't at all surprised that Muffin knew where she lived. On several occasions he'd stayed overnight with her when Sophie had had to leave Happy Hounds for various reasons. She could count on one finger how many clients she'd done this for. But Sophie—and Muffin—had always been special.

Muffin huffed through her door, dragging his blanket in his wake. He moved directly to the middle of her living room and dropped it, then sat down and stared at her mulishly, as if daring her to question his presence.

She followed him into the living room and knelt beside him. "I take it you're not a happy camper."

He remained stubbornly mute.

"Does Jake know you're here?" she asked, stroking his back soothingly.

Muffin looked away with a snort.

"We have to tell him, you know. He'll be worried sick."

He snorted louder.

"I know that your party ended rather abruptly, but that really wasn't Jake's fault." She couldn't believe she was excusing the worm. But her personal opinion aside, Muffin and Jake had a long future together, and she wasn't about to support Muffin's antagonism.

"Okay, so he's not a world-class human, but he's all you've got, and he really did seem to be trying there. And in his defense, his fiancée's showing up was most definitely a surprise to him, too." *That*, she could assure Muffin without reservation. Had he had any inkling his betrothed was headed his way, she sincerely doubted he would have made plans to be with another woman. He was a cheat and a slug but he wasn't stupid.

"How about a rawhide?" she asked.

Muffin kept his face averted, but his eyes slid sideways to look at her.

LeAnne smiled and stood, then went to the kitchen to grab a rawhide chew. She took it out to Muffin, who forgot his indignation in light of the treat. He'd stood back up and his stump of a tail wagged. "Here you go, sweetheart."

He instantly dropped down and got into some serious gnawing. LeAnne left him to it, and went for her phone.

She dialed the number to Jake's bungalow, but it was busy, so she called the concierge desk. Sure enough, Jake was on the other line, frantically demanding her number. So she instructed Tim to tell Jake to hang up and she'd call. At this point she wanted Jake Donnelly to have her number about as much as she wanted to get run over by a train.

She waited about twenty seconds, then dialed his number again. He answered on the first ring. "LeAnne?"

"Yes, it's me."

"Muffin's missing," he said. The panic in his voice was obvious, and would almost be endearing if he were anyone else. "Somehow the door was open, and he took off. Can we form a patrol to look for him?"

"We could do that, but it's not really necessary."

"Not necessary?" he barked. "Do you realize how many freaking acres you have here, lady? He could be anywhere!"

"He could, but he's not. He's right here, Jake."

187

"There? As in, your place?"

"That's right. He showed up about ten minutes ago."

"Is he all right?"

"He's fine, Jake."

He sucked in an audible breath. "Good." Then he seemed to gather himself and he added, "I'm going to kill that mutt when I get my hands on him."

"Now settle down. Muffin was upset."

"Upset? I'll show him upset."

"In your current state, I think it would be best if Muffin spent the night here."

"Not a chance. That mongrel comes home and faces the music. Where do you live?"

"Not a chance," she said right back at him. "We can meet tomorrow morning and I'll hand him over. But I'm not bringing him back to you in your current mood."

"You don't need to bring him back; just tell me where you live."

"No."

"LeAnne—"

"No, Jake. I'm not telling you where I live and I'm not returning him tonight."

He swore. Twice. *Nope, make that three times.*

"Besides," she said, in her sweetest, most reasonable voice, "this'll give you a chance to spend time alone with your fiancée."

"Listen, LeAnne, about that—"

"I don't want to hear it."

"It's not what you—"

"I mean it, Jake."

He took another noisy breath. "Muffin and I need a session tomorrow."

"When pigs fly."

"Look, my dog has just run away. You don't think that's grounds for counseling?"

It was an excellent reason for counseling. The professional side of her warred with the personal. No way in hell did she want to be alone with Jake. Even with Muffin there as a buffer, she considered the prospect dangerous. Besides, it might traumatize Muffin to witness LeAnne ripping out the jerk's heart.

She sighed. "What's Muffin's schedule tomorrow?"

Papers rustled on his end of the line. "He has obedience training at nine—and trust me, he's not missing that one—and his pedicure at ten. Pedicure. Sheesh. It'll be a miracle if he doesn't leave here a sissy."

"This might come as a real surprise, but male dogs' nails grow, too, you know."

He ignored that. "The rest of the day's free. How about yours?"

Unfortunately, Fridays were fairly light days, as many of the residents took long weekends to sightsee outside the resort. "I'll meet you in front of the hotel at eight-fifty to hand him over. Then how about we meet at the pool at eleven?"

"The pool? Won't it be crowded?"

Exactly. "It won't be too bad."

"Are we going swimming?"

"You two are." She, on the other hand, was burning that Speedo. Never again could she wear it without being reminded of his hands all over it.

"Well, okay. See you tomorrow."

"Tomorrow."

"And LeAnne?"

"Yes?"

"I never lied to you."

Before she could conjure an appropriate and cutting retort, he hung up.

Since Jake's soon-to-be wife had been plastered by his side earlier that morning when he'd come to pick up Muffin, LeAnne was somewhat surprised that she was nowhere in sight when he arrived at the pool.

Muffin was obviously still angry with Jake, as he first lagged behind, then ran ahead, fighting the leash with every step. LeAnne didn't even want to hear how obedience class had gone.

A full-fledged scowl graced Jake's face, and LeAnne could tell he was ready to strangle the dog. She jumped up quickly from the lounge chair and greeted them.

Jake had the nerve to look scrumptious in his black swim trunks and a pale blue Oxford shirt, completely unbuttoned, sleeves rolled. Tantalizing glimpses of his chest were absolutely not what she needed at the moment.

Of course, it had been her stupid idea to meet here in the first place, so she couldn't exactly expect him to show up in a snowsuit. But why hadn't she kept in mind that swimming meant bare skin? Lots of it.

Muffin was obviously still a little miffed at LeAnne, too. He apparently felt she'd betrayed him by turning him back over to the evil Jake. This dog sure knew how to hold a grudge.

"You ready to play, Muffin?" LeAnne asked, bending to pet him.

Muffin sniffed, but his eyes turned longingly to the pool. It was disgustingly devoid of guests and their pets, but at least the lifeguard was there to witness events. And to keep Jake from trying to explain himself where no explanation could get him off the hook.

But she had to wonder at his declaration last night that he'd never lied to her. The only way that *that* statement was true would be if he'd distinguished between girlfriend and fiancée. And she wasn't about to let him get off on that technicality.

Between Jake's shirt and the brilliant sky behind him, his eyes shone a dazzling blue. Sparked with irritation at his dog, they blazed almost indigo. He'd also obviously forgone saying howdy to his razor this morning, and the dark stubble on his face made his strong jaw look even more solid, masculine, and formidable.

And she shouldn't be noticing.

LeAnne dragged her thoughts from him and concentrated on a stubborn Muffin. "Okay, young man, let's begin with your attitude."

"Hey! I don't have an attitude!" Jake protested.

LeAnne and Muffin scoffed in unison. "I wasn't talking to you," LeAnne said. "And besides, you're not that young. But, yes, you do have an attitude."

His smile could bring torpedoes to a screaming halt. "I'll forgive the 'not that young' remark, seeing as you're forgetting that Muffin's older than I am, if you're multiplying right. And he's still acting like a spoiled brat. And I showed considerable restraint this morning when what he deserved was a good old-fashioned dog-whooping."

She glanced up at him. "Oh, so you believe in violence as a form of education?" she asked with all the sarcasm she could muster.

She wasn't prepared for his reaction in the least. He went stiff and his face took on the quality of stone. His eyes went blank. The muscles in his neck corded. And as far as she could tell, he'd stopped breathing.

"Jake?" She touched his arm. "I was teasing."

It was a good ten seconds before he sucked in a breath. "I'd never hit him," he said in a low, tortured tone.

LeAnne's heart melted more than it should.

He stated it so quietly, so meaningfully, she knew she'd struck a horrible nerve. "Of course you wouldn't. If I thought you would, I'd demand custody of him instantly."

Jake blinked several times. And he seemed to return to the present; she was sure he'd been visiting a not-so-happy memory. Or memories. "Jake," she said softly, "Muffin isn't afraid of you. He trusts you not to hurt him physically. I can tell that right away. He's afraid of you emotionally. He doesn't trust that you love him. So he's acting out."

And in that moment she realized she and Muffin had a lot in common. Which was a scary thought.

Jake ran a hand through his hair, then rubbed that prizewinning jaw. "Look, I know you mean well. But I'm not sure I'll ever replace Aunt Sophie in his eyes. He's going to resent me forever for not being her."

LeAnne wanted to applaud him for finally understanding you could get into an animal's head. And she wanted to kiss him for getting into it right. He might be a pure creep in the people department, but he was beginning to understand his dog.

"You know, he's not going to resent you forever," she said. "He's going to start adapting to your way of loving him, which is different than Sophie's was. And he'll discover it's the best love he can imagine."

He digested that for a moment, then leaned toward her, smiling. "How I'd like to show you the best love you can imagine."

She wobbled for about two seconds. Then she came to her senses. Leaning into him, she smiled her best smile. "Oh, yeah?" she said, pushing just hard enough to make him take a couple of steps back. "You think so?"

"Lady, you're lethal."

"No kidding," she said, right before shoving him with all her might. The huge splash as he hit the water was tremendously satisfying.

"Would you look at that?" Jimmy said to the driver of the car. "She just pushed Donnelly into the pool."

"You're the one with the binoculars, Bun," Horace "the Python" Walters replied.

"Don't call me that!" Jimmy snapped. It pissed him off to high heaven that a dweeb named Horace Walters got a cool name, just because he was good at squeezing money out of "customers." Hell, he hadn't once done a hit. As far as Jimmy was concerned, that made him a rank amateur.

"Well, it explains why Colson brought her to this place. Donnelly was already here waiting for them."

The night before, they hadn't seen Colson enter this place with his charge, but they'd been shocked as hell sitting outside the gates, hidden in a police speed trap, when Colson had left. By himself.

They'd broken the locked gate and entered in the middle of the night to scope out the place. Then they had stayed neatly inconspicuous sitting in the front visitors' parking lot, hoping to spot their mark. Instead, Jimmy had been shocked to see Colson's partner, walking by himself into the hotel earlier that morning.

So the two Feds had played tag team.

After driving around the grounds so as not to cause suspicion just sitting in the lot all morning, they'd returned to find Donnelly and their mark out in the open together. This was going to be a piece of cake. They just needed to time it perfectly. He'd have to wait for Donnelly to get out of the pool, though. Too easy to miss or not make a lethal shot in water.

"The girl dyed her hair," he commented. "But man, she's still a looker."

"Let me see."

Jimmy handed over the binoculars and Horace took a look. "Looks shorter than I remember from her pictures."

"Pictures don't mean squat. Ever seen Sylvester Stallone in person?"

"Wonder why she's not in a bathing suit?" Horace said, and he sounded real disappointed. Jimmy wouldn't have minded seeing her in something skimpy himself, but he was too professional to say so.

Jimmy snatched the binoculars back, then again aimed them at his targets. Just then movement at the woman's feet snatched his attention, and he looked down. "Holy shit! What the hell kind of dog is that?"

Horace grabbed the binoculars again. "Damn, Jimmy. Didn't you ever go to school? Half the damn schools in the country have bulldogs for mascots."

Jimmy grabbed the binoculars again, trying to keep his temper under control. He didn't like being reminded he had an eighth-grade education. "Course I knew that! Sure are peculiar-looking dogs. That one looks mean, too," he said, shuddering. Jimmy considered himself a brave man, but he sure as hell didn't like dogs. Wasn't afraid of them, of course. Just liked to avoid them.

"Whatever you do, don't hit the dog."

"If it gets in the way, that's its problem."

"I mean it, Bunny. You shoot that dog and I'm driving you straight to the nearest cops."

Jimmy rolled his eyes. Not only a rank amateur, but a wimp, too. But Jimmy also had no doubt that Horace would do it. He had his own sense of right and wrong, and Jimmy had seen his temper when he thought he'd encountered wrong. A wimp, maybe. But a mean wimp when provoked.

"I won't hit the dog."

* * *

Jake surfaced, sputtering, his shirt now plastered to his chest, and his hair dripping water down his face and neck. He was the sexiest wet guy she'd ever laid eyes on.

"Feel better?" he asked, swiping his hair back from his forehead.

"Much."

He glanced over at Muffin. "And you're probably ecstatic."

Muffin yipped and his back end wiggled.

"Not so fast, young man," LeAnne scolded while trying valiantly to stifle a grin. She picked up a small rubber ball from a basket and tossed it over Jake's head into the pool. "Fetch!"

Muffin sailed through the air and landed with an admirable splash. She watched for Jake's reaction and was pleased to see him tense and prepare to take action if necessary, even though he'd already seen proof that Muffin was a good swimmer.

For the next twenty minutes LeAnne directed them in various games, some pitting them in competition with each other, some requiring them to cooperate to accomplish the goal.

LeAnne watched their antagonism melt away and a quiet contentment filled her. The two didn't know it, but they were going to be just fine. It was really endearing how often Jake slowed his pace to allow Muffin to win a race to the ball, and then grumbled about losing after Muffin gave him a superior *woof*.

Jake tossed her the ball, then cradled Muffin in his arms and waded to the side of the pool. "I think he's getting tired."

"You're probably right. Let's take a break."

Jake lifted Muffin out of the pool, then dragged himself out as well. He grabbed his towel and dried off, then bent and ran it over Muffin's back.

"By the way," LeAnne said, "how does Muffin get along with . . . your fiancée?"

Jake straightened abruptly. "Umm, well, they haven't really . . . spent much time together yet."

"Does she like dogs?"

'Umm, yes, I think so."

"You *think* so?"

"I mean, she does. She likes dogs."

"Where is she, anyway?"

"She . . . uh, had a headache. She decided to stay in bed."

The image of him lying next to the woman popped into LeAnne's head involuntarily. And her stomach clenched. Which was really dumb. She didn't care one way or another.

LeAnne noticed that he couldn't make eye contact with her. He was either lying about something, or embarrassed. Or both. She turned away from him because she had a sudden very unprofessional desire to slug the man.

Just then a loud bang sounded, and LeAnne's

head whirled in the direction of the noise. Her first thought was that Mrs. Merriweather was popping balloons again. But instead she saw a dark car slowly cruising by and an ominous black thing sticking out from a lowered tinted window.

She didn't have time to assimilate it all, though, because in that same instant she found herself flying into the pool.

When she surfaced she saw Jake crouched down. "Get down to that end of the pool!" he barked and pointed. "Keep your head low!"

LeAnne wasn't about to question him. She dove and swam for all she was worth, and when she came up for air, she came up just high enough to drag air into her lungs. And to hear another loud bang. Realization hit. They were being *shot at!*

She looked over at Jake, still crouched, and still way too exposed as he sidled along the edge of the pool, on full alert, scoping out the car. "Jake, get in here!" she screamed, suddenly terrified for him.

"Shh!" he hissed. "Just stay down!"

He made it to the cabana that flanked the left side of the gate, and LeAnne breathed a sigh of relief that he was at least covered that much. Muffin must have sensed the danger, because he took off like a rocket through the gate, barking wildly.

"Muffin, no!" Jake and she yelled at the same time.

In horror LeAnne watched Muffin chase after the car, and she waited for the inevitable shot to ring out and drop him. Instead, to her utter amazement, the black metal rod, which was obviously the front of a big gun, disappeared inside the car window, and the vehicle's tires squealed as the driver gunned it.

Jake glanced back at her and pointed. "Don't you move. Not a muscle." Then he skulked around the cabana and out the gate. "Muffin, get back here! Now!"

She watched as Muffin skidded to a halt but gave one long last look at the receding vehicle, before turning around and trotting back to Jake with a jauntiness in his step that indicated he was quite proud of himself.

Jake dropped to his knees and quickly checked Muffin for injury, then picked him up and strode back toward LeAnne. "Of all the stupid, idiotic . . ." As he hit the safety of the cabana he set Muffin down. "You sure you're all right?"

Muffin woofed.

Still staying low, he made it to the lip of the pool. "Are you all right?"

LeAnne nodded her head.

"The car took off. But we need to move."

"What is going on?" LeAnne asked, her voice a shaky squeak. "Why is someone shooting at us?"

"No time to explain right now. I need to get you two out of here." He glanced around. "We can't go back to my bungalow. We'd be exposing ourselves too much if they come back. Where's your place?"

"To the west of the employee parking lot."

"Perfect. We can make a run through the clubhouse and out the back." He scowled as he squinted off in the direction the shots had been fired from. "Damn it, I should have had my gun." He held out his hand. "Come on. We need to hurry."

LeAnne didn't know what was going on, but she knew who the expert was in this crowd, and she let him drag her from the pool without further explanation.

Buzz came pounding up the road from the direction of the front gate, his face a study in panic. For a big man, he sure could run.

"I thought Mrs. Merriweather was popping balloons," he said when he halted before them. "But then that car raced out of here like a bat out of hell. Was that gunfire?"

"Some . . . someone shot at us."

Buzz turned accusing eyes on Jake. "I ought to—"

"Yell at me later. Right now we need to take cover and plan."

They scurried to the clubhouse, which Jake insisted on checking out before he let the rest of them enter. He turned immediately to Buzz. "Did they leave the property?"

"Hit the exit at about ninety."

"Did you get a license number?"

"New York plates. That's it. Now what the hell—"

"Make and model of car?"

"Ford Taurus."

Jake nodded and picked up the phone on the wall. He punched in three digits, which meant he was dialing a spa number. "It's me," he said. "Listen carefully. I'm sending Buzz over. You know who Buzz is? He's a big, handsome black man. Bald. One gold tooth. He's wearing"—he glanced over at Buzz—"a dark green short-sleeved shirt and khaki pants. Let him in and do exactly as he says. Got it?" After a moment he said, "You *have* trust him. You *have* to trust him."

He hung up and turned back to them. "Okay, here's what I want you to do. Go to my bunga-low and call us from there. We'll be at LeAnne's place. Whatever you do, don't let Elisa leave there until I give you the next instructions. Don't let her out of your sight."

"Look, you son of a—"

LeAnne grabbed Buzz's arm. "Please, Buzz. I . . . d-don't know wh-what this is all about. But let Jake make the decisions for now. Please."

Muffin barked.

All three of them stared down at him. Muffin gave Buzz the sternest look LeAnne had ever seen. She'd appreciate the switch of allegiance if she weren't shivering with cold and fear.

Buzz gave Jake another scathing look, but then nodded. "Call soon."

"I will. We need to move fast."

Buzz turned to go, but Jake stopped him. "Buzz, keep an eye open all around you."

"I always do."

Jake led LeAnne and Muffin to the back entrance of the clubhouse, peered out in all directions, then waved for them to follow. Neither protested, and they soon made it to LeAnne's bungalow. At her door he shielded LeAnne with his body while she fumbled with her card key.

They stumbled inside, and Jake immediately locked and bolted the door. "Close all shutters and curtains," he commanded.

LeAnne didn't question him, just moved around the bungalow, doing as he asked. Her heart was still racing, her mind a jumble of confusion and adrenaline-laced fear.

After closing the curtains in her bedroom, she returned to the living room.

"Now tell me what's going on."

Jake frowned. "Just let me call Mark first; then I'll explain."

"Phone's there," she said, pointing to her side table.

He nodded, then strode to the phone and grabbed it. Jabbing a number into it, he mumbled, "You'd better have your phone on, buddy." Impatiently he tapped his fingers on the table while he waited, his expression grim. When the other party answered, he didn't bother with niceties. "They found us." He listened for a moment, then said, "Damnit, a tracker? What are you, some kind of rookie?"

He gave the other person about a tenth of a second to answer before obviously cutting him off. "Two of them. Blue Ford Taurus. New York plates. We didn't get the number. They probably left the premises, but you can bet your ass they're not gone for good."

He paused. "Yes, I'm calling the cops. I want them securing this property." Another pause. "Okay, what's your ETA?"

Again he listened, then pulled the phone from his head. "You have a back entrance to this place?" he asked LeAnne.

She nodded. The adrenaline was slowly seeping out of her, but she feared it was being replaced by delayed shock. She felt numb and stupid.

He peered at her as if he could read her mind. "Look, I'm sorry all this happened, but now's not the time to go spacey on me, okay? Just buck up for another hour, and everything will be okay. I promise. The cavalry's coming."

LeAnne blinked and shook her head. She took a deep, bracing breath, then nodded again.

"Good girl." He thrust the phone at her. "Give Mark directions to your place using the back entrance."

She did it automatically, sounding to her own ears like a robot. The air-conditioning in her place, combined with her wet clothes, started to get to her. By the time she'd finished rattling off directions, her teeth had begun to chatter.

Jake took the phone back from her and barked a few more things into it before disconnecting. Then he immediately dialed nine for an outside line, then three numbers. He waited a moment, then explained their situation to a 911 operator.

Once that was completed, he put the phone down for a moment and moved to her, taking her shoulders. "You need to take a hot shower and get into some dry clothes."

A shower sounded wonderful. She nodded again, her teeth clacking.

"Good. Go."

Her voice still shaky and squeaky, she asked, "What . . . what's going on, Jake?"

He sighed. "Shower first; then we'll talk."

"I'm not really in the mood to take a shower while there are armed and dangerous men roaming around my resort. My God, Jake, my guests are in danger!"

"Those people are only after one person, LeAnne. They aren't out to shoot randomly."

"They . . . they're after you?"

"No."

Well, she sure as heck didn't think they were after Muffin. And since the lifeguard had taken lunch several minutes before the shooting, that left her. "Oh, my God! Why are they after me? What did I do?"

"You had the nerve to be standing next to me."

"What?"

"I'll explain after your shower. The cops are on their way. And don't worry, I'm here. No one is going to get past me to you." He cocked his head toward her bedroom. "Now please, go shower and get into clean clothes."

Her feet felt like lead blocks, but she started toward the shower. From behind her, Jake said, "And when you're done, pack some clothes."

She turned and gaped at him. "What?"

"I said pack some clothes. I'm afraid you're coming with me."

Chapter Nine

"Not a chance I'm leaving here," LeAnne said twenty minutes later. She hadn't argued with him before her shower because she'd known she needed to be dry and in control again before confronting the turkey.

"I'm sorry, but you are. You are now in danger and I'm not leaving you here."

"Why am I in danger? I don't know a thing about what's going on!"

"I'm guessing they mistook you for Elisa."

"Who is Elisa?"

"The woman who arrived last night."

"Your fiancée? I don't look a thing like her!"

"Well, it would be real nice if I had a phone number where I could call them and straighten that out, but since I don't, at the moment they're assuming you're her. And even if they somehow straightened that out all on their own, you are now a witness, no matter how little you think you saw. You're a witness, and trust me, they are beginning to *hate* witnesses."

LeAnne's first concern was the safety of her guests. And for that reason she wanted to know why this big jerk of a man had brought danger to her haven. "You tell me, right now, what is going on," she demanded.

He sighed, even as, for the hundredth time, he surreptitiously glanced out the window. Then he turned back to her. "The less you know, the better."

"No way. I've been shot at today, dumped in a pool, and now I'm being threatened with kidnapping. I have a right to know why."

Jake glanced out the window again, then turned back to her. Actually, right now he thought it a good idea—not to mention fair to her—to explain what was going on. Because once Mark learned the details of the incident today, he'd have no choice but to agree that she *had* to come with him when he blew this pop stand. And he wasn't about to leave her here.

He'd bet his badge the shooter today had a scope on his rifle. Which meant he'd gotten a real good look at LeAnne. The question was, how had he mistaken her for Elisa? In Jake's mind, the two looked nothing alike. Well, they had something of the same build, although Elisa was a good three inches taller. But from their position about fifty feet away, they wouldn't have been measuring. And they'd probably assumed she'd dyed her hair.

So there was only one damning conclusion: they'd mistaken her for Elisa because she was in his company.

He was furious that his job had brought this danger to LeAnne's doorstep. She worked so hard to make this place a sanctuary, where people came to relax and forget about the pressures awaiting them back home. And all that had been shattered for her today. Because of him.

"Jake?"

He shook his head and smiled grimly. LeAnne had changed into butter yellow shorts and a yellow, lime green, and sky blue cotton short-sleeved shirt. She'd originally emerged from her bedroom wearing sandals, but he'd sent her back to put on sneakers instead, claiming they were more practical. But from the narrowed gleam in her eyes, he knew she'd figured out why he wanted her to change shoes. Sneakers were easier to run in than sandals.

She crossed her arms and tapped her foot. "Well?"

He took a deep breath. "Elisa isn't my fiancée."

If he'd expected her to jump for joy at that news, he was sadly mistaken. Her eyes narrowed even further. "No? Then who is she?"

"She's a witness in one of my cases."

"I see. A prosecution witness, I take it?"

"Yes."

"And the defendants aren't real happy about that, huh?"

"You catch on real quick."

"So you bring a woman who's being chased by deadly thugs to *my* resort?"

"I had no idea Mark was bringing her here. I swear."

"But you didn't send them packing."

He lifted his arms helplessly. "It seemed like a good plan once Mark spelled it out. No one knew I was here but Mark."

Her glare slowly faded. "She's obviously not safe here any longer. We have to get her out of here."

"That's the plan."

"But I'm not going anywhere."

"I'm afraid you are," he said as gently as he could. He hated himself for getting her embroiled in this mess, but he wasn't about to leave her behind now.

"You can't force me to leave."

"Lady, I'll haul you out of here bodily if you don't want to leave under your own power."

"That's kidnapping."

"I prefer to call it keeping you alive."

"I'll bring charges against you."

There wasn't a court in the world that would indict. "LeAnne, be reasonable. It's only for a few days until we're certain that Winston's thugs have abandoned the search for Elisa here."

"Why am I not safe, while the rest of the guests are?"

"They think you're her! If they return and see you, they'll shoot at you again. And even if they *do* figure out their mistake, you're still a loose thread."

"But I don't know anything!" she cried.

"They don't know that."

There was a knock at her door, and Jake pointed. "In the bedroom."

A mulish expression crossed her face, but then she blew out an exasperated breath and whirled, marching to her room. Jake kind of mourned the fact that he couldn't take time to appreciate the sway of her slim hips. He moved to the door and glanced through the peephole. Buzz was standing there whistling, acting as if he didn't have a care in the world. Elisa, beside him, was obviously shaken.

Jake opened the door with the chain still in place until he could make certain Buzz and Elisa were alone. They were, and Jake quickly let them in.

Buzz strolled in carrying Jake's duffel bag and Elisa's suitcase. As soon as the door shut his whistling halted and he glared at Jake. "What business you got bringing trouble to LeAnne's door?"

"Trust me, Buzz, that's the last thing I'd

want to do. And I'm doing everything I can to rectify it."

"What is going on?"

LeAnne came bounding out of her bedroom. "Buzz! This turkey's trying to kidnap me! You have to stop him!"

While she'd been in the shower, he'd briefed the police. They were now patrolling the entire area, and staking out both entrances. But he hadn't had time to fill Buzz in, only to give him basic instructions.

"It's my fault," Elisa said.

"No," Jake responded. "It's not. Buzz, this is important. I need your support on this."

"Give me one good reason."

"I'll give you several. Elisa is not my fiancée. She's a witness in a trial set to start in a few weeks. She's under federal protection until then. Somehow the thugs tracked her here. Unfortunately, they spotted LeAnne with me and decided she must be Elisa. Right now they've got a picture of LeAnne in their minds as their target. She's not safe here until we ascertain that they've stopped looking here for their mark. Until then I want to get her away from the resort."

Buzz digested that for a moment. Then he turned to his boss, and Jake could see in his face how hard it was to overrule her. "I'm sorry, LeAnne. Got to figure Jake knows what he's doing, much as I hate to admit it. He got you in this mess; you let him make it right."

Her jaw dropped; then she glared at Jake. "You're a jerk."

"First-class," Jake agreed, hating that he'd had to persuade her treasured and trusted employee into seemingly betraying her. As far as he could tell, Jake's appearance in LeAnne's life was about the worst thing that had ever happened to her. And that stung for some reason.

Not twenty-four hours earlier he'd fully planned to be the *best* thing ever to happen to LeAnne Crosby. Or have fun trying.

She seemed to deflate. "You *will* take charge, Buzz?"

"Absolutely."

"How are we going to explain my sudden absence?"

"Death in the family," Jake said.

"No!" LeAnne practically shouted. "I won't even *pretend* that someone in my family has passed away. Absolutely not."

"It's just an excuse."

"No. It's like a jinx. No. I won't use my family that way."

"Okay. You have a friend who's been overseas for years and finally got to come home for a few days, so you went to visit her."

She shook her head. "Not good enough. The people here would still consider that abandonment. They pay good money and they expect *all* the services we've promised."

"Okay. How about the wildly generic 'family emergency'? After all, it is one. You're your family, and the emergency is you want to keep breathing."

She thought about that. "All right," she finally conceded. "But I'm going on record as being really ticked off."

Elisa stepped forward. "I can't tell you how sorry I am about all this," she said softly.

"LeAnne Crosby, Elisa Johnson," Jake introduced. "Elisa, this is LeAnne."

They shook hands and LeAnne said, "It's not your fault," then glared at Jake. She looked back at Elisa and studied her, and a reluctant smile tipped up her lips. "How in the world could *anyone* mistake me for you? You're beautiful."

Buzz apparently agreed with LeAnne, if the expression on his face when he turned his eyes on Elisa was any indication. The simmering anger disappeared, and something of a moony look showed up instead. *Oh, boy. Now this is interesting.*

"That's probably the exact reason they mistook you," Jake surmised. "They saw you were with me, they saw a beautiful woman, and they thought it had to be Elisa."

The startled expression that crossed LeAnne's face was endearing. The woman apparently had no idea that she was about the most beautiful creature he'd ever seen. That was cute. He'd love to think of all the ways he could come up with to show her just how beautiful she was, but he had more pressing things to think about at the moment. He turned to Buzz. "Did you pack everything I asked for?"

"Think so. Not real happy about you bringing a gun onto the property, though."

"A gun?" LeAnne practically shrieked.

"I'm a federal agent," he explained to both of them. "I'm required to keep it with me. In fact, I should have had it on me when the gunmen showed up. But I left it in the room in deference to LeAnne and her guests."

That explanation didn't seem to appease either of them, but he didn't have time to worry about it.

He opened the duffel, and sure enough, Buzz had packed all of his toiletries and several pairs of socks, briefs, shorts, and shirts. If he needed anything else, they'd get it on the road.

"And the money?

Buzz unzipped a side pocket to reveal a wad of bills that could choke a rhino.

"Thanks," Jake said. "Mark will make out a receipt for reimbursement."

"What else can I do?" Buzz asked.

"Keep an eye out, keep the police informed, and don't tell *anyone* the truth about LeAnne. She's had a family emergency."

Buzz nodded, but he frowned at Jake. "When you get back here, we're going to have us a nice long chat about how you got LeAnne into this."

Elisa laid a hand on Buzz's arm. "He didn't do it. He truly didn't. He had no idea we were coming here."

LeAnne took notice. Buzz was a big guy with a big Adam's apples—which was suddenly wobbling as he stared at her soft white hand draped over his dark skin. It was a beautiful sight to LeAnne, two colors that contrasted, yet complemented each other.

She glanced at Buzz's face in time to find him gazing longingly at Elisa. This was such a new thing, Buzz in puppy love, LeAnne was almost sorry all of them were leaving and taking away his chance to get to know her.

Impulsively, she said to Elisa, "The moment this ordeal's over with, come back and have a week on us."

Elisa and Buzz both smiled at her as if she'd just bestowed upon them the key to heaven. Jake had a decidedly different reaction. He stared at her as though she'd just grown horns.

LeAnne ignored him, in the interest of potential matchmaking. She'd always felt Buzz had put his huge heart on freeze in order to give his all to Happy Hounds. It was about time he found a little romance.

Buzz closed up the duffel. He glanced at LeAnne. "Don't you worry. Things will be just fine." His gaze marched to Jake. "You take care of them or you answer to me. You got a lot of making up to do."

LeAnne didn't know why her defensive instincts kicked in, but they did. "Buzz, he saved my life today. If he hadn't tossed me in the pool, I might be dead."

"Oh, God," Elisa whispered, her face stricken.

"But probably not!" LeAnne rushed to assure her.

"It *is* my fault, Buzz," Jake said. "And I'm terribly sorry. I'll make it up to you all somehow."

"You do that by keeping them safe," Buzz said in a tone that promised retribution if Jake didn't come through. And then he looked at Elisa. "Godspeed, miss. Hope to see you back here soon, under better circumstances." He pulled a dog biscuit out of his pocket and bent to give it to Muffin. "Let's go, Muffin."

"What?" Jake asked.

Buzz straightened. "I assumed Muffin's staying here."

"You assumed wrong. He's coming with us."

"You didn't tell me to pack any of his things."

A guilty flush bloomed on Jake's cheeks. "Damn. I have *got* to learn to be a better parent. I forgot all about it."

"He's welcome to stay here," Buzz said. "I'll look after him."

"No, I want him with me," Jake said stubbornly, and LeAnne almost broke out in applause. When Jake looked at her and saw her smile, he added gruffly, "Where I can keep an eye on him." He apparently didn't want to look as though he cared *too* much. "We'll stop along the way and pick up everything he needs."

Buzz nodded, giving Muffin the bone anyway. With a final pat on Muffin's head, he said,

"See you soon, little man. You take care of all of them, you hear?"

Muffin barked and the bone flew out of his mouth. He quickly retrieved it.

With one final shy smile at Elisa, Buzz took his leave, beginning to whistle tunelessly and swagger in a carefree way, even before he made it through the door.

"What happens now?" LeAnne asked Jake.

"We sit tight and wait for Mark."

They didn't have to wait long, maybe twenty minutes, but to LeAnne it felt like hours. With reluctance and after a barrage of nagging on Jake's part, she packed some clothes in the duffel, blushing furiously as she stuffed her underwear inside.

There was something so personal about sharing a clothing bag with a man. Panties side by side with briefs. His and hers toothbrushes. Small T-shirts stacked neatly on top of large ones. It suggested intimacy, as if they were off on a weekend tryst.

Mark entered cheerfully, as if they were heading for Walt Disney World or something. LeAnne wanted to dislike him just on principle. After all, this mess *was* all his fault. But when he directed a dimpled smile at her, she had a hard time scowling at him properly.

Mark and Jake strolled casually into the kitchen, as if they were just going for a bite to eat, rather than plotting their next move in private. LeAnne and Elisa exchanged exasperated looks and LeAnne said, "Spies have an overblown sense of the dramatic, don't you think?"

"We are *not* spies!" Jake called from the kitchen.

"Not to mention really good hearing," Elisa added with a grin. Then her smile faded. "I really am so sorry you got dragged into all this."

All of LeAnne's anger at the situation faded. "Please, don't feel bad. I admire your bravery, actually. It can't be easy being the target of thugs."

Elisa's blue eyes hardened. "It'll be worth it to see the Winstons behind bars."

LeAnne's curiosity was piqued, but she figured Jake wouldn't appreciate her prying into the case. And she figured if just being in the vicinity of this woman was enough to put her life in danger, then knowing details about the criminals was probably not a good move on her part.

Mark and Jake emerged from the kitchen five minutes later, Mark having helped himself to a root beer from her refrigerator.

"Finished packing?" Jake asked.

LeAnne nodded. "I even managed to dig up another heart blanket for Muffin."

His eyes lit up a little. Apparently he wasn't

219

as down on heart blankets as he had once been. "We'll stop along the way and pick up whatever else Muffin needs."

"Along the way where?" she asked. "Where are we going?"

"I'll tell you when we're on the road," Jake said. He turned to Mark. "You two want to go first or second?"

LeAnne's mouth dropped open. "We're not all going together?"

"No, Ms. Crosby," Mark answered her. "We're splitting up. You and Jake first."

And then it hit her. She was going away with Jake. Alone. Well, they were taking Muffin with them, but what kind of a buffer could a dog be? And what was the reason she needed a buffer again?

Oh, yeah, he was a cheating slimeball. Except he wasn't any longer. At least not the cheating part. But the prospect of running away with the sexiest man she'd ever met was unnerving.

She made a last-ditch effort to appeal to their common sense. She looked at Mark. "Is it absolutely necessary for me to leave? I just don't feel I'm in any danger."

Mark's cheerful smile vanished. "These people are desperate. And we've seen what's happened to people left behind when we've fled to a new location. I know it's inconvenient, and I'm sorry I got you involved at all, but Jake's right. You're safest with him and away from here until we're certain they've given up the search in this location. We promise to get you back here as soon as possible."

She finally gave in to the inevitable. She was running away with Jake Donnelly.

Just to impress upon Jake how unhappy she was with the situation, LeAnne gave him the silent treatment for a good half hour. He didn't seem to mind, however. In fact, he was quite content to drum his fingers on the steering wheel in time with the classic rock music pounding from the speakers.

But she wasn't fooled. His eyes were shifting constantly, checking the mirrors and scanning the road ahead. The first few minutes of the ride he took side roads at random and at times retraced their path. Apparently satisfied that no one was following them, he finally got on I-95 north and stayed on it.

LeAnne couldn't stand keeping quiet any longer. "Where are we going? D.C.?"

"No."

Silence.

LeAnne growled. "New York? Philadelphia? Istanbul?"

"I don't suppose you'd just let it be a surprise?" he asked.

"I'd like an idea of how long we're going to be on the road."

"Do you get carsick?" he asked, effectively avoiding her question again.

"Never before," she retorted, "but I wouldn't rule it out today."

He had the nerve to laugh. "Is it the company? If so, I'm afraid you'll hurt Muffin's feelings."

Not deigning to answer, she lifted her nose and sniffed loudly, but she had the feeling the sentiment got lost among the guitar riffs banging around the interior of the car.

Nonetheless, she reverted to the silent treatment again.

An hour later Jake took the Fredericksburg exit, then drove around seemingly aimlessly until he came upon a Kmart. There he pulled into the lot. "I'm going to pick up some stuff for Muffin and some snacks for us. Anything you want?"

"I'm not hungry, but I could use some bottled water. And so could Muffin."

"Gotcha."

"Make sure to pick up a pooper-scooper, too. I'll take Muffin for a walk while you shop, and my bet is you'll need it."

"Right."

Jake shut off the engine and pulled out the keys, making it impossible for LeAnne to take off and leave him stranded. *Too bad.* She grabbed Muffin's leash and slid out of the car. They met at the back of the station wagon and Jake opened the tailgate. Muffin leaped out in a mass of wrinkles, then pranced in place as he scoped out the area.

Jake slammed the door shut as LeAnne

attached the leash. "Back in a flash," Jake said, then started for the entrance.

"Jake?"

He wheeled around but started walking backward, obviously impatient to get back on the road. "Yeah?"

"Can you pick me up a book?"

"Sure, what kind?"

LeAnne's favorites were mysteries and legal thrillers. "A romance novel."

That stopped him. "You want *me* to buy a romance novel?"

"Yes, please," she said sweetly. "Maybe two."

He frowned. "Fine," he said tersely.

"And a *National Enquirer.*" She'd never read that rag in her life.

Now he turned a little green around the gills. *Good.* Before he could protest, she turned to Muffin. "Come on, sweet guy. Let's go stretch our legs."

Jake would bet a year's salary that LeAnne Crosby had never read a *National Enquirer* in her life. So the altruistic dog lover had a sadistic streak, it seemed.

He considered just telling her they were sold out, but decided the better revenge was to pick one up and force her to read it. He left the store pushing a cart, proud he hadn't blushed *too* much as the clerk scanned his purchases. Of course, he'd quickly said, "For my sister," when the woman had picked up the magazine. And to offset the girly selections he'd also included a Grisham and a King book, as well as a *Sports Illustrated*.

He looked around the parking lot and at first didn't spot LeAnne and Muffin. Panic set in. He'd taken every precaution possible to make certain they hadn't been followed, including a roadblock by the police that would prevent anyone from leaving the resort from the back entrance for at least an hour after he and LeAnne departed. And there was no way for anyone leaving from the front entrance to see them leave from the back. After that he'd taken so many detours that it would be next to impossible for anyone to find them. Next to impossible was not *completely* impossible, however, and all he could think of was that LeAnne and his dog had been abducted.

He loped to the station wagon, unlocked the passenger side door, and reached back to unlock the backseat door. He yanked it open and tossed the bags inside. If a thorough search of the area didn't reveal Muffin and LeAnne, he'd have the state police set up road-blocks both to the north and south on 95. He sincerely doubted any other drop-dead gorgeous females riding with butt-ugly bulldogs would be riding on 95 at this exact moment.

Heart pounding, he slammed the door closed, then glanced around to search for potential witnesses. What he found was

LeAnne and Muffin turning the corner at the far end of the store.

Relief turned to aggravation quickly. Jake *hated* feeling frightened and he *hated* feeling that he'd lost control of a situation. He pulled open the door again and dug out the pooper-scooper. He waved at LeAnne to get her attention, then held it up questioningly. She shook her head no, which was just as well. After that scare he'd just as soon get this show back on the road as soon as possible.

He tossed the scooper back into the car, then sifted through the bags and pulled out one of the two dog dishes he'd bought. He grabbed one bottle of water and squirted it into the dish.

LeAnne and Muffin sauntered up as if they hadn't just given him a minor coronary. "Don't do that again!" he barked, and LeAnne's head snapped toward him in surprise.

"Do what?"

"Walk out of my sight."

"Walk out of your sight?" she repeated as Muffin started slurping the water. "For goodness sake, you were in the store. *Way* out of sight."

"Just don't do it again."

She sighed. "Jake, the only grass within a mile of here was at the side of the building."

Okay, so he was being a little unreasonable. But he was still too aggravated to admit it. So instead he rummaged through the bags again and brought out fancy bottled water for her and a Yoo-Hoo for him.

After Muffin stopped drinking, Jake handed him a dog bone and let him chew and take a final slug of water before opening the tailgate and dumping him on his heart blanket again. By the time he'd finished that, LeAnne had tossed the water and stuck the bowl in the back on the seat.

He opened her door for her, grabbed a couple more things from the bags, then jogged around the car to the driver's side. He slid behind the wheel, then made a big deal out of presenting her with the rag mag and the two books. "What the lady asks for, the lady gets."

She wrinkled her nose in distaste for a moment, but quickly masked it. "Oh, wonderful!"

He tapped the magazine. "Real good article on several reliable Frank Sinatra sightings. Ol' Blue Eyes is apparently alive and well and singing in a lounge in Tahoe."

"Who submitted the story? The Lake Tahoe Visitors' Bureau?"

Despite his still-simmering irritation, he chuckled as he started the car and put it in drive. "I bought some rawhides for Muffin, if you want to grab one and toss it back to him."

"That was nice," she murmured in a way that indicated surprise.

Which of course irritated him all over again.

He slapped his sunglasses on his face. "I *can* be nice, you know."

"I've witnessed rare instances of it, sure," she agreed.

Before he could think up an appropriate retort, she reached behind her and started groping for the bags. Out of the corner of his eye he watched the material of the shirt stretch tight over her breasts, and his mouth went Sahara dry.

He'd been dreaming of those breasts ever since Scooter and Bob, the T-shirt guinea pigs, had made an appearance at his door back at the resort. His interest had intensified to obsession by the time he'd kissed her out in the parking lot, with those breasts pressing against his ribs.

Apparently having failed at grasping the bag, LeAnne unbuckled her seat belt and scooted around. She draped herself over the seat back and started rooting through the bags.

Her butt poked high up in the air, with her incredible legs bent at the knees. Jake nearly ran them off the road ogling her. He straightened the car out and drastically adjusted his rearview mirror to the left.

And what a rearview it was.

A fantasy kicked in: One of her tearing off her clothes while he pulled into a rest stop and adjusted his seat back a foot. Of her unzipping his pants and exposing his hard-on, then straddling him, sinking down onto him. Of her thrusting her breast into his mouth as she moaned and milked him. Of her coming all around him, driving him over the edge with her pulsing and crying out.

God, he wanted his hands on that softly curving tush. He wanted his lips gliding up and down those creamy thighs. He wanted to possess that body every which way.

"Got it!" she said, which had him scrambling to return the mirror to a less incriminating angle. "Look, Muffin!" she said, "Catch!" Then she sent the rawhide chew flying to the back of the car.

In the rearview mirror Jake watched Muffin catch the bone in his mouth, and Jake stifled a smile. Why, he couldn't say.

LeAnne settled herself and buckled up. She picked up her bottled water, and out of the corner of his eye he watched her tip her head back and sip. Her profile was breathtaking, too. She had a cute nose. He'd noticed before, but hadn't realized until now that it wasn't really straight, but tipped up a little. And those lips. And her lashes were longer and more lush than he'd realized, too. Probably because when he was looking at her he was usually concentrating on her bottomless eyes.

"Let's see what we have here," she said, sticking her water bottle in the cup holder and grabbing the magazine.

Uh-oh. She wouldn't dare—

"Oh, boy. Trouble on the home front for Antonio and Melanie."

She would.

"And look here! Pamela's considering implants again. That ought to make you happy."

"You really don't need to share."

"Oh, but it's only fair, seeing as you were kind enough to buy it for me."

"No, really. You go ahead and enjoy that all by yourself."

"Demi's pregnant again, but the father's in prison."

"LeAnne . . ."

She laughed and tossed the paper on the floor. "Well, it's the least you deserve for buying it."

"That was the least you deserve for asking for it."

"True," she agreed cheerfully.

Jake was immensely relieved that her good humor had been restored. He didn't like upsetting her. And since that was about all he'd done since she'd met him, he decided she had a very forgiving nature.

But then she sobered and said, "Do you think Elisa's going to be all right?"

"Well, she's in Mark's hands, and Mark's the best."

"Oh, really? Then how did they manage to find her at Happy Hounds?"

229

Trish Jensen

"The bad guys put a tracking device on his car, then followed him there, apparently."

"So what's to stop them from doing something like that again?"

"We've checked the car thoroughly. And now Mark knows not to let *anyone* know where he's taking her. Not even me."

"Why not?"

"The bad guys have been incredibly lucky finding Elisa. It doesn't feel right."

"Are you saying you have a traitor in your ranks?"

He glanced over at her. "You know, you're very perceptive."

"Not really. I just know a little about that kind of thing from a corporate viewpoint."

"You've had trouble at Happy Hounds?" he said, but was pretty sure that was not what she'd been talking about. He was curious whether she'd skirt the issue or fib.

"No. My husband did at his company."

Well, that answered that. Blunt honesty. He tried to look shocked and aggravated. "You said you weren't involved, much less married."

"I'm not. Not anymore. I'm a widow."

"Oh. I'm so sorry."

She started plucking at the hem of her shorts. "Yes, well, thank you. I'm sorry he died, too. I'm *not* sorry I'm not married, however."

"To him, or to any man?"

He was bracing himself for her to tell him it was none of his business. But he also wasn't surprised when she answered. LeAnne was proving to be a very up-front lady.

"At this point, to any man. But I have to say, it was Stephen who taught me that married life isn't always a picnic."

"Nothing worthwhile is," Jake said, then wondered where that had come from. The last thing he'd classify marriage as was worthwhile, if his folks were any indication.

"I know. You're right. And I also know that marriage to another man wouldn't necessarily turn out like my first marriage."

Jake finished off his Yoo-Hoo before asking, "If you don't mind my asking, what was the problem?"

She hesitated, then sighed. "Well, I think the first problem was that he was quite a bit older than I was. It didn't seem like an obstacle at first. I mean, it certainly didn't matter to me. But as time went on, I think it began to bother him. He started worrying that I was looking for someone younger. I wasn't, but nothing I could say or do would convince him. He started having me followed. Over time his accusations and lack of trust just got to be too much."

"I'll bet," he said quietly. "But you know, that sounds more like an exception than the norm."

He didn't know why, but the thought of LeAnne going through the rest of her life without having a happy, fulfilling relationship bothered him. He'd seen her in action. She had a huge heart and plenty of love to give. It would be such a waste to lavish it all strictly on animals. Which brought him to another thing he was curious about. But before he could ask, she answered his last comment.

"I know. It borders on irrational. I just can't seem to shake the thought that it might happen again. I can't deal with a man who doesn't have faith in my love for him."

Stephen Latimer had been known as an absolute genius. Right now Jake considered him about the biggest fool he'd ever heard of. "I'm sorry. But you know, my guess is the day you meet the next Mr. LeAnne Crosby, you'll know it."

"You think so?" she asked, turning wide eyes to him.

Something in his chest just melted at the almost hopeful expression on her face. She might like to fool herself into thinking she was better off alone, but that look gave her away.

Then the weird melting gave way to a twinge of irritation. How come she hadn't considered him her next relationship? She sure as hell had kissed like she wanted something with him. Okay, so he'd been thinking short-term. But it was a blow to his male pride that she hadn't been envisioning white picket fences and babies while he'd been ravishing her lips and touching her body.

He mentally slapped a hand upside his head. Was he going bonkers? He wanted to think of getting into a relationship with a woman about as much as he wanted to get into a relationship with . . . a dog.

Okay, less than with a dog. Because he was getting used to that situation. He could handle Muffin's needs. It hadn't been easy, and it wasn't going to suddenly become easier because he understood Muffin a little better these days. But he was beginning to understand that commitment.

Commitment to a woman still scared the bejesus out of him. He was pretty sure they were a lot more trouble than Muffin. That was saying plenty, because Muffin was a pain in the ass.

"I think," he finally answered, "that any man would be lucky to have you."

She laughed, the sound warming every cell in his body. "My guess is you think I'm the biggest pain you've ever met."

"Funny, I was thinking the same thing about you meeting me." Their eyes locked and Jake felt a little lost. "I've done nothing but cause you trouble."

"True. You've definitely been a pain."

That stung more than it should. "For someone who has a burning love for dogs," he said, deciding to change the subject, "you have an amazing lack of them in your own place."

Again she chuckled, a truly musical sound. "I have six at the moment."

"Where are they?"

"With my brother, in the Shenandoah Valley.

He owns a horse farm. He takes them during the season."

"Why?"

"I learned early on that I couldn't pay them the attention they needed during the season. He has six kids. Three sets of twins. They more than keep my babies happy and occupied." She grinned. "In fact, I think the dogs are relieved to come home. They get a breather."

"You love them."

"Of course," she said, looking at him as if he were a loon. "Just like you love Muffin."

"Technically, I'm not in love."

"Personally, you are."

"He hates me."

"He wants to love you."

Jake was sure he shouldn't care. But he couldn't stop himself, regardless. "Do you think he, you know, likes me? I mean, I know that he's resigned himself to living with me. But do you think he's starting to be okay with it?"

"How many times have you let him sleep on the bed?"

"Just twice! And that second time was just because he was afraid of the storm. And last night I slept on the couch, which really didn't matter because he was with you."

Okay, Donnelly, too much information. Why had he felt the need to let her know his sleeping arrangements last night?

"He likes you." She shifted toward him.

"Jake, he knows you are clueless in the dog department."

"I'm trying."

"He knows that, too."

"He has every reason to hate me, though. I've been shitty to him."

"He knows that you're providing him with what he needs. Now you're learning to provide him with what he wants. Jake, he's learning. Like you are."

"Bottom line being . . . ?"

"You two are in good shape."

The lull of the car engine put LeAnne to sleep. But she woke in time to see the "Welcome to Pennsylvania" sign. She yawned. "Are we heading to Canada?"

"Nope, we'll be there in a couple hours."

"Where?"

"Aunt Sophie's."

"I thought Sophie lived in Rhode Island."

"Not during the summers, she didn't."

"The cabin," LeAnne said. "Of course. Sophie talked about it a bit. Didn't you stay with her there?"

"Yes. To tell you the truth, as far as I'm concerned, it was the only home I had."

Chapter Ten

Jake's "home" was a beautifully rustic lakeside cabin in the middle of nowhere.

The cabin—made of wood, of course—didn't fit the picture of any hideaway cabin LeAnne would have imagined. Built into a hill, it was a multilevel construction that could have been part of the woods around it. Looking at it, she was sure it had been formed there, rather than made. A porch ran the entire length of the front of the house.

She glanced at him as he soaked it in, stepping out of the car with a reverence that was almost spooky. Most definitely, this was home to him. His eyes caressed the cabin like a lover.

"You really do love this place," she said.

Jake's eyes cleared to a royal blue. "Yes."

Trish Jensen

She let it go while they got settled. But she was dying to ask him about his childhood. She knew about his life with Sophie, or as much as Sophie had revealed. But she wanted to know the rest.

The cabin was amazing. Rustic on the outside, pure comfort within. They walked into a great room that featured a central fireplace, and off of that a screened-in porch that looked out on the lake. The kitchen was state-of-the-art. But the walls and floors were of hand-tooled wood.

It blended modern convenience and antiquated charm. And it was beautiful.

Jake brought in what little they had while Muffin ran straight for the couch in the great room. Obviously Sophie had allowed Muffin on the furniture, seeing as how he jumped on the couch as if he owned it.

Their clothes were packed together. It was embarrassing to ask him, but she wanted to know. "Which one is my room?"

"Same one as mine. So you choose."

"I want my own room."

"Nope."

"I'm not sleeping with you."

"You're sleeping beside me."

"You'll take advantage of the situation."

"Not if you don't want me to."

"I don't want you to."

He nodded. "Fine. We'll revisit the issue when this is all over."

238

"Fat chance."

He shrugged as if he couldn't care less either way. "Look, you don't want me touching you, I won't touch you. But this place doesn't have a security system, and I don't trust thugs to mess up twice. Wherever you want to sleep is fine by me, but wherever that's going to be, I want me between you and the door."

"Are there any rooms with two beds?"

"Not since Aunt Sophie traded in my bunk beds when I was twelve."

"I'm *not* sleeping with you."

"Then I'll sleep in a chair by the door."

"I couldn't let you do that."

"Think back real carefully, LeAnne. I didn't ask for permission."

"If I'd known this was now it was going to be, I'd never have agreed to come."

He sighed. "Are you going to be this difficult the whole time we're here?"

"Look, you . . . you *spy*—"

"Now you're just calling me that to be contrary."

"I didn't ask to be here in the first place."

"I recognize that." He ran his hands through his hair, leaving it mussed in a way that would be sexy if she weren't so angry. "Okay, how about this? I'll set up a booby trap at the bottom of the stairs so anyone trying to come up will make a racket."

"That'll work!" she said, cheering instantly. She didn't like being difficult and she hated being mad. But she wasn't about to allow this man to climb in bed with her. For a certainty, she'd be all over him.

Okay, so she admitted it. She was hot for the FBI guy, even though he'd done nothing but cause her grief.

And kiss her senseless.

And turn her life upside down.

And make her feel lust for the first time in years.

"One other thing I'd like you to do," he said, interrupting her list of pros and cons.

"If it's reasonable."

"*Everything* I say is reasonable!"

Muffin beat her to a satisfying snort of disbelief.

They both turned to him, Jake glowering. "I'll deal with you in a minute."

Muffin sniffed and graced him with a haughty look. LeAnne made a mental note that she needed to work on that attitude.

Jake swung back to LeAnne. "When you go to bed at night, you put a chair under your doorknob."

"Gladly."

"You let no one in except me. And not even me if I say, 'LeAnne, let me in.'"

"What will you say instead?"

He thought about that. "How about, LeAnne, I want you." He smiled that zillion-watt smile.

"Cute," she said, ignoring the man as best she could by focusing on the floor. "But not really effective. I'll just assume you're attempting to sweet-talk me again. How about, 'The bat drives at midnight'?"

He laughed so hard, she felt all gooey and happy. Ridiculous, but she loved the idea of making him laugh that much.

"Lady," he said, lifting the duffel, "you'd make a really bad spy."

"I'll take this room," LeAnne told Jake, after he'd given her a tour of all three in the cabin. Considering that Sophie had transformed it into almost a monument to Jake, he felt both honored and disappointed. He'd have loved to spend time exploring it all over again.

The rough wood walls were covered with pictures of him. From his first steps to his graduation from Quantico, she had his first twenty-five years of life covered. And she'd saved every toy and memento he'd left here. They littered the bureaus, the side tables, even the floor.

Most of it was pretty embarrassing. But he had to admit that he was shocked and happy that Aunt Sophie had decorated his old room like this. Last he remembered, this room had been a shrine to Bachman Turner Overdrive and the Grateful Dead.

The furnishings were the same as he remembered—heavy oak. The comforter was still the same maroon, navy, and cream. His pitiful pine desk still sat in the corner.

After dumping the duffel on the queen-size bed, he walked over to the desk, running his fingers over the ridiculously uneven finish. The legs wobbled under his touch. "My first major project," he told her.

"You built that masterpiece?" she asked with a grin.

"There's a false bottom in one of the drawers no one will ever find," he boasted.

She found it in less than two minutes.

"That's real emasculating, you know," he commented dryly. "Just how effective a shrink are you?"

She laughed. "My middle brother tried to build one of these. His was worse than yours."

"Thank you very much."

"He's now a carpenter."

He lifted an eyebrow. "That's real encouraging. I hope he's improved."

"A little."

They grinned at each other, but the smiles faded fast. She was close and she was beautiful and she was attracted to him, no matter her protests.

They'd gone through a hellish day together. Jake had experienced moments of mortal danger before. More times than he cared to remember, actually. They were *never* fun. But LeAnne's ability to bounce back, instead of collapsing into a shaking mass of putty, had won his admiration.

Her gazing up at him now won more than

that. He couldn't help it; he wanted to touch her flesh, those lips. His fingers grazed her jaw; his thumb skimmed over her lower lip, then the upper. Both were soft and pink and needing attention. "I've got to keep focused here."

"Yes," she said, her breath whispering over his fingertips.

"Concentrate on your safety."

"Yes."

"Not think about making love to you."

"That would probably be best."

"I want to keep you alive."

"I completely support that goal."

His hand dropped. "So you see why I have to stop picturing you naked."

She chuckled softly. "I'll stop picturing you if you stop picturing me."

His breath hitched. "You've pictured me naked?"

"It wasn't a real stretch when I've seen you in nothing but swim trunks."

Okay, he was stupidly flattered. And of course, saying they were going to stop fantasizing about naked flesh was the same as saying they'd stop thinking about that elephant standing on the coffee table.

But Jake had a job to do, with the most important stakes he could remember: the safety of this woman. So he cupped her face and kissed her senseless for about ten seconds. Then he let her go and stepped back, just for a moment enjoying the dazed look in her eyes.

Then he cleared his throat, cleared his head, and got down to business.

"So, you want this room?"

She looked at him as if he'd just spoken in tongues. "What?"

He waved toward the bed. "You want to sleep here?"

"Oh. Oh, yes, this'll be fine."

"Good, well I'll let you go ahead and unpack your things."

"Fine."

They might have continued to stare at each other for moments longer, if not for the deafening crash that sounded from below.

Jimmy was sweating like a pig. The last few hours had been a nightmare, dodging the patrol cars suddenly littering southern Virginia. They'd had to ditch the rifle in a rural pond, then abandon the car in a cornfield. At this time of year the corn wasn't tall enough to do much more than conceal the wheels, but they didn't have time to look for a better place.

They'd frantically wiped the car down to the best of their ability, then set out on foot toward the small town where they'd parked their backup vehicle.

Then they'd cautiously made their way back toward the dog place, only to find more cops milling around than at a doughnut shop.

They'd driven right on by and had kept going until they made it to Richmond and rented a room in a Motel 6. And now the news from D.C. really sucked.

"What do you mean, they're gone?" Jimmy nearly shrieked at their FBI insider, the Rat.

"Just what I said. They bugged out almost immediately."

"Where are they headed?"

"Don't have a clue."

"*What?* It's your damn job to have a clue!"

"Not this time. Colson obviously suspects someone on the inside. He's not telling *anyone* where he's taking the Johnson woman. Even the director couldn't get it out of him. Not that he tried."

"You mean Donnelly."

"Nope. Colson."

"Colson wasn't there."

"Here's the real funny part, Bunny," the man said, in an aggravatingly amused voice. "Neither was the Johnson woman. You shot at the wrong target."

"Impossible," he said, but the sweat was now running in rivers down his neck, chest, and back.

"Not only possible, but a fact. You screwed up big-time, Bunny."

"Stop calling me that!" he screamed.

"You came real close to shooting the owner of the club."

Jimmy swore viciously. "How was I to know? She looked just like the woman, and she was with Donnelly."

"I think your best bet is to find a real safe rabbit hole and jump in. I know I'm about to take an extended vacation."

"I've got to find them!" he shouted, not even trying to hide the panic in his voice. "You *have* to find out where they went!"

"Bunny, this operation is about to bust wide open. Colson called in just long enough to say they were leaving, and he wouldn't be in contact with *anyone* at the Bureau until he was certain the people after the Johnson woman had stopped the search or he had her in such deep cover God Himself couldn't locate her."

"I've *got* to find them."

"You're not a real good listener, are you, Bunny?"

Jimmy's legs gave out on him and he slumped down onto the bed. "What am I gonna do?"

"My suggestion? Buy a one way ticket to the Caymans."

Following on the heels of the crash came Muffin's excited barking. Jake pulled his weapon at the same time he shoved LeAnne deeper into the room. "Close this door and put the desk chair under the knob."

As he strode to the stairs with all the stealth his training had taught him, he checked the Glock's magazine. He took the steps sideways, his back pressed to the wall, the gun leading the way. At the bottom of the steps he stopped, double-handed the gun, and spun.

All he saw was an overturned lamp and Muffin barking at a terrified mouse, shaking inside one of several Havahart traps Jake had automatically placed around the cabin. He took a deep breath to release some of the adrenaline coursing through him and clicked on the safety. "Damn it, Muffin, you scared the hell out of me."

Muffin glanced back at him with a goofy bulldog smile, obviously thinking he'd just found a new friend. Jake had the feeling the mouse would heartily disagree.

He swung on his heel and headed back upstairs. At the door to his room he tried to enter, and was happy to see he couldn't. She'd followed his instructions. He knocked. "All clear. Let me in."

"Those aren't the right words."

He tried to think back. "I want you, LeAnne."

"Nice sentiment, wrong words."

He racked his brain. Oh, yeah. "The bat drives at midnight."

He heard her husky chuckle and then the scrape of the chair on the floor. She swung open the door. "No intruder?"

"Oh, definitely an intruder. But I bravely caught him and contained him. Want to see my prisoner?"

"Is he dangerous?"

"Very. But I have him under control."

She followed him downstairs, and Muffin, on seeing her, came bounding over with a happy yip, then whirled and raced back to the mousetrap, wanting to show off his new companion.

LeAnne walked over to it and hunkered down. "Well, hello, little fellow!"

Considering her profession, Jake shouldn't have been surprised that LeAnne didn't squeal and jump up on the furniture. Still, it pleased him inordinately that a small, harmless critter didn't freak her out. Uncle George and Aunt Sophie had tremendous respect for all creatures, and would no more consider killing a mouse than they'd shoot at a raccoon or a bird. They'd passed that respect on to Jake, and he loved that LeAnne felt the same way.

"How about we give this perp his freedom, then make some supper?" he suggested.

"Sounds good. I'm starved."

It was close to eight at night, and he realized neither of them had eaten since morning. They'd fed Muffin at one of the rest stops, but he'd been so anxious to reach their destination, he hadn't thought to offer her sustenance, other than the candy bars they'd picked up along the way. Sheesh, when it came to LeAnne, could he do *anything* right?

Dusk had settled in over central Pennsylvania, and slate gray clouds made the evening darker, moodier. Jake hadn't wanted to turn on too many outdoor lights. Even though the nearest residence was miles away, he didn't want any beacons for anyone who might stumble upon the cabin.

But he turned one on now, so LeAnne could see where she was walking. The stones that passed for a sidewalk were a little uneven now, more so than when he was younger.

Muffin bounded down the steps, running from one place to another, obviously familiar with the surroundings and happy to be home. And though there'd never been a dog here while Jake was growing up, it seemed so natural now, as if he couldn't imagine the cabin without the dog.

LeAnne glanced around the front of the cabin as if she had never seen it before. Which made sense, since he'd hustled her inside so fast upon their arrival, she probably hadn't had time to take it all in.

Jake tried to see the place through fresh eyes—LeAnne's eyes. Aunt Sophie had been a flower nut, and Jake had made sure that her gardener kept up the flowery splendor. Impatiens, marigolds, petunias, and a whole bunch of others he couldn't name brought a colorful riot to the front of the cabin.

He led her down the stone path to the side of the house, where a bubbling goldfish pond lay surrounded by even more flowers.

"This place is so Sophie," LeAnne said from behind him.

"That it is," he agreed quietly.

"The first year I opened Happy Hounds, she arrived, looked around, and announced that what the place needed was more flowers. I kept adding flowers in various places and every year she'd point out another spot and say, 'Flowers would really spruce that up.'"

Jake chuckled. "So *she's* the one responsible."

"Yes, and I'm grateful. That's something nearly every guest comments on." She was quiet for a moment. "Who takes care of this place? I noticed that all the bedding inside smelled fresh and there wasn't a dust mote to be found."

"Leo and Lila Paxton. Leo takes care of the outside; Lila cleans the house. They come once a week."

They continued in silence, Jake breathing in deeply the air of the place he loved most in the world. He led her down to the lake, to his favorite spot.

"It's beautiful," LeAnne said softly. "What mountain is that?" she asked, pointing across the lake.

"Lyon's Mountain," Jake said. "And yes, it's beautiful, every season of the year."

"I was under the impression you came here only in summer."

"I did, for the most part. But when my mother died in March of my sophomore year in high school, Aunt Sophie offered to let me come live with her year-round until I graduated and went to college. I begged to stay here instead of Rhode Island, and she and Uncle George agreed."

He pointed at the mountain. "In the winter, it's snowcapped. In the spring you come out every day and watch as the mountain trees start to bloom, and it's a real pretty light green. Like mint green or something. It always looks like a fresh start. I love spring. And then in the summer the leaves get really lush and dark. The fall's spectacular, too. The mountain looks like it's on fire. There are so many different kinds of maples on it that it turns bright red and yellow and orange. It's amazing."

He flushed when he met her gaze and saw her soft smile. He hadn't meant to get all worked up over scenery. "Sorry," he mumbled.

"No, no, it sounds beautiful." She stuck her hands in her shorts pockets. "Was your father already deceased by then?"

"No," he said gruffly.

"Didn't he protest your moving out?"

Jake bent and set the trap on the ground. "Well, he was probably unhappy that he'd no longer experience the satisfaction of making it clear how much I'd ruined his life, but in the end he was just as relieved to be rid of me as I was to go."

"Oh, Jake," she whispered.

He shrugged as he freed the mouse, which immediately scurried out and ran for cover. "Ancient history."

"Is your father still alive?"

"Last I heard. Of course, I haven't inquired in the last five years, so who knows?"

"How did you supposedly ruin his life, Jake?"

He continued fiddling with the trap for no reason other than that he didn't want to be looking at her when he answered. He was pretty amazed he was answering her at all. But for some reason her tone wasn't pitying or full of fake concern. She just seemed to want to know. Probably the shrink in her, trying to dissect his psyche. "Let's just say I came along long before he was ready to marry and settle down."

"Like that's your fault?"

"In his mind. My fault and my mother's, both. From the day I was born to the day I walked out of his house forever, he blamed my mother and me for every single failure in his life. If it hadn't been for us, he'd have been rich and successful and happy."

"You didn't buy into that theory, did you?"

He finally surged to his feet. "Let's go," he said, tugging her hand. She willingly followed, and because her hand felt so good in his, he didn't drop it.

"Jake," she said, "tell me you didn't buy that theory."

He shook his head. "I'd say I bought into it when I was younger. After all, every father's word is law, right?

"But when I was about seven or eight, I overheard an argument between my parents. It happened after my father slapped me for bringing home a friend without asking. My father was yelling that if we kept feeding every little vagabond I dragged home, we'd be living in the streets before long. My mother told him that just like the last million times she'd offered, she'd happily help him pack. He could leave anytime he liked. He could walk away and never look back and she'd never ask a thing of him. He then slapped her and told her he didn't shirk his responsibilities, no matter how distasteful they were."

"Oh, Jake. That's horrible," she said, her tone equal parts anger and disgust.

"Like I said," he repeated while his thumb caressed her soft palm, "ancient history."

Jimmy decided that running for his life was the better part of sanity. If he called in to the boss and reported the disaster earlier that day, his life wouldn't be worth a plug nickel.

He couldn't understand how everything had gone wrong with this job. They'd had everything going for them: enough capital to call on unlimited resources, a mole in the Bureau who had access to the information they needed to track the girl down, and his own smarts and cunning. How could they have failed?

Well, he'd have a long time to ponder that question, seeing as he planned to retire—right now, tonight—and disappear. Good thing he'd been building a nest egg for just this eventuality.

Now to get rid of Horace, get to a bank machine, and get the hell out of Dodge.

"Don't you think it's about time to call in, Bunny?" Horace said.

"Yeah, yeah, I'm just trying to think of our next move before I report in. You know, have a Plan B."

"Isn't this about Plan T by now?"

"It's not my fault!"

"It's your fault you missed."

Horace had been out gassing up the car when he'd talked to the Rat, so he didn't know about the little mistaken identity problem. And Jimmy decided to keep it that way. "I think the rifle was faulty," he complained.

"Right," Horace said, with a smirk that Jimmy'd like to wipe off with his fist.

"And I could make the case that your driving screwed us up."

Horace's smirk vanished, and a beady-eyed look that was eerily reminiscent of his nickname took its place. "Don't even try that shit with me, Bunny."

He didn't need to be a genius to know that until he could get safely away from this idiot, it wouldn't be a good idea to piss him off. "Hey, I was just teasing," he said jovially, slapping Horace on the shoulder. "Are you hungry?"

"A little."

Jimmy pulled his wallet out of his pocket. "How about you run pick us up some burgers?"

"Oh, no, you don't. I'm not having you calling

in while I'm gone and trying to blame me for your screw-up."

Jimmy was offended. Running away was one thing. The only practical solution. Squealing on a colleague went against his code of ethics. "Take the motel phone with you, if you don't believe me."

"And out would pop that cell phone in your pocket."

"I'm giving you my word," Jimmy said with all the sincerity he could muster.

Horace's laugh was nasty and insulting. "You're coming with me."

Damn. Well, they couldn't do anything more tonight anyway. Jimmy would sneak out during the night. Right after he treated Horace to about a dozen rounds of drinks. "Fine," he said, masking his irritation. "Well, if we're both going, no need for cheap takeout. Let's find ourselves a nice steakhouse."

Since the Paxtons hadn't known Jake was coming, the kitchen cupboards were empty except for a few spices, and the refrigerator held nothing but a box of baking soda. Since Domino's didn't deliver, Jake had had to make a grocery run. The list of precautions he'd forced on her before he'd left had almost been laughable.

The closest grocery store was a twenty-minute drive, so by the time he arrived back at the cabin, it was fairly late in the evening and she was ravenous.

"I'll cook," she offered, wanting to be able to eat it.

He cut a narrow gaze at her while he put away the last of the groceries. "No need. I'll do it."

"No, really, I'd be happy to work for my keep."

He leaned back against the counter and crossed his arms and his legs. "You don't believe I can cook."

"I didn't say that."

"Then step aside. I'm chef du jour."

"Is there anything I can do?" she asked.

"Yes. Go down to the cellar and pick us out a bottle of wine."

"Where's the cellar?"

He pointed to the door beyond the pantry.

"Are there creepy-crawly things down there?"

"It's as clean as the rest of the place."

LeAnne turned on the light and descended. Jake had been right. The basement was as spotless as the rest of the house.

The main room contained a washer, dryer, and workbench, with more tools hanging on the wall than Tim Taylor possessed on *Home Improvement*. There were two doors off the main room. She opened the first door, and sure enough, cool, musty air kissed her skin. The light came on automatically and she encountered enough racks of wine to inebriate a small platoon.

She perused the labels for a while, impressed

at the selection, before finally choosing a '94 California cabernet. After closing the door, she headed toward the stairs, but a bout of curiosity had her reversing her steps and going to the other door. She opened it and peeked in. The light didn't come on in this one, so she groped until she found the switch and flipped it on.

She wasn't sure, but it looked like a darkroom. Not being too familiar with darkrooms except those she'd seen in movies, she didn't know if it was state-of-the-art, but it certainly seemed to contain a lot of gadgets, square buckets and tongs, among other things. She was about to flip off the light when she spotted a file cabinet that was labeled FINISHED PRINTS.

Of course it was none of her business. And at this point, the cabinet was most likely empty, anyway. But she couldn't help just checking. She figured if the cabinet was locked, that was her signal not to snoop.

It wasn't locked. There were several file folders, but the one that grabbed her attention first was marked CRITTERS. She pulled it out and opened it. The file was filled with nature shots. Striking black-and-white nature shots.

She was drawn to them, to their stark beauty. One of a raccoon feeding her baby. One of two squirrels at play. A duck gliding across a lake with five babies paddling in her wake.

The photographs were incredibly moving for some reason she couldn't put her finger on. Maybe it was the sense of being dropped right into nature's lap. But it was more than that. They allowed one to experience the simple beauty of wild animals as they went about their daily routines, totally unaware of and undisturbed by the person capturing that moment in time.

She knew for a fact that Sophie was a disposable-camera type of gal, so she doubted this had been her hobby. But she recognized the view of Lyon's Mountain from that clearing by the lake, so the photos must have been taken around here. Maybe her husband had been a camera buff.

She was so caught up in absorbing the details, she didn't hear Jake approach. So when he said, "What are you doing?" she jumped about a foot.

She whirled guiltily, the file pressed to her chest. "I'm sorry!" she said. "I . . . I just opened the door out of curiosity and I . . . well, snooped."

His blue eyes traveled the room and something subtle changed in his expression. He seemed both peaceful and angry all at once. Probably peaceful at the wonderful memories and angry that she'd sullied them.

"I really am sorry. It's just that these pictures are so beautiful. They should be hanging upstairs, not sitting down here stuffed in a drawer."

"You really think they're good?"

"Oh, absolutely! I'd pay for these."

He cocked his head as he perused each one in turn. "Actually, these were the rejects, but my uncle couldn't stand to part with them."

"He was amazingly talented, Jake. You can see what a creative, poetic soul he was."

For some reason that made him flush, and a niggling feeling hit her. The way Jake had described the mountain today hadn't exactly been lyrical, but it was poetic in its passion and simplicity. "Or was he?" she asked, following up on her hunch.

He remained stoically silent.

"Did you take these pictures?"

He waved. "It was a hobby once."

"Once? Why did you stop? Jake, you have real talent!"

"It was a kid thing, really. When you spend summers in a cabin with no TV, you learn to amuse yourself any way you can."

She didn't buy that. She'd seen the spark of love and pride in his eyes as he'd glanced at the photographs. She'd seen a tic in his jaw that betrayed tension and a history he was avoiding discussing.

Stepping up to him, she laid a hand on his chest. "Tell me," she said, and she wasn't using her clinical voice, either. She wanted to know this man, but not just so she could analyze him, could classify him.

His head dropped as he stared at her hand, lying directly over his strongly beating heart. Then he looked up, and the heat in his eyes kicked the pace of her own pulse into over-drive. She attempted to keep her voice level as she said, "Who taught you to take pictures?"

"Uncle George."

"Did he teach you to develop them as well?"

"Actually," he said, his voice almost hoarse, "we learned together. We spent an entire summer studying all about it, and taking a class. This room used to be a large storage closet. We converted it together."

"Why did you give it up?"

The tic returned. "I grew up. I had better things to do than waste my time taking pictures of animals."

Her hand dropped from his chest. "That," she said, waving at the photos, "is not a waste of time. It's a thing of beauty."

"Yeah? Well, according to my old man, it was a thing for sissies. He said that, of course, right before he trashed the Leica Uncle George gave me for my sixteenth birthday."

"Excuse my language, but your old man was a bastard."

His chuckle was only slightly strained. "Is that your professional assessment, Doc?"

She nodded. "A completely clinical analysis."

"Then it must be true."

"Of course."

"Want to hear a self-diagnosis?" he asked as his hand went to the back of her neck.

She almost dropped the bottle of wine. "Yes."

"I'm experiencing an alarming case of the raging hots for you."

"I think that can be treated," she whispered as his mouth lowered.

"Me, too," he said, "like this."

LeAnne's senses went into a tailspin as his mouth settled on hers. Any protest she might have uttered died a quick, merciful death as she returned the kiss with a fervor that would have alarmed her if it didn't feel so good.

His mouth moved over hers, pressing and teasing and playing, until her lips tingled and spread pure lust through her body. She stopped thinking and gave herself over to sensation.

Once again, the man didn't touch her where she needed him. He pulled her against him, and she loved the feel of his big, hard body pressed to her smaller, softer one. But his hands refused to take liberties, and she was beginning to resent it.

She broke the kiss. "Why won't you touch me?" she asked in a fog.

He blinked. "I *am* touching you."

"Not where I want."

His smile was slow. "Why don't you tell me where you want me to touch you?"

She was hot and frustrated and needy as hell. But also just a little inhibited. Women didn't beg to be ravished. "I shouldn't have to tell you."

The hand on the back of her neck thrust

261

upward into her hair, and he pulled her to him and kissed her again. "According to Aunt Sophie, a man never travels anyplace unless a woman gives him directions."

She was just about to give him a free pass for an around-the-world trip when a strident and shrill constant beep interrupted. Jake went stiff, then cursed. "The bacon!"

And while she stood there with hormones bouncing around her body, he turned, ran out, and pounded up the stairs.

"Bring the wine!" he called over his shoulder.

LeAnne helped Jake clean up the mess of incinerated bacon while the cabernet breathed and LeAnne calmed her raging heart. Muffin, after the initial excitement—and his failed attempt to be fed the blackened bacon—had settled down to snore softly in the corner by the back door.

Once Jake started over, he gave his all to cooking their supper. She decided it was normal to feel a little slighted that he could turn off that fast and head in a totally different direction.

She poured them each a glass of wine, then sat down at the kitchen table and watched him work. He chopped and stirred and sautéed with a sexy efficiency that had her thinking totally wicked thoughts. Her curse, she decided, after a sip of wonderful wine, was that she couldn't keep her feelings bottled.

"Jake?"

"Hmmm?" he said without turning around.

"Do you always . . . is it always . . . is it easy for you to just . . . *stop?*"

"Stop what?" he asked, shredding potatoes.

"Please don't play coy with me. It's hard enough for me to ask you this."

He stopped shredding and turned to her. "I honestly don't know what you mean. And I *never* play coy."

"About intimacy. You just seem to be able to turn it on and off at will."

He dropped the potato on the cutting board and picked up his wine, taking a sip. Then he looked at her, and most of her stomach melted.

"Well, I have to say the possibility of a fire tends to grab my attention."

She swirled a finger around the lip of her goblet, but kept her eyes level with his. "But this isn't the first time. You seem to be able to do that anytime you like. You act like you're interested, but any distraction and you forget I'm there."

"Trust me, Doc, I *never* forget you're there."

"What do you want from me, Jake?"

He returned to obliterating the potato, and for a few seconds she thought he wouldn't answer. When he did, it was with a question. "Are you always this blunt?"

"Always," she said, nodding, even if he couldn't see it.

"What do you think I want?"

"You tell me."

He laughed. "Always the shrink."

"No," she said softly, "right now I'm asking as a woman."

The remains of the potato fell from his hands. He stood for a second, his back to her; then he turned. "You want to know what I want? Okay. One, I want to keep you safe. That's primary. I got you into this mess and I need to make sure you come out of it alive. Two, I want to make love to you. Over and over and over until you're begging for mercy. Or better yet, begging for more." He took a deep breath. "Blunt enough for you?"

Her wineglass almost slipped through her fingers. "Yes," was all she could manage to squeak out.

"Now it's your turn. What do you want from me?"

She swallowed, then glugged down a healthy sip of wine. "In any particular order?"

"You have a long list, do you?"

"Somewhat longer than yours."

He dumped the shredded potatoes into a saucepan, and they instantly sizzled. Then he worked over the beaten eggs again. "Well?"

"Do you want them in order of importance or just as they showed up on the list?"

"Importance."

She had to shuffle the cards in her head. "One, I want you to do what you have to do to keep Elisa safe."

"Working on it."

"Two, I want you to bond completely with Muffin."

"Working on it."

"Three, I want you to get back into photography."

"Why?"

"Because it's obvious you loved it, and it's obvious you were wonderful at it."

"That's not a professional wish." He started chopping onions with a vengeance.

"No, you're right, I forgot to mention we moved from the professional to the personal. Heck, I'd hire you as the professional photographer at Happy Hounds. You're that good."

"I don't even have a camera anymore. But I'll think about it."

"Good."

"Any more?" he asked, testy. "Because you're really getting bossy."

She took a deep breath. "I want you to touch me all over and make love to me over and over and over until I beg for mercy. Or beg for more."

He didn't say a word, just went still for a moment before slowly turning off all the burners and the oven with precise, measured movements. He washed his hands with the liquid soap, then dried them so slowly she wanted to scream.

Finally he turned to face her. "This is a bad

idea. I need to be keeping an eye out for bad guys."

"The bad guys don't have a clue where we are."

He weighed it all, then made up his mind. "I've got ten bucks on you begging for more."

"I've got twenty on *you* begging for your life."

Chapter Eleven

"I'd have to say professionally that this isn't a good idea, LeAnne," Jake said, while he allowed himself to be tugged upstairs.

"I'd have to agree with you, for a totally different reason."

"So why are we doing this?"

"Are all you FBI spies this dumb?"

"I'm not . . ." He thought better of it. "Yes, we are."

"I figured as much." She dragged him into his old bedroom and pushed him down on the bed. "Now make me beg."

"You're pretty much a little tiger when you get your hormones in an uproar."

She smiled a cat smile that had him worried and crazily aroused at the same time.

"This is about the worst idea we've come up with," he said, dragging her to him by hooking his fingers in her shorts.

"I know. It stinks," she said, helping him open her zipper.

"We should have more restraint."

"I know. It's shameful." She dropped her shorts, and when he saw the wispy, lacy light purple panties, he forgot what the word *restraint* meant. In front of him was a creamy, flat abdomen that wanted to be kissed.

He lost all sanity. He grabbed her hips and laid his lips on her belly, breathing in her scent, soaking in her softness. She groaned and her muscles tensed and she responded like a woman starved.

He planned to give her a feast.

Jake stopped thinking and just felt. He undressed her completely and held her away so he could just look at her standing before him. Staying seated on the bed, he caressed her with his eyes, then with his fingers and his mouth. He kept her standing while he touched her breasts, probed between her thighs. He kissed her skin everywhere he could reach without moving.

More than the excitement of having a sexy female body naked before him was that it was LeAnne's sexy female body. And she was *so* responsive to his touch, so willing to signal her desires and likes, he was about to come just touching her.

He stroked her and she almost collapsed. "Jake," she whispered, "this is what I wanted."

"This is what you get, baby. And so much more."

He stood and grasped her, then laid her on the bed.

"Show me."

Her legs spread, and she looked up at him with a glazed and needful expression that nearly made his knees buckle. "Touch me. Now," she demanded.

Oh, he wanted more than that. He wanted to taste her, to bring her to a writhing frenzy with his mouth. He quickly shed the rest of his clothes and lay down over her, kissing her lush mouth, inhaling her scent, trying to stay in control while his body was thrumming.

He took his time meandering down her body, teasing her breasts and suckling her belly. Her response was so sexy, he couldn't help kissing other hot spots.

He'd never been with a woman who talked so much during sex, and couldn't believe what it did to him. If it had been anyone else, he'd probably kiss her mouth shut. With LeAnne, he wouldn't stop her to save his life.

"Oh, Jake, that feels so good. . . . Your mouth on me, ohhh . . . Oh, please don't stop. . . ."

He was so excited, he wanted to burst out of his skin, wanted to burst inside her. Wanted to be inside her. When he couldn't stand it any longer, he moved up to take her, but she pushed him away with amazing strength and said, "Now *you* get it."

And he found himself on his back while she played with him completely and worshiped his body as no woman had ever done. And she talked more while he was utterly mute.

"Your chest is so beautiful," she whispered as she laid kisses all over him. "And stomach and hips," she added as she devoured him and had him dying to plunge into her.

She was driving him wild as he'd never been driven.

"Touch me," she said, and he struggled out of a sea of need to give her what she wanted. Then she surpassed every fantasy he'd ever conjured when she brought them both to a crashing orgasm while he stroked her and she stroked him and he fell into oblivion.

"You owe me twenty bucks," LeAnne reminded Jake, even as she snuggled against his sweaty chest.

"I'm not done with you yet," he said with a gasp, and hoped she believed it. If she made him prove it again, he was a dead man. The woman was insatiable.

He was beginning to love that about her.

When he'd finally sunk himself inside her, he'd felt so good, so at home, so ready to make this woman his own, he'd pretty much gone crazy and started talking back. It hadn't shut her up, and it had been the sexiest experience of his life.

He might have concluded that having a woman analyze how good he was in bed would be about the least enticing thing he could imagine. No way. Her crying out "You're making me crazy" was about the sexiest psychobabble he'd ever heard.

"I'm not sure I thanked you for saving my life," LeAnne said softly against his highly sensitized skin.

"I'm not sure I've apologized properly for putting it in jeopardy."

Hiking herself up onto her elbow, she looked down at him solemnly. "Jake, I know that wasn't your fault."

His hand lifted to her face, then shoved through her hair to the back of her neck. "Lady, you are so beautiful."

Her lashes lowered and her cheeks went rosy. "I'm glad you think so."

"You are so much more than any fantasy I've had about you."

Her eyes widened. "You've had fantasies about me?"

"Oh, lady, you have no idea how many fantasies I've had about you. None of them come close to the real thing."

Her color rose even higher. "Well, I have to say, I . . . never realized . . ." Her voice trailed off.

271

Jake hid a grin. "Are you going to let me stay here tonight?" he asked, then held his breath.

She laughed softly. "It'd be sort of pointless to make you leave, don't you think?"

"Good." He grasped her small waist and lifted her bodily over him while she let out a small squeak. "Me closest to the door, remember?" He stood up and strolled naked to the guest room, where he'd left his gun. Muffin was lying on his blanket, but he wasn't asleep. He glanced up at Jake with an expression that looked like a combination of accusation and envy. Jake shrugged. "Don't give me any guff, mutt. I didn't force her."

Muffin growled.

Jake turned to the door, but then turned back. "I'm going back to that room. You want to join us?"

Muffin jumped up and grabbed a corner of the blanket in his mouth.

"Don't even think about trying to get up on the bed, dog. Two's company; three's a crowd."

The next morning Jake woke to the warmth of LeAnne's soft, naked body pressed against his back, her arm draped over his waist. Her breath puffed in and out rhythmically and silently on his shoulder blade, letting him know she was still deep in slumber.

No surprise there. They'd had a busy, wonderful night—easily the best night of his life. LeAnne was an incredible woman: giving, loving, and sexy. Yet at times he'd recognized her amazement when the things he did to her obviously surprised and delighted her. Married or not, she was obviously not vastly experienced. He'd loved making her come every which way but loose.

A contentment he'd never felt in his life stole over him, and he took a moment to savor it. He could get used to this. Although he'd had women stay an entire night before, it had always been something of a nuisance. Right now he felt that he could happily spend a year in bed with this one.

He listened to the morning sounds that drifted in through the window screen: the birdsong, the chatter of squirrels, and the occasional chirps of chipmunks at play. Smiling, he let happy memories wash over him—memories he'd buried with Sophie, too painful to think about until now.

He missed her like crazy, but until now he'd refused to let himself feel it. Every once in a while her loss would steal up on him and blindside him when he least expected it. Then he'd firmly suppress the feelings, shove them into a corner of himself.

And up until now, he hadn't allowed himself to remember the love and acceptance Aunt Sophie and Uncle George had given him unconditionally. It just hurt too much to realize that there wasn't a person left on earth who cared about him the way they had.

But being here with LeAnne, surrounded by childhood memories, he recognized his right to grieve, but also to realize that Sophie would always be in his heart and soul. She would never die there.

It hadn't hurt at all to share his past with LeAnne. He'd enjoyed taking her to his favorite spot, enjoyed watching her reaction to his childhood hobby. Maybe someday he'd get himself another camera. He knew he'd love to take about twelve dozen rolls of LeAnne. If there was anyone who stood as a testament to Mother Nature's generosity, she was it.

LeAnne murmured something in her sleep, and with a smile Jake gently turned over and took her in his arms. Her lashes fanned out above her cheeks, and her skin glowed in the morning light.

But what really zapped his heart was her mouth. Kiss-swollen lips, reddened chin and cheeks, her mouth was proof of their wild night together. He rubbed his bristly jaw and grimaced, feeling sort of bad. Then he bent and feathered soothing kisses on and around her mouth.

Her silky hair fell over her eyes and he brushed it back, taking the time to enjoy the creamy softness of her skin. God, she was exquisite, and last night she'd been all his.

He didn't have any illusions about their future. After his vacation he'd be back at work, traveling at a moment's notice to all parts of the country, chasing bad guys, tracking down leads and witnesses. It wasn't the kind of life he'd ask any woman to put up with, especially a woman like LeAnne. She deserved so much more than he had to offer her.

But he also knew that she'd never be completely out of his life. In fact, he couldn't now imagine a life without LeAnne in some part of it. Even if they were just friends, he wanted some kind of relationship with her. He found it hard to imagine that there had ever been a time he hadn't known her. And this just after having known her for barely a week.

He wished he'd listened more closely when Aunt Sophie had raved about her. Stupid him. He'd assumed she was just another in the long line of women Aunt Sophie had considered marriage material.

Well, Aunt Sophie had hit the nail on the head this time. LeAnne Crosby was definitely marriage material. Too bad he wasn't.

He leaned down and kissed her again. She stirred just a little and her arm tightened around his waist as she pressed even closer to him. He glanced down at her incredible breasts, flattened a bit against his chest. He had things to do, but he couldn't leave her without tasting her one final time. So he pulled back a bit, then lowered his head and took her nipple into his mouth, sucking gently. She moaned softly, her hand moving to the back of his head, threading through his hair.

Jake wondered if he could bring her to orgasm without waking her. It was a challenge that appealed to him on just about every level. His hand drifted down her waist to her hip, then slipped between her legs.

She was still moist, and he loved the way her body responded to his stimulation. Her thighs spread for him, and he entered her with his finger, while still stroking her with his thumb. His mouth went to her other breast and he suckled it even more fervently.

Her lips parted and a tiny gasp sounded from between them. Her head started moving from side to side and her hand tightened on his head reflexively.

Jake was hard as a rock but he ignored it, just wanting the enjoyment of giving her explosive pleasure. He kissed his way down her belly to the hollow of her hips and then he tasted her.

She moaned some more as his tongue glided over her, as his finger slid in and out of her. Her body began shaking and she arched up, crying out his name. He didn't stop until he'd wrung every convulsion of her muscles from her. Then he kissed his way up her body again, to find her boneless and smiling.

And awake.

"Good morning," he said, smiling sleepily down at her.

"Oh, it definitely is," she replied, wrapping

her thighs around his hips, drawing him to her. "Make it better."

LeAnne insisted on cooking breakfast, and Jake readily agreed, as he had some things to take care of.

He got a pad of paper and a pen and took them into the kitchen, Muffin hot on his heels. LeAnne handed him a mug of coffee prepared exactly the way he liked it. He gave her points for noticing the morning they dined together at Happy Hounds. Very little got by the good doctor.

Jake slumped into a chair and sipped gratefully. She turned back to beating pancake batter, and he took a moment to admire the view. She was wearing denim shorts and a red tank top today. He ogled her sweetly rounded bottom and those incredible legs that just minutes before had been wrapped tightly around his hips.

Jake couldn't believe it when he felt himself swell with desire once again. As it was they'd made love most of the night. And here he was wanting her again.

He shook his head. He had some work to get done. "Does Buzz live on the premises?" he asked LeAnne.

She glanced over her shoulder at him. "Yes, year-round. Why?"

"Give me the name of one or two employees you have who don't live at the resort."

"Most of them don't, Jake," she said.

"Do you know any of their home numbers by heart?"

She scrunched up her nose. "Let's see. I know Darla's. And I know Michael's. He's the head concierge."

"Can both of them be trusted?"

"With what?"

"With passing a message on to Buzz."

"Why don't you just call Buzz?"

"I don't trust that the bad guys aren't now monitoring incoming and outgoing calls."

She spun on her heel, outrage written all over her face. "Can they do that?"

"Legally, no, but those people have friends in all the right places."

"This stinks," she said.

"I know. I'm so sorry."

The anger drained from her face. "I know you are." And just like that, she forgave him. In her shoes, he knew he wouldn't be so generous. He marveled at her ability to be fair-minded. She was one hell of a woman.

"Both of them can be trusted," she commented. Then she rattled off their numbers.

"I don't suppose you know if either of them is working right now?"

"It's Saturday, so Darla's off. I don't remember the concierge schedule. Michael sets it."

"Okay, I'll start with Darla."

He took the pad and his coffee into Uncle

George's old den. Even after all this time there was still a hint of cherry pipe smoke in the air. Jake glanced around, smiling. So many good memories here. Uncle George had been a huge fan of reading, and Jake was sure that he'd read every single one of the two hundred or so classic books lining the shelves, some several times over.

Before Jake could read, Uncle George would read a chapter a night to him—sometimes more when Jake could wheedle him into it. After Jake learned to read, Uncle George sat and listened quietly, a smile of contentment on his face while Jake struggled over the big words. Uncle George had had the patience of Job for a few years there.

If Jake ever did have any kids—an outside chance at best—he knew he'd pass on that reading tradition to them. As the image formed in his mind, he was shocked to see LeAnne in the role of mother, holding their child on her lap while Jake read *Huckleberry Finn* with gusto.

Funny, whenever he'd conjured that image in the past, the only woman in sight had always been Aunt Sophie. Somehow he'd managed to create imaginary children without a woman.

He shook his head to clear the image and sat down at the desk. Picking up the old-fashioned rotary phone, he dialed Darla's number and mentally crossed his fingers.

Luck was with him. Her mother called her to the phone. "Darla, my name's Jake Donnelly. I don't know if you remember me—"

"Sure, you're the hunk."

He chuckled. "Well . . . uh, thank you."

"What can I do for you? If you're looking for LeAnne, I'm afraid I can't help you. She had to go away on a family emergency."

"Actually, I'm looking for Buzz."

"You can call the front desk. They'll page him and call you back."

"Listen carefully, Darla. I need a very, very important favor from you."

She paused. "Okay," she said, drawing out the word. "If I can."

"I need you to take a message to Buzz. I know it's inconvenient on your day off, but it's vital, and I promise I will reward you generously for it."

"I can't just call him?" she asked.

"No, it has to be delivered in person."

"When?"

He checked his watch. It was nine-thirty. "As soon as possible? Say, within the next hour?"

"Well, I was planning on going to the ten o'clock aerobics class at the resort anyway. So it's no problem."

"Darla, you're a lifesaver. Truly, this is so important, and I'm so glad to be able to trust you with it."

"Does this have something to do with LeAnne?"

He hesitated. "Indirectly."

"Oh, no! She's not in trouble, is she? I knew something was wrong—"

"No, no! She's not in any trouble. I promise. She should be back any day now. But I need to discuss something with Buzz."

"Okay, hold on." A few seconds later she returned. "Okay, I've got a pad and pen. Hit me."

"I want you to tell Buzz that I need him to call me at this number"—he repeated Sophie's number to her twice—"at noon today."

"Okay. Got it."

"Wait, there's more. Tell him I don't want him calling me from his place. Tell him I want him to leave the resort and drive to a pay phone and call me from there."

"What's going on?"

"I'll explain it all soon. I promise, it'll all make sense."

"Are you sure LeAnne isn't in danger?"

"She's perfectly safe. And she'll stay that way as long as you pass that message on to Buzz just as I asked."

"Will do."

"And Darla? Please, whatever you do, do not mention this to *anyone* but Buzz. Not the number, not the message."

"Do you promise me this is in LeAnne's best interests?"

"I promise, I guarantee, I give you my word. You're going to be a hero by the time LeAnne gets back."

She giggled for a moment. "In that case, I'll do it exactly the way you said."

"Thank you so much. You have no idea how much I appreciate it."

Jake hadn't realized how tightly he'd been gripping the phone until he went to hang it up and felt the stiffness in his knuckles.

He glanced up to find LeAnne standing in the doorway, smiling. "Poor Darla. She's probably dying of curiosity."

"I'm sure she is. But her first loyalty is to you, and she'll do exactly as I asked."

She gazed at him for a long moment, and her eyes slid down to his mouth, lingered, then moved back up again. She swallowed hard. "Breakfast is almost ready."

He stood. "Good, I'm starving," he said, then gave her a sweeping once-over. "For food, too."

Jimmy was furious. Horace was being a real pain in the ass. He kept insisting Jimmy call the boss and check in, and Jimmy was running out of stall tactics.

The Richmond paper had surprisingly not reported the story of the shooting at that fancy-schmancy club yesterday. He couldn't decide if that was a good or bad thing. Either the club people had somehow managed to hush it up to save their reputation, or worse, the FBI had suppressed it so Jimmy wouldn't know just how much *they* knew.

His fondest desire at the moment was to

climb onto the first plane out of the country. But he'd overplayed his hand last night, buying drinks one after another until he was falling asleep on the drive back from the bar. He didn't even remember Horace getting him inside their room. The next thing he knew it was morning, and when Jimmy managed to crack open his eyes Horace was already up and busy trimming his nails.

So now he was stuck until he could find some other way to get away from the snake, as he'd come to think of Horace.

"No more stalling, Bunny," Horace stated flatly. "Call in."

Jimmy scowled at him. "What's your hurry? And if you're so hell-bent on talking to the boss, call him yourself."

"Okay," Horace said calmly and moved toward the phone.

"No, wait!" Jimmy bellowed. He had the feeling Horace didn't know how to put a spin on a story. Or at least not the type of spin that would be beneficial to Jimmy.

Reluctantly he punched in the numbers, nervous enough that he had to stop and start over twice. He was hoping for a busy signal or an answering machine, but he didn't get either.

"Bunny, I'm not a happy man."

"The rifle jammed," he said desperately.

"A bolt-action rifle jammed?" the man asked blandly.

"I mean, it misfired."

"Bunny, Bunny, Bunny," the man said in such a condescending voice, Jimmy wanted to beat the phone on the side table. "Please don't insult my intelligence."

Jimmy glanced up and Horace was smirking at him. Suddenly he hated this job, hated these people. He wanted out. He wanted sun and sand and salt water. "I figure Colson's taken the girl and headed west."

"How do you figure that?"

"Well, that's been his modus operandi so far," he said, always proud when he got to use those cool legal terms. He should have gone to law school. If he was a lawyer, *no one* would be calling him Bunny.

"You have two more days, Bunny. Forty-eight hours. You don't get the job done, we're going to be *very* disappointed."

Sweat beaded his upper lip, both in relief and fear: relief that he'd been given a reprieve, fear because he didn't have a clue what to do next.

"We'll get it done," he said, infusing his tone with confidence he didn't feel for a second.

"See that you do."

Bunny disconnected before any more veiled threats could be tossed his way.

Without looking at Horace he quickly punched in the number for the Rat. He breathed relief when the man answered. "Tell me you got something."

"Maybe."

"Tell me!" he said, then lowered his voice to a growl to disguise his panic. "It better be good."

"Call this my parting gift."

"What is it?"

"I've been keeping track of family connections to all the parties involved."

"Yeah? And?"

"A long-distance phone call was placed an hour ago."

"So?"

"It was placed from one of your Feds' listed places of residence for his next of kin. Not your main mark, by the way, but close enough to be curious."

"So?"

"He no longer has next of kin."

"So? If they're gone, the number's probably been given to someone else."

"Nope, still listed in his family's name. The bills are routed to a lawyer's office for payment, but the listing hasn't changed."

"I don't get the big deal here. So someone made a call from that place."

The Rat sighed. "First activity in months."

"So?"

"Want to know where they called?"

"Where?"

"Call was placed to a residence in the town right outside of that resort you visited yesterday."

Jimmy didn't like sounding dumb, but he didn't get it. "You think someone's at the Virginia place?"

"No, you idiot. They'd be too smart to call the resort itself. So they'd call someone nearby."

"So we should go shake up those people for some info?"

"Where'd you graduate? Moron U? Follow the bouncing witness, Bunny."

"Huh?"

"One long-distance call from a residence where nobody lives, but which is listed as the address of next of kin to one of the Feds assigned to this case. That call is placed to a location near where that same Fed was as of yesterday."

Understanding dawned. Jimmy could have kissed the guy. "Give me the address."

LeAnne was already experiencing cabin fever. Although it was a lovely place, she was not used to being cooped up inside all day long.

As she handed Jake the final pan to dry, she presented him with her best smile. "Could we take a walk or something? I'm going a little stir-crazy."

Jake stared at her. "Damn, woman, that smile could sell a sports car to an Amish guy."

She'd never used wiles before in her life, but she really, really liked the way she affected him. She waited until he finished drying the pan and set it in the rack before stepping up to him and spreading her hands over his chest. "Could it sell a nature walk to an FBI spy?"

"It could probably make this FBI spy sell national secrets to China."

She laughed. "Make sure the exchange rate is good Hunan chicken." She drummed her fingers against his chest. "Please, can we go for a walk?"

"We can go for a walk. But first I need to run out and buy a couple of newspapers."

"Why?"

"I want to see if we got any press."

It took longer than Darla expected to meet up with Buzz. That was strange. The man materialized out of nowhere all the time. Why he took so long to answer his page this time had her worried.

When he finally showed up at the gym, she grinned and cut out of the aerobics class.

"What's going on?" he asked.

She dragged him out of the gym, past the locker rooms to the back entrance. "Okay, here we go," she said in a conspiratorial whisper. Then she took a good look at his face.

She'd worked for LeAnne for three years, and she'd known Buzz all that time. The man never had a bad day. He was always cheerful, friendly, happy—the best. But there was something very different about him today—something she couldn't stick a name on.

"What's up with you?" she asked.

"Whaddaya mean?"

"You look like, I don't know, a little out of it."

He slapped a cool look on his face, but she wasn't fooled. Buzz was in love. She'd know that expression anywhere. The problem was, he didn't look happy about it. She'd grill him if she weren't so intent on following Mr. Donnelly's instructions. She stuck her finger down her leotard and sports bra.

Buzz's eyes grew big as saucers, then narrowed. "Little lady, you don't do that in front of no man, you hear me?"

She rolled her eyes. "I didn't have anyplace else to keep it, silly." She passed on the phone number to him.

"What's this?"

She lowered her voice to a whisper and relayed the instructions Mr. Donnelly had given her.

Buzz took it all in, made her repeat it twice, then nodded. "You did a good thing," he said. "Thank you."

Darla felt excited and happy at once. She didn't have a clue what was going on here, but she knew she'd carried off her assignment right. And she couldn't wait to find out what it all meant.

LeAnne had given her a chance when no one else would. She had a juvenile record for shoplifting, and most people in town had told her to forget it when she'd applied for jobs.

Only LeAnne had shown faith that Darla wouldn't repeat that offense. She would adore LeAnne forever for letting her prove she'd changed.

And she loved this place—the people, the employees, the animals, and especially Buzz and LeAnne. They were family.

"Is LeAnne okay?" she asked.

"LeAnne's in good hands."

"When is she coming home?"

"Soon, I'm hoping." He got real serious. "Don't tell a soul, hear me? It matters."

"I hear you."

Buzz started to leave, but she stopped him. "And when this is all over, I *have* to know who your new love is."

"Look at this," Jake said, tugging at LeAnne's hand and pointing at the ground. "Those are deer tracks."

"One adult, two fawns."

His head shot up. "That's right!"

She grinned. "The question is, how did *you* know that?"

He straightened and looked around, feeling a sense of serenity in this place that had shaped him. "My Uncle George. He taught me all about tracking animals, observing their habits."

Muffin trotted happily ahead of them, obviously familiar with the territory. Jake watched and let the dog go so far, then called him back. He got a dumb, melting feeling inside when Muffin listened and trotted back to them. He dropped a small Milk-Bone to the dog—something he'd learned from LeAnne. Reward the good. He'd learned to carry the treats wherever they went.

LeAnne tugged at him until he turned to face her. "I think you were really lucky to have Sophie and George," she said, obviously not ready to drop the subject.

"I really was," he admitted.

"Tell me about your mother. You've never talked about her."

Jake picked up a couple of flattened pebbles and started skipping them across the lake. "She was Aunt Sophie's sister."

"Was she like Sophie?" she persisted.

For the first time he thought about that. "In a lot of ways, yes, she was. In many ways, she wasn't. Aunt Sophie would never have stayed with my father."

"Why do you think your mother did?"

He sent another pebble flying. "Is this a session, Dr. Crosby? Am I going to be receiving a bill?"

A hurt expression passed over her face. "Sorry. I wasn't trying to analyze you. I was just interested."

Jake felt like a heel. He dropped the rest of the pebbles and pulled her close. "No, my fault. I'm just a little touchy about the family thing."

"I shouldn't have pried. I was just . . . interested."

"Pry all you want," he said, and strangely enough, he meant it. "I might not always answer, but I'll never get angry that you asked."

"I'll tell you what," she said, brightening considerably and doing indecent things to his body. "If I ever ask something you don't want to answer, just say, 'The weasel dies at dawn.'"

He broke out laughing. He couldn't help it. "You're really into this spy stuff, hmm?"

"I'm really into spies. Can't help it. I'm fatally attracted to them."

He stared down at her beautiful, glowing eyes and felt lost. "Have I mentioned I'm a spy?"

Muffin snorted.

Muffin got no treat for that one.

Jake shot him a dark look, then picked up a pebble and skipped it way out into the lake. "Fetch!"

Muffin snorted.

Jake had to cut the walk short to make it home for Buzz's call. Which was too bad. He'd loved sharing this land with LeAnne, who never failed to amaze him. If he didn't have to be constantly on guard, this would seem like an idyllic vacation with the woman of his dreams.

On the stroll home he held her hand, and an odd fulfillment engulfed him. He had a dog by his side he'd never wanted, a woman he'd never expected to trust, and this property that he'd never expected to share. Yet mix them together and he was an utterly too-happy guy.

Mark would dig him a grave if he could see him now.

Almost at the walkway to the house, he heard the distant sound of a motor vehicle approaching. Instinctively he shoved LeAnne into the foliage on their left and barked, "Come!" to Muffin.

The dog almost never responded to that tone of voice, but he responded now, following and hiding, but growling low and menacingly.

"What is it?" LeAnne whispered.

"Shhh," he said to both of them.

His view was obstructed, but he could see enough to tell that the vehicle was a minivan. Strange vehicle for thugs. Or a very smart choice.

Jake stuck his face in Muffin's. "I appreciate it," he said in a whispered growl, "but cut it out."

Muffin went silent, but continued to bristle.

A man climbed out. He left the door open, and the howl of a child from inside the vehicle reached them.

"Don't you think they need something?" LeAnne whispered in his ear.

"Shhh . . . we'll see."

Jake watched as the man approached the cabin too cautiously, watched him try to peer in both windows before he knocked on the door. The back of the man's right hand resting on the back of his hip wasn't casual enough, and his stepping to the side of the door while he waited for an answer was a dead giveaway.

The sound of the baby crying continued, and Jake recognized a pattern to the wails. As it repeated over and over, it became obvious that it wasn't a real baby, but a tape of a baby.

Whether or not Jake had any question about the stranger before, the man's testing the door and finding it locked pretty much sealed the guy's fate.

Jake systematically filed details about the man's appearance in his mind. White. Mid-thirties. About six feet tall. Dark hair sticking out from below a maroon baseball cap.

The man walked the length of the porch, testing all the windows, then hurried down the steps and headed back to consult with the other person in the van. Jake couldn't make out any details of the man's cohort.

After a minute or so the guy quickly headed for the back of the cabin.

Muffin jumped up, the fur on his neck standing on end. Jake grabbed the dog before he could leap and held him down. "Stop," he said in a hiss. "Quiet!"

He took LeAnne's hand and wrapped it around Muffin's collar. It didn't escape his notice that she was shaking. He'd give anything

293

to hold her and reassure her that he'd *never* let anything happen to her, but he didn't have the luxury of time to do that now.

He looked into her eyes. "Stay still. Keep Muffin quiet."

She grabbed his shirt. "Don't go out there! Please!"

"Honey, I'll be fine. I've got to catch this guy and find out how he discovered this place."

He had to pry her fingers from his T-shirt and ignore the terror in her eyes. He kissed her hard. "Stay put."

"I'd like to ask you to do the same."

"I'll be back before you know it."

The crying baby tape was a godsend. It effectively covered the sounds of breaking twigs and crackling leaves as he made his way among the pines and oaks toward the back of the cabin.

He found the man trying to pick the lock on the door to the kitchen. Jake moved about ten yards past the man, then approached him from behind, his gun drawn and pointed straight at his back. Just as the guy managed to beat the lock and push open the door he barked, "Freeze or die, bozo."

The guy chose to freeze.

"Hands up and free of anything I might misconstrue as a weapon, or I'll have to blow you away in self-defense."

The man dropped two lock-picking tools and raised his hands.

Jake patted him down, relieving him of a .22 and a knife. The weapon told him immediately that this was no professional thug or anyone from the Bureau. He was a common thief.

"Start talking."

"I . . . didn't mean any harm, man. I'd gotten the word this place was empty."

"Then what's to steal?"

"Not steal. Just to hang out, you know."

"Hang out, eh? What's wrong with your own place?" Jake asked, pulling the guy's wallet. The man had three IDs with three different names from three different states. "Any of these really you?"

"Just a precaution, man."

Jake was reasonably certain that this guy was just some two-bit crook running from the law. His dilemma was how to turn the guy and his companion in without calling attention to himself and LeAnne.

"Put your hands behind your head," Jake suggested, emphasizing the importance of cooperating by poking the muzzle of his gun against the man's spine.

The man was in a cooperative mood.

Jake grabbed the back of the man's grungy shirt and directed him back toward the front of the cabin. "Who all's in that van with you?"

"Who *are* you?" the guy asked.

"Jimmy Hoffa. How many in the van?"

"Just my buddy and me."

"That baby crying is a tape, right?" He wasn't about to let them go if there was a kid in there.

"Yeah, yeah. Works real good."

"Oh, yeah, I was fooled for almost five seconds. Your buddy armed? And don't lie to me now, 'cause Bessy here gets real testy when people lie to me."

"He doesn't carry squat. I don't let him. Don't trust him with them. He's my boy."

"It's always heartwarming to see father and son breaking and entering together."

They rounded the corner of the cabin and walked toward the van. When the passenger saw what was happening, he threw open his door, jumped out, and hit the ground running.

"Stop him."

"James, come back now!" the man shouted, but the kid wasn't in the mood to listen to dear old Dad.

Muffin shot out of the woods and began barreling toward the boy, who couldn't be older than twelve or thirteen. Before Jake could call him back, the dog ran in front of the kid and tripped him up. Then Muffin circled around him and took a big bite out of the buttocks section of the kid's shorts and hung on.

"Don't let him hurt my boy!" the guy said. "Please!"

Jake rolled his eyes. "Muffin, let go!"

"Muffin? What kind of pansy—"

Jake cut him off with another poke of the gun. "Don't be making any disparaging remarks about my dog, okay? Really tends to tick me off."

LeAnne also emerged from the woods, and Jake groaned. Didn't anyone listen to him anymore? She ran to the kid and got Muffin to release him. Then she helped the boy up and marched him back toward them.

"What *is* this? *The Mod Squad* or something?"

"Any more weapons inside your van?"

"No. I swear. We're not violent or nothing. I just wanted my boy."

Child abduction.

They all met on the passenger side of the van, Muffin and LeAnne looking more pleased with themselves than they should. Jake was going to give them a good dressing-down later.

The boy was in tears and LeAnne was consoling him. Jake felt bad for the kid, but didn't have time to worry about it. "Listen up. Here's how it's going to be. Seeing as Mr. Smith or Mr. Roberts or Mr. Thomas here didn't actually do any harm, we're going to let them drive on out of here."

LeAnne and Muffin both looked at him as if he'd lost his mind.

He ignored that. "LeAnne, check the van for any more weapons."

She hesitated, then climbed in and searched. "Nothing," she said, jumping out. "Unless you consider a Happy Meal lethal."

Jake nodded at the kid. "Get in and buckle up."

The kid scrambled to comply.

Then Jake led the man to the driver side. "Get in."

The man did, the expression on his face slobberingly grateful. It wouldn't stay that way for long. Jake handed him his wallet, intact. "Hope you don't mind my keeping your gun and knife."

The man shook his head rapidly.

"Good. Get out of here. Don't bother to turn the vehicle around. Just back right up."

The man nodded and Jake pulled LeAnne to the side of the road, calling Muffin. They stood there as the guy started the engine, twisted around in his seat, and peeled out, backward. Jake repeated the license number silently to himself over and over to make sure he remembered.

Once the van disappeared around the bend, LeAnne turned to him, an expression of pure disbelief on her face. "What the heck just happened here?"

He checked his watch, then swore softly. That little incident had made them ten minutes late for Buzz's call. Grabbing her arm he said, "Come on, I'll explain later."

As they jogged to the cabin with Muffin trotting beside them, Jake said, "That man thought we were the contemporary *Mod Squad*."

"Really?" LeAnne said, a dazzlingly pleased smile on her face.

298

Jake reached down and patted Muffin's side. "Who do you think you are? J. Edgar Woofer?"

Muffin barked twice.

As Jake fished the door key from his pocket, he glanced first at LeAnne, then Muffin. "You both did great."

Muffin yipped.

LeAnne punched a fist in the air.

"I'll kill you both for it later."

Chapter Twelve

"I'm still a little fuzzy on why you let that man go," LeAnne said as they closed and locked the door behind them.

"Oh, no. I just gave him a reprieve until the cops can earn their keep."

He went to the kitchen to retrieve his cell phone and punched in 911. As an anonymous, concerned citizen he reported an attempted break-in at one of the cabins on Lyon's Pride Lane. Luckily he'd stumbled upon the thieves before they could complete the break-in, and they fled, heading east down the road toward 322. He described the van, gave them the license number and mentioned there was a boy in the vehicle who looked like he was being held against his will. He disconnected before they could get any personal information on him.

By that time it was almost twelve-twenty and the cabin phone hadn't rung since they'd returned. If Buzz had given up on them, Jake might hunt that burglar down and dish out punishment himself.

There was a downside to having used his cell phone: anyone tracking its use would now be able to get a general idea of their location. Not exact, but too close for comfort. They had to move, but he desperately needed to touch base with Buzz first.

LeAnne, who'd been listening in on his conversation with the emergency operator, stared at him solemnly. "You think that man had abducted his son?"

"Sure looks that way."

"If we'd held them until the police arrived, we'd be certain he was caught and the boy was returned to his mother."

"And the police would learn who we are and that we're here."

"Isn't that boy's safety more important?"

He took her shoulders. "Sweetheart, the boy isn't in any danger from his father, other than possibly picking up some really nasty habits. And trust me, the Pennsylvania State Police are good. They'll get him."

"I'm not going to feel good about this until I know the boy's safe."

"I'll keep checking in with them, then."

"Thank you."

He almost blurted out, "I'd do anything for you," but bit it back just in time. "You're welcome."

The phone's shrill ring startled them both, and Jake gave her a quick kiss. "I need to take this privately, sweetheart. Stay away from windows in case the cops patrol back here looking for damage."

Before she could respond, he turned and jogged to the den, closing the door. He answered on the third ring. "Yeah?"

"It's me," Buzz said quietly.

"I'm so glad you didn't give up. Sorry for being late."

"Scared me half out of my head. Is LeAnne all right?"

"She's absolutely fine. What's going on there?"

"Here? What do you mean?"

"Well, for starters, did our two friends make it away okay?"

There was a pause. "Yes."

"Seen any more bad guys?"

"If they've come back around, they didn't stop for a chat with the cops swarming the entrance."

"They're still on guard there?"

"Yes."

"Good."

"Well, good and bad. Our guests are leaving

in droves, scared to death of what might have happened to LeAnne, why the cops are all over the place, harassing them as they try to go in and out. This is a mess."

LeAnne was *not* going to be happy about that. Which meant he wasn't going to tell her until absolutely necessary. He was sure she'd insist on returning before it was healthy. "I know. I'm sorry. It'll be over soon."

"Not soon enough for me."

"What kind of publicity is this getting?"

"None that I've seen, and I been looking."

"Good." That meant Mark must have checked in before they took off and given orders. "Okay, listen, we're not staying here, so this number won't do you any good. Give me the number of that phone booth."

Buzz rattled it off.

"Can you be there tomorrow morning about nine?"

"Of course."

"I'll call you tomorrow."

"Fine."

Jake replaced the receiver and pocketed the number. He strode out the door to find LeAnne on the floor, giving Muffin a massage. When they weren't in such a hurry, he was going to ask for one of those massages.

"Okay, folks, hop to."

"What's going on?"

"Road trip."

* * *

"Face it, Bun, you're lost."

"Shut up," Jimmy said, slowing down his rental car as a side road came into view. "How the hell is anyone supposed to find anything in this godforsaken state? Ain't they ever heard of road signs?"

"Or is it you can't read a map?"

Bunny had had it up to his eyeballs with Horace. Completely. The man was absolutely useless. All he was good for was sarcasm and criticism, and Bunny hated his guts. Time to dump this guy for good.

He took the next exit.

"What are you doing?" Horace said.

"We need gas."

Horace leaned over and looked at the controls. "It's half-full!"

"We need a full tank after we make the hit. Besides, I gotta take a leak."

He pulled into a Mobil station. "Make yourself useful and fill her up."

He headed toward the bathroom, but when he glanced back and saw that Horace's attention was elsewhere, he veered off and headed inside the station. He quickly asked the clerk for directions to the street he was looking for, and luckily the clerk knew.

Then he made use of the facilities and headed back to the car, climbing in while Horace recapped the tank. He started the engine, then rolled down the window and held out a fifty. "Pay for the gas and get yourself something to drink. Get me a Snapple. I think I have this puppy figured out."

Horace looked annoyed but he took the bill. Bunny waited about five seconds before peeling out. The last he heard over the sound of his own laughter was Horace screaming like a woman.

Feeling a whole lot better, Jimmy got back on 322 and headed for his target. No one was going to blame him for dumping Horace when he reported he'd accomplished the task all on his own.

Jimmy found the road—one he'd passed at least three times—and took it. He slowed down while he patted his holster to reassure himself he was prepared. He found the cabin about two miles farther on but he didn't stop there. He cruised by, parking another quarter mile up the road without ever having passed another residence, which was good. The only witnesses out here would be the wild kind.

Approaching the cabin from the rear, he noted that things seemed awfully still. Of course, he didn't expect people hiding out to be holding a party.

Hoping for the element of surprise, he skulked up to the back door, then peeked in the window. No one there. He quickly picked the lock and entered, wincing when the door squealed ever so slightly. He sure wished his marks would take better care of their homes.

He listened intently, but heard no signs of life. So he tiptoed farther into the kitchen. That was when he saw the handwritten note on the counter. He snatched it up, even as he kept his gun trained on the doorway, in case anyone entered.

Mrs. Paxton,
*   Used the cabin for a couple of days. The place was in great shape. Help yourself to any of the food left in the refrigerator and pantry. I don't expect to be back in the near future.*

Best regards,
Jake

Jimmy swore savagely. He'd missed them again. That damn Donnelly was a slippery son of a bitch.

What was he gonna do now? He had no idea how long ago Donnelly had bugged out or in what direction he'd gone. He stalked through the entire place anyway, just in case the note was a fake, but the cabin remained disgustingly devoid of humans to blow away.

He returned to the first floor, and with the danger of a confrontation passed, he took time to appreciate the place a little better. Now this was the kind of cabin he'd dreamed of retiring in. He took in details so that when he did finally get out—which at current calculations was going to be soon—he'd be able to build something just like this.

Picking up the phone in the small library-type room, he dialed the Rat's number. His jaw dropped when a mechanical operator told him the line had been disconnected. To be sure he hadn't dialed wrong—after all, this was that old kind of phone you rarely saw anymore—he tried twice more, with the same result. Damn, the Rat really *had* bugged out. That thought terrified him. No more leads. None. Donnelly could have gone anywhere—north, west, east, south—to the moon, for all he knew.

He was a dead man. It was time for him to bug out, too. Unless a miracle dropped in his lap in the next forty or so hours, he didn't stand a chance. Time to disappear.

He looked around and a thought occurred to him. The only other person who knew the location of this place was the Rat, and he was gone. Even Horace never saw the exact address.

Why not stick around awhile? Donnelly wasn't planning on coming back. He could enjoy this place for a few days while the shit hit the fan, then died down. And that would give him time to plan his next move.

Congratulating himself on his brilliance, Jimmy went out the back door and practically skipped his way to his car. As he passed a pretty lake, he wondered how the fish were, and if Jake Donnelly had been nice enough to leave a fishing pole behind.

Never again would *anyone* call him Bunny.

"Damn," Jake muttered as they crossed the border into Maryland.

"What's wrong?" LeAnne asked.

"I forgot to pick up the Havahart traps."

"What's wrong with that?"

"You can't leave them down when people come by only once a week. The point is to capture the mice alive and release them. A week without food and water rather defeats the purpose."

LeAnne stifled a smile. The more she learned about this man, the more she liked him. He might be a big, bad FBI guy, but underneath, his heart was pure mush.

His body isn't bad, either, she thought, laughing inwardly at the understatement. She'd never, ever been with a man the way she had been with Jake. She didn't know if it was the realization that this was merely a fling—so she didn't have any long-term stakes—or if it was just how sexy she found him, but every inhibition she'd ever harbored had disappeared last night.

And she'd experienced the greatest sex of her life.

She was going to miss it when they parted ways, no doubt about it. She studied his profile, so strong and hard edged. He was a truly handsome beast, and he'd just given her the best night of her life.

She was definitely going to miss him . . . er, the lovemaking.

"Why are you staring at me?" he asked, catching her in midogle.

She jerked her gaze away from him, willing herself not to blush. "No reason."

He chuckled. "Dr. 'Honest Abe' Crosby, prevaricating?"

"I . . . well, you're pretty good-looking."

From the back of the car, Muffin snorted.

Jake directed a quick glare in the rearview mirror, then glanced back at her. "You think so?"

"I said so, didn't I?" she replied testily. Then she took a breath and changed the subject. "Isn't Aunt Sophie's housekeeper due to show up at the house soon? Maybe she could pick up the traps and set free any critters that might have wandered in."

"Well, I think the Paxtons come on Thursdays. At least they used to. Still too long a time." He pointed at the glove compartment. "Get the cell phone out of there, will you?"

She did, and handed it over.

Jake unfolded it and his eyes jumped from road to phone as he punched in a number.

LeAnne noticed that he did almost everything well: efficiently, precisely, with instant decision-making skills that she had to admire. Although she sure wouldn't want to have to rely on him if her car broke down.

"What are you grinning about now?" he asked, and she found herself caught again. The man missed almost nothing.

She considered fibbing about it, but he seemed pretty good at reading her, too. "I was just thinking, if we ever make it back to Happy Hounds, remind me to give you a lesson on opening the hood of a car."

He frowned, then opened his mouth to retort, but it was cut short when he jerked the bottom of the phone to his lips. His gorgeous lips. "Mrs. Paxton? Hello, it's Jake Donnelly. . . . I'm doing okay, how are you? . . . That's wonderful. . . . Mrs. Paxton, I have a favor to ask. I visited the cabin over the weekend, and just realized I left without picking up the Havaharts. Is there any way you or Mr. Paxton could drop by in the next day or two and pick them up?"

He was silent for a while, his lips turning down into a frown. "No, we left over two hours ago. . . . What kind of car? . . . Mrs. Paxton, that's not mine. . . . No, I didn't offer the cabin to any friends."

He sliced a look at LeAnne that spelled trouble. "Mrs. Paxton, listen to me carefully. . . . No! I don't want you going over there. Whoever that is, it's no friend of mine or Aunt Sophie's. I want you to promise to stay away. Don't even drive by the place. . . . No, don't call the police; I'll do it. Just sit tight, and I promise to contact you the minute I know what's going on. Thank you. And my best to Mr. Paxton. Tell him the grounds look beautiful. Good-bye, Mrs. Paxton."

He disconnected, and LeAnne stared at his grim expression worriedly. "What?"

"Looks like we have visitors at the cabin. How could they possibly have pinpointed the location that fast, from just a single call?"

She didn't have a clue what he was talking about. "The call from Buzz?"

"No, I don't think so. Buzz was calling from a pay phone. It must have been the call to the police. They did it awfully fast, though. Cell phone calls can be traced to a general location, but not to an exact location without very sophisticated equipment."

He dialed information while he said to her, in a growl "Get something to write on and with." He asked for the Pennsylvania State Police office located in Mifflin County. Barking a number at her, which she scrambled to get down right, he then clicked off unceremoniously, then reconnected and said, "Dial that number," thrusting the phone at her.

She did, then handed the phone back. He hit the "send" button. LeAnne sat in astonishment as he insisted on being forwarded to whoever was in charge, identified himself as an FBI Special Agent, gave the police the location, and demanded they proceed to Sophie's cabin and look for an intruder. He instructed them to interrogate the person or persons and impressed upon the police the stakes involved.

"Under no circumstances release any people you find there. Charge them with trespassing, breaking and entering, looking stupid. I don't care what. Just do not release them. Dispatch that instantly; then come back on the line."

LeAnne wanted to ask what was going on, but his attention was already divided between the road and the phone. So she kept silent and just watched his face and listened to the *thump, thump, thump* of his thumb drumming on the steering wheel impatiently.

Finally someone must have come back on the line. "Okay, now check on something else for me. Any arrests today in Mifflin County of a man driving a minivan with a kidnapped child?" He nodded, thanked the person, and disconnected.

Folding the phone, he tossed it high in the air and right into her hands. "Richard Thomas is in custody, his son James well on his way to being reunited with his mother in State College."

LeAnne gaped at him, so amazed that in the

midst of yet another crisis of sorts, he'd thought about her and her wishes.

He glanced over, then did a double take. "What now?"

She blurted out the only thought in her head. "You know, spy guy, you could really make a girl fall in love."

Jimmy, formerly known as Bunny, was fishing when the heat arrived. He'd found fishing poles and a rowboat in the shed behind the house and had known this was a sign that his fortunes had turned.

He'd just finished reeling in a nice-size trout when he heard the first motor vehicle approach. It hadn't occurred to him that it might be the cops, seeing as there wasn't a single siren. It wasn't until six cars screeched to a halt near his launch site that he realized he was trapped.

He'd glanced around wildly, wondering if he could row to safety, but the cop with the bull-horn had assured him his boat would be plugged full of holes. Jimmy wasn't dumb enough to miss the unstated implication: he could be plugged full of holes, too. Besides that, he couldn't swim. Even if they missed him, he'd drown out there.

With all of his dreams dashed, he paddled back to land, not even attempting to go for his gun. Not with at least eight rifles trained on him.

As he neared the shore, two cops waded into

the lake, guns still leveled right at his racing heart. He held up his hands. "If you promise not to call me Bunny, I'll tell you everything I know."

As they hit the D.C. beltway, Jake's mind was racing. And in a really lousy direction. While he would have loved to explore LeAnne's last comment, he had too many things weighing on his mind, too many facts leading to very bad conclusions.

Professional or not, he wanted LeAnne's opinion. "I need advice," he said softly.

"Hit me," she said, matching his tone.

"Only two people know about Aunt Sophie's cabin. My boss, officially, for 'next of kin' purposes in case anything happened to me."

"And the other?"

He cleared his clogged throat. "Mark. Same reason, only for personal purposes."

"You can't believe Mark would do this."

He shook his head. "I can't. But I'd be a fool not to consider all the possibilities."

"Talk it through."

"Mark has been keeping Elisa safe for over a month, ever since the prosecution had to reveal through discovery that she was going to testify. He's had plenty of opportunities to get rid of her if he were on the take. But how much more brilliant to keep looking like he was just one step ahead of the bad guys? He's known how long it would be until trial from the beginning. He could keep her alive until the day before the trial and still be in good shape."

"Why would he bring her to you, then? He also knows how good a spy you are."

"I'm not a—" He laughed. "Right. I'm a hell of a spy, which, by the way, you find real sexy."

"True. Back to the replay."

He nodded again. "How much more brilliant on Mark's part to bring her to me? If the gunmen had done anything right, it would look like Elisa died on my watch, not his."

"Mark had no idea you were heading to the cabin, Jake."

"Absolutely true. He also didn't have fast access to cell phone information."

"Cell phone information?"

"To get the approximate location of my phone call to the police today. To put two and two together and get four."

"Who did?"

"My boss."

"Is he suspect number two?"

"Yes. He's the only other person who knows about the cabin."

"Do you trust your boss?"

"I've never liked him, but never had any reason not to trust him. Although thinking back on it, he always hated that Mark and I refused to offer information about each other's whereabouts when we were hiding witnesses, or like when I didn't want anyone to know I was at Happy Hounds." He glanced over at her. "No offense."

"Almost none taken."

"Against regulations, and all that," he continued. "But we'd plead ignorance, even though he knew we were lying. We'd tell him we'd figure out how to find a way to contact each other if it were an emergency. Since we always came through, he never called us on it."

LeAnne was silent for a few minutes. Jake glanced over at her and found her deep in thought. The woman looked irresistible deep in thought. In the midst of a crisis, Jake found his body hardening, and decided he was a pervert—at least where she was concerned. He had the feeling she could turn him on in the middle of a war zone.

"How many times has Mark saved your life, Jake?" she asked finally.

Each and every time was ingrained in his head. "Six, big-time. Several more getting me out of scrapes."

"How many times have you saved his?"

He was uncomfortable with the calculation, because they added up to more. "About the same," he said.

"Do you trust him with your life?"

"Yes. Well, I thought so until just now. And you have no idea how much I hate not trusting him right now."

She laid a hand on his thigh, and grabbed his attention for a second. "I know it stinks to second-guess all you believe to be true." She took a breath. "Did Muffin like Mark?"

"Instantly. Even before Mark started spoiling him like a nephew or something."

"Did Muffin like your boss?"

"He never met my boss." Jake thought for a moment. "But you know what? The only thing Muffin has ever destroyed was my favorite Garth Brooks CD. And that was the day after I brought it home, after lending it to my boss."

"Let's go to the expert." She turned her head toward the back of the car. "Muffin? Got a question."

In the rearview mirror Jake watched Muffin pop up.

"Muffin, do you like Mark?" she asked.

Muffin yipped.

"Do you like Garth Brooks?"

Silence.

"That dog has no taste in music," Jake complained.

"But great instincts about people," LeAnne pointed out. "There's your answer."

Jake nodded. Without delving too deeply into the idea that he was basing a hunch as much on the opinion of a dog as his own instincts, he held out his hand. "May I have the phone again, please?"

"Who are you calling now?"

"My boss's boss."

She scrambled for it, unfolded it, and handed it to him.

As he punched in the number with his thumb, he commented, "You know, shrink lady, you could really make a guy fall in love."

Chapter Thirteen

There were enough hotels and motels along the Route 7 corridor of Tyson's Corner, Virginia, to house a small nation. However, finding one that allowed animals was a chore. By the time they'd settled into a less-than-Trump-Tower-style room, Jake was outraged on Muffin's behalf.

"This dog is cleaner than most humans I know," he griped. "I can't believe the discrimination against animals around here."

LeAnne smiled. The man wasn't aware of it, but he'd fallen hard for his dog. On the trip south he'd started out scolding the two of them for not following his orders that morning. He'd complained that they—mere citizens—had placed themselves in danger and compromised his handling of the situation. Somehow that slid into, "Did you see Muffin stop that kid? Was he great or what?"

She hadn't once had to remind Jake to stop and give Muffin a break. He hadn't allowed her to pour Muffin water or give him a treat. He wanted to do it all.

Yes, indeed, the man had fallen for his dog.

For his part, Muffin had begun shadowing Jake as though they were tied to one another. Whenever LeAnne gave him a command, Muffin now looked to Jake to see if *he* expected Muffin to obey.

She'd be a little insulted if she weren't so happy for the two of them.

Yet she was a little envious, too, she admitted privately. Oh, how much she'd love to feel Jake's devotion directed at her. Oh, how much she was beginning to feel the void of having no man in her life dedicated to loving and keeping her.

After Stephen, she'd thought she'd never want that kind of commitment again. It had turned so ugly, so suffocating, that complete independence had become her mantra.

But lately—a little too lately—she'd allowed herself to look beyond her relationship with Stephen. To look at other couples, devoted to each other without suffocating one another. Her parents, for example. Her oldest brother, Nick. He was so crazy in love with his wife, Lanie, it was almost disgusting. Her two other brothers had yet to find love everlasting, but it was only a matter of time. Both had huge hearts.

"Earth to Doc."

LeAnne glanced up, startled. She hadn't realized she'd been so deep in thought. She'd been standing there with her toothbrush in her hand.

Jake shot her a roguish grin. "Engaging in a little daydreaming, Doc?"

That was another thing that had changed. When she'd first met this man, every time the word *doctor* passed his lips in relation to her, there was barely concealed sarcasm underscoring each syllable. Now he called her that most of the time, and seemed to do it with at least a little admiration.

She blinked. "I . . . well, yes."

"Care to share?" he asked as he spread Muffin's blanket on one of the two double beds in the room.

Which meant that he fully intended to share the other bed with her. She might have been offended that he took the sleeping arrangements for granted if she weren't so eager for bedtime to arrive.

"No," she told him. She didn't think he'd be real thrilled to hear she was thinking romantic thoughts. In fact, he'd probably run screaming from the room.

He shot her another knowing grin. "Psychologically, I don't believe it's good for one's mental health to suppress emotions."

Since she wasn't about to answer him, she just wrinkled her nose at him and sailed into the bathroom to brush her teeth.

When she emerged, Jake was on the phone. The frown on his face was stern, but when he looked up, there was a twinkle in his eye. After a final and curt, "Good," he hung up, strode over to her, and picked her up and swung her around.

She gasped in surprise, but when he set her down and she witnessed the most amazing smile on his face, she laughed. "Win the lottery?"

"Close. They busted Jimmy Delaney at the cabin."

"Who's Jimmy Delaney?"

"Nickname Bunny. He's one of Trenton Pierce's rent-a-thugs."

"Who's Trenton Pierce?"

"A real sleazebag. He literally makes his living selling the services of his 'boys.' They're a real talented bunch. Arson, blackmail, murder. You name it, he's got someone who can get it done for you."

"I'm confused."

"Suffice it to say that the people Elisa is testifying against became desperate enough to hire Trenton Pierce. After all, they're racketeers and money launderers, but they hadn't stooped to murder. At least not directly. So they hired Trenton Pierce to get it done for them, and he put one of his goons on it."

"Bunny."

"Bunny."

"Is he the one who shot at me?"

"Probably, although I don't know that for sure. All I know is that he is squealing like a pig. Bagging him, we not only have the Winstons on additional charges of solicitation of murder, we have Trenton Pierce and his merry band of thugs. And we have my boss. They picked him up at Dulles, boarding a plane for the Caymans."

"So Mark is in the clear."

"Of course he's in the clear! He's my partner and best friend!"

Muffin growled.

"My best *human* friend," he amended for Muffin. Then he glanced at LeAnne and slid a knuckle down her cheek. "My best human *male* friend."

Her heart tripped. Oh, yes, she loved the idea of being Jake's friend. Honesty would have her admit she'd love to be more than that. But she'd settle for friend. And for now, lover. "What does this mean?"

"This means," he said, pausing to kiss her, "we can go home."

"Home" meant Jake's small ranch house in a neat little neighborhood in Vienna, Virginia. They'd circled the block twice before pulling into his driveway, Jake wanting to make certain no bad guys were hanging around.

Jake had apologized for not being able to

take LeAnne directly back to Happy Hounds. But he had a meeting with one of the head honchos the next morning at his office to discuss all the implications. But he promised to have her back in her own home by late afternoon Sunday.

LeAnne was anxious to get home, but not as anxious as she would have expected. And for whatever reason, she was excited to see where Jake and Muffin lived.

The interior of the house was so neat, LeAnne had a strong suspicion that Jake had a cleaning service or person. She just couldn't picture him pushing a vacuum cleaner.

Muffin appeared happy to be back, running around the house yipping, reacquainting himself with the familiar. Even Jake seemed surprised and then delighted by Muffin's reaction to coming home.

House Beautiful wouldn't be begging for a spread on his place anytime soon, but really it wasn't too bad for a bachelor's digs. Most of the furnishing matched something else in the rooms. The two things that stood out were the number of houseplants he had and the framed pictures on the walls.

They were all blown-up nature photos, and they were all spectacular. LeAnne would have bet Happy Hounds that they'd all been taken by Jake.

While he moved around the house turning on lights, LeAnne stepped from one picture to another in awe. They were breathtakingly beautiful—some stark, some rich in contrasts of light and dark. She was absolutely certain they'd win awards.

"Would you like a glass of wine? Or tea or something?" Jake asked from behind her.

"You have to take up photography again, Jake," she blurted out as she studied a picture of a deer sipping water delicately from a stream.

She sensed him stiffening behind her. She turned to him and saw him struggle to maintain a stoic expression. "I don't really have the time any longer."

"You are too good not to use this kind of talent," she said, waving a hand at the photo.

"Do you want some wine or not?"

"Yes, please," she said, then followed him through a small dining room to an even more compact but efficient kitchen.

He had a wooden wine rack sitting on one end of the kitchen counter and he pulled a bottle of cabernet from it. While he uncorked it, she said quietly, "Don't let your father take it away from you, Jake."

"Look, I don't even have the equipment any longer," he said, handing her the wine.

And in that moment, LeAnne knew what she would be doing while Jake went to his meeting tomorrow.

LeAnne woke with Jake's arm firmly anchoring her to him. In just two nights of sleeping with this man, she had the feeling she'd become addicted to him like a potent drug.

She'd forgotten how good it felt to be in a man's arms. Or maybe it had never felt this good with Stephen. She had a hard time remembering. But she knew without a doubt that making love had never been this good. And she had a sinking feeling she knew why. It wasn't just Jake's skill as a lover, or his obsessive need to bring her pleasure, or his uncanny ability to hone in on the most sensitive parts of her body.

It was the sharing, the intimacy, the joining.

It was the love.

Okay, there, she'd admitted it. She was halfway—or maybe more than halfway—in love with this man. Which was pretty darn stupid. Because she had good instincts, and her instincts told her he wasn't a forever kind of guy.

Yet the way he'd made love to her last night felt special, as though he was worshiping her rather than just using a body to slake a need. And some of the things he'd said in the throes of ecstasy had been more than words of lust.

She didn't know where all this was leading, but she firmly believed in accepting and enjoying the gifts that fell from heaven. And right now, he was a gift. And boy did she enjoy unwrapping him.

LeAnne giggled softly, and felt his arm tighten around her. His hand, which had been gently cupping her breast all night, started kneading it. Then he tugged her onto her back.

Oh, man, he was gorgeous sleep-tousled and drowsy. His blue eyes were heavy-lidded and his hair was in disarray. But his lips lifted in a smile. "Want to share the joke?" he asked in a sleep-growly voice.

Not really. But honesty compelled her. "I was just picturing you as a gift and me unwrapping you."

His eyes widened. "A gift?"

"Uh-huh."

His hand cupped her cheek. "Lady, I've done nothing but tear your life apart since I walked into it."

"That's not true. Yes, upheaval followed in your wake, but none of it was your fault. You did the very best you could to overcome a lot of bad situations."

He stared at her for a moment, then shook his head. "You know, you are the most forgiving woman I've ever met, Doc. You have every right to hate me."

"As a general rule, I usually don't sleep with men I hate."

His thumb, stroking her cheek, went still. "Can I ask you something?"

"Of course."

"Where do you see all this headed?"

She gave a small shake of her head. "I don't know."

He flopped onto his back. "I don't, either."

Missing his warmth, she turned and cuddled against his chest, her head resting on his shoulder. "Do we have to analyze it?"

"I thought analyzing things was what you did for a living," he said as his fingertips glided up and down her spine deliciously.

"Sometimes you just have to go with the flow."

He kissed the top of her head. "LeAnne?"

"Yes?"

"I can tell you this much. I don't want it to end when I come back to D.C."

Those were the most thrilling words she'd ever heard in her life. "I don't, either."

LeAnne paced back and forth in Jake's house, waiting excitedly for him to return. Although she'd broken the rules when she'd hopped a cab to Tyson's Corner to go shopping, she was still anticipating his reaction to her gift.

The doorbell rang twice, his signal. She ran to it and opened it a crack, leaving the chain in place. "What's the password?"

He chuckled. "The bat drives at midnight."

"Nope, that's the old password. What's the new one?"

He paused for a moment. "LeAnne, I want you?" he guessed.

She opened the door, laughing. "You're good."

"Well, they say honesty's the best policy," he

retorted as he walked in, kicked closed the door, and treated her to a breath-stealing kiss. "Damn, woman, you *do* turn me on."

Since her heart had flipped into high gear, she happily agreed with that sentiment.

Muffin came bounding into the foyer from the kitchen, where he'd been decimating a rawhide chew toy. "Hey, mutt," Jake said, bending and petting him. "Did you behave for LeAnne?"

Muffin yipped.

Jake straightened, grinning. "Well, Doc, ready to go home?" he asked.

"Almost." She grabbed his hand and tugged him into the living room, where his present sat on the coffee table.

He saw it immediately and narrowed his eyes. "Where'd that come from?"

"Don't go getting all macho on me. I'm here and I'm fine."

"You *went out?*"

"For an hour, tops. Open it."

He opened his mouth to complain some more, then shut it. "That's for me?"

"No, it's for Bunny the hit man. Of course it's for you!"

"You bought me a present? What for?"

"To thank you for all the excitement the last few days."

"Is it ticking?"

She grinned. "Only one way to find out."

She could tell by the conflict in his eyes that

331

he was torn between yelling at her some more and wanting to rip the wrapping off. A story Sophie had related to her once about Jake pierced her heart. Sophie had said that when Jake had been a boy, she and George had bought him a two-wheeler mountain bike. His father had made him return it to them with the explanation that he didn't know how to ride a two-wheeler. He'd been nine.

Little did his father know that George had taught him to ride a two-wheeler the summer Jake was six.

LeAnne couldn't remember in what context that conversation had come up. She hadn't absorbed Sophie's stories then as much as she should have. She hadn't known the man, and she'd assumed anyone subjected to that much abuse as a kid would probably turn out to have plenty of issues as a man.

Yet she'd watched him this last week, and seen someone who'd come away from it all absorbing all the tidbits of good in his life and rejecting the bad. He had his faults, but meanness wasn't one of them.

She loved him even more for that.

"Go on, open it," she said, trying to keep her wobbly voice from giving away emotion.

"I didn't get you anything," he said, looking a little stricken.

LeAnne laughed. "Jake, it's not our anniversary. This is a selfish gift. Given for no good reason but that *I* wanted you to have it. Open it."

He sat down heavily, looking stunned. He started out carefully pulling the colorful paper apart, but quickly got caught up and started tearing at it. When he pulled out the box, he went perfectly, utterly still.

LeAnne stood tensely, wondering if she'd made a huge mistake. But when she saw him blink several times fast and open the box reverently, she knew it had been the right choice.

"A camera," he said softly. He pulled it from the casing, his fingers brushing over it.

"I couldn't find a Leica, but the guy at the store said this one was pretty good."

"It's more than good." He glanced up, his blue eyes slightly misty. "You shouldn't have done this."

"Why not?"

"Why?" he countered.

"Because you have an incredible talent, and I can't stand your wasting it."

"I don't deserve this."

"Hey, I didn't buy you all the fixings. That's your problem. But you most definitely deserve the camera."

"LeAnne?"

"Yes?"

"I'm really angry you left here today."

Her heart sank. "I was careful."

"LeAnne?"

"Yes?"

"I'm in love with you."

* * *

The ride to Happy Hounds was interrupted by a few events, the first being Jake stopping off for some special film, the second Muffin making it known he wanted a reprieve, and the third Jake needing badly just to neck with LeAnne.

He was so shocked by the admission he'd blurted out earlier, he'd almost forgotten how to drive a car. But he knew it was true. He was in love with LeAnne Crosby.

She was so beautiful. So free with her love that she shined with it. So much fun to be with. And so damn sexy he got hard just looking at her. For the first time in his life, Jake considered forever.

He'd been fighting it from the moment he'd exploded inside her and felt as if he'd found home. He'd fought it every time he was away from her for even a shower, then got to be with her again. He'd fought it even as he'd briefed his superior and talked too damn long about the woman and dog who'd come to the rescue when he'd needed them.

But he couldn't fight the gift of the camera.

It wasn't the gift that mattered, but the sentiment behind it. She'd found his weakness, his love, and she wouldn't let it go. She'd shoved him back into something that had been a dead void. He'd filled that void by driving himself forward into what he'd considered his life's mission: to demand justice for those who didn't have the power to seek it for themselves.

Yet he'd never forgotten the high of snatching moments in time, of capturing nature in its raw beauty. He'd always known the shots were good, but he'd never expected them to touch another soul the way they affected him. And just seeing the look in LeAnne's eyes when she'd gazed at them had told him she felt what he did when he saw them.

His father had made him feel like a fool for loving photography. He'd called him lazy and stupid for Jake's willingness to wait minutes, sometimes hours, to get just the perfect shot.

But LeAnne understood.

God, he was crazy about her.

They reached Happy Hounds at a little before five in the evening. Buzz was waiting for them at the gate, as he'd said he would when Jake spoke with him this morning.

LeAnne jumped out of the car and with a happy squeal ran around to Buzz and let him envelop her in a bear hug. They looked at each other with matching ear-to-ear grins. Then they checked each other over as if searching for injury.

When both were satisfied that all was well, they pulled apart. "You sure you're okay?" Buzz asked.

"I'm fantastic."

"No worse for wear?"

"What, you mean on LeAnne and Jake's excellent adventure?"

Buzz grabbed her shoulders and held her at

arm's length, subjecting her to more intense scrutiny. "There's something different about you."

Uh-oh. Jake decided a little intervention was in order. He climbed out of the car just as LeAnne stammered, "I . . . don't know what you mean."

Jake stuck his hand out. "Good to see you again, Buzz."

Buzz hesitated, obviously not as thrilled to see him. Finally he shook Jake's hand. "Well, as long as you brought her back safe."

"I see the police have backed off."

"Considering there's almost no one here to protect, it seemed like a waste."

"What?" LeAnne whispered.

Buzz glared at Jake. "You didn't tell her?"

"I didn't want to upset her."

"How many people have left?" LeAnne asked.

"About half," Buzz said. "Worse than that, the newcomers just turned right around and canceled their reservations when they saw all the cops."

"Oh, no," LeAnne said, turning stricken eyes on Jake.

The look in her eyes nearly sliced him in two. Not three hours ago she'd given him back his passion. Three hours later, he'd destroyed hers. "I'm so sorry," he said softly, fighting off the burning need to hold her. "I'll make it right somehow. I promise."

"Damn straight, you will," Buzz said.

LeAnne blinked rapidly and swallowed hard. "It'll be fine."

"It will," Jake said, nodding. "I'll make it fine. I swear." He returned his gaze to Buzz. "Okay, well, we need to go and get settled. I need to contact Mark."

"Yeah?" Buzz said, moving to the back door of the car. "Then I suggest you give me a ride and I'll give you directions."

"Huh?"

"You want to see Mark, I'll take you to Mark."

"Are you saying—"

"Yep, he and Elisa have been here the whole time."

"Hide in plain sight," Mark said cheerfully, when Jake, LeAnne, Muffin, and Buzz entered Buzz's bungalow.

"You mean to tell me we've been running around being chased by bad guys for the last couple of days while you two hung around here in the lap of luxury?"

Elisa looked back and forth between the two men, her blue eyes troubled.

"Not exactly the lap of luxury," Mark said, unperturbed. "Until this morning we've been holed up in a bunker on the property."

"A bunker?" Jake and LeAnne said at the same time.

Buzz shrugged. "I happened to get my hands on the old prison layout a year or so ago. On

the north end of the property I noticed a soli-
tary-confinement holding cell. I was curious, so
I checked it out, and it was still there. Real well
hidden."

"It was Buzz's idea to have us stay," Elisa
said, and Jake didn't miss the pride in her tone,
or the look she gave Buzz.

Oh, boy. Jake and LeAnne exchanged
glances, and it was obvious she'd seen their
looks, too. He hadn't been the only one to fall
in love in the last couple of days.

But somehow he didn't think LeAnne had
joined the club. When he'd told her he loved
her, she hadn't returned the sentiment. In fact,
she'd just stared at him, shocked, then thrown
herself at him and kissed his face, laughing
happily. At least he'd hoped it was happily. The
kisses turned hotter and they'd ended up
spending almost an hour making love before
leaving D.C.

It had been their most explosive union yet,
and he'd marveled at how much more emo-
tional the experience was when he realized he
loved the woman he was loving.

But she had yet to speak those words to him.
And the way things were going, he wasn't
going to hold his breath. Having her return to
find her business in shambles was just another
checkmark on a long list of ways he'd screwed
up her life.

He didn't miss the irony of it all. Finally he'd
met a woman who had him fantasizing about

white picket fences and rugrats running around, and everything he'd done from the moment he'd met her had messed with all she held dear. He could just hear his father laughing at him, calling him an idiot.

"Well, folks," LeAnne said into the silence. "While this has been real fun, I need to get back to my place and settle in, then go assess the damage."

"I'll take you and we can sort out our things," Jake said. "Buzz, do I still have my bungalow?"

"That one, or the pick of plenty of others, now," Buzz responded.

"Thanks, I needed that reminder," Jake retorted.

"Look, it's my fault," Elisa said. "Not Jake's."

"Not yours, either," Jake and LeAnne said at once.

Jake stared at LeAnne. The woman's capacity for forgiveness knew no bounds. He just wished he'd stop doing things she needed to forgive him for.

LeAnne touched Elisa's arm. "I'm just glad we could provide safe haven for you."

"I'll never be able to thank you enough."

"Put the bad guys in jail," LeAnne said. "That'll be thanks enough."

Jake and LeAnne finished digging her things out of the duffel bag, and he could tell she was anxious to get him gone and get back to business.

"Can I see you later tonight?" he asked her.

LeAnne shook her head. "I can't guarantee that, Jake. I might be engaged in a good bit of damage control."

"I can't tell you how sorry I am about all this."

"I know you are."

"And I mean it. I'm going to make it right."

She smiled. "Spy to spy? I'm pretty sure time will take care of it. And even if business doesn't pick up this year, it will next year."

"Can you afford that?"

"I'll survive," she said, still smiling. "Jake, please stop worrying about it. Truly. I'll be fine; Happy Hounds will be fine."

"Okay. Well, if you are free tonight, call me? Or just stop by, all right?"

"I will."

He kissed her. And although she returned the kiss fervently, she cut it short a lot sooner than he'd have liked.

Suppressing the urge to tell her he loved her again, he touched her face one last time, then called to Muffin. As he and Muffin left, he couldn't shake the feeling that he was going to lose her. If he hadn't already.

Mark arrived at Jake's bungalow a little over an hour later, a six-pack of Milwaukee's finest and his briefcase in tow.

Jake nodded his thanks as he twisted the top off the bottle and took a long pull. For the next hour he briefed Mark on the events of the last couple of days, leaving out a few details, like the fact that he and LeAnne had become intimate.

Mark wasn't astonished at the events, because as soon as Buzz had given him the all-clear, he'd put a call into the office and heard about it from their new temporary boss.

Still, they were both in shock at the betrayal. The man they'd looked to for guidance had done everything in his power to get them killed.

"When's the arraignment?" Mark asked.

"Tomorrow."

"Chance of bail?"

"Absolutely none."

"Good." Mark shook his head. "Just amazing."

Jake stood and went to the refrigerator, pulling two more beers from it. Returning, he handed one to Mark. "What's the deal with Buzz and Elisa?"

Mark stretched out his legs and crossed them at the ankles. "Exactly what it looks like. Love at first sight." He took a swig of beer. "I think that's another reason why Buzz suggested we stay here. That way he could help watch over her. But you have to admit it was brilliant."

Jake nodded. "I'm surprised you didn't think of it first."

"I would have!" Mark defended indignantly.

"You know, I'm really bugged by what all this has done to LeAnne."

341

"I know. Me, too. I'm really sorry I ever brought Elisa here."

Aside from the harm to her business, Jake couldn't decide if he was all that sorry. If they'd never had to flee, there were a lot of things he probably never would have learned about LeAnne. Like her grit in the face of adversity. Like her bravery in the face of danger. Like her nonstop sex talk while he made love to her.

Dragging his thoughts from dangerous territory, he said, "I sure hope this doesn't kill her financially."

Mark sat up and said, "Little chance of that." He grabbed his briefcase and snapped it open. Pulling out a manila file folder, he handed it to Jake. Jake glanced at the tab. It read, LATIMER.

"Interesting stuff in there," Mark said.

Jake wanted to burn the damn thing. In fact, he *might* burn the damn thing. He stood and walked to the table by the sliding glass door. He tossed the file on it. "I don't need that. Anything I want to know about the guy I can ask LeAnne."

Mark was silent for a moment and his eyebrows rose slowly. "Oh. It's like that, is it?"

Jake avoided looking at his partner. "Well, I'm not exactly sure what it's like. But I *do* know that she's about the most open, honest person I've ever met. Anything I want to know, she'd tell me."

Except for whether she loves me or not.

"Do I hear wedding bells?"

He turned around and finally faced Mark. "What do I have to offer a woman like that? She's sweet and kind and she makes a living digging into dogs' minds. I make my living schlepping across the country tracking down the scum of the earth. The two just don't go together."

He started pacing. "And look what happened to her just by meeting me. She's had nothing but trouble since I drove through her gates."

"She didn't exactly look the worse for wear," Mark commented dryly. "In fact, she looked pretty damn content."

Jake stifled a proud grin. "She always looks that way. I've never met a woman in my life who's so content in her own skin."

Mark stood, dangling the now empty beer bottle in his fingers. "Well, time to get back to our witness." He checked his watch. "Think I gave them enough time?"

"Probably not," Jake said, remembering his first two nights with LeAnne. "But I'm surprised you left her alone at all."

"Are you kidding? With Buzz? I think he'd tear apart any person who'd dare threaten her." He shrugged. "Besides, we're heading out tonight, and they're not going to get a chance to be together until after the trial. I couldn't deny them some time alone."

Jake laughed. "Are my ears deceiving me? Did you just let it slip that there's a romantic heart under there somewhere?"

Mark appeared utterly indignant. "Not a chance. I just know better than to mess with Buzz."

Jake walked Mark to the door. "Keep in touch."

"Will do."

As soon as Mark left, Jake dropped his beer bottle in the recycle bin in the kitchen, then returned to the suite. He glanced at the TV but that held no appeal. Neither did reading. He looked at the camera, sitting on the dresser. Then he strode to the sliding glass door and opened it. "Muffin, want to go for a walk?"

Muffin yipped and came galloping through the door.

Jake loaded the camera with film. "Let's go."

Chapter Fourteen

LeAnne spent the hours after Jake's departure making certain that the remaining guests spotted her and assured themselves that she was fine and all was well. She dropped in at every restaurant, since it was suppertime for many; she visited the pool, tennis courts, and paddocks, which were still busy with early evening obedience training classes.

And although she was glad to reconnect with her guests, she still found herself searching for Jake, hoping to run into him.

The official party line they'd come up with was that there had been reports of an escaped convict in the area, and she'd been so concerned about her guests while she'd had to be away for a bit that she'd requested police protection for her visitors.

Lying really got to her, but she understood the reasons for it. She was grateful that it hadn't gotten around she'd been shot at on the premises. Definitely not good public relations.

LeAnne left the gym after stopping for a chat with Mrs. Merriweather—who'd obviously been extremely worried about her.

She meandered through the lobby of the hotel and out into the early evening breeze. She could probably go home now and take a long, luxurious bubble bath.

Yet as she walked she found herself heading in the direction opposite her bungalow. She found herself heading straight to Jake's. Just assuring herself that he and Muffin had settled in again, she decided.

Who was she kidding? She wanted to see him, touch him, kiss him. Just a couple of hours out of his company and she missed him like crazy. This wasn't a good thing.

At least, it wasn't for their long-term future. She had no illusions. Jake was a mover and a shaker. He liked the thrill of the hunt, the rush he got from bringing bad men and women to justice.

LeAnne was at heart a homebody. She liked deep roots, a settled existence. Although she had to admit that the last couple of days with him had been exciting in many ways. Nothing she'd like to experience on a regular basis, but still . . . stimulating.

He was an amazing man. So macho, yet sensitive. She had the feeling he'd be insulted by that observation. He didn't see what she saw, or at least he didn't interpret his own actions the same way. He had no idea how much the photos he took revealed his inner soul.

And he'd told her he loved her. He'd meant it; she had no doubt about that. The wonder in his face as he realized what he'd said revealed plenty. If she was any judge of human nature—which in her line of work, she sure hoped she was—she'd venture to guess it was one phrase that hadn't passed his lips very frequently in his life.

And she loved him, too. No doubt about it. When he'd said those words to her, she'd been so overwhelmed with joy that there couldn't be a question about that. Still, on the drive home, she'd come to recognize all of the obstacles before them. Some, unfortunately, seemed insurmountable.

LeAnne arrived at Jake's door and sucked in a deep breath, her pulse racing. She licked her lips and then knocked.

No answer.

She knocked again, just in case he hadn't heard the first. But still no one came to the door. Feeling more disappointed than she could have imagined, she turned and began heading back to her place.

And ran right into Buzz.

"Oh!" she said with a squeal, feeling a little silly that he'd caught her chasing after Jake. "I . . . I . . . just wanted to say good night."

"Good," he said, sounding distracted. "Then you can give the man this from Mark." He thrust an envelope at her.

"Well, he's not here."

"Got your master key card?" Buzz asked.

"Yes, but I can't—"

"Mark said it shouldn't be left outside. Something important, I guess."

For the first time LeAnne noticed the sad light in Buzz's eyes. "They left?" she asked softly.

"Yeah."

"You'll see her again."

Buzz's Adam's apple wobbled. "I just don't like not being able to protect her."

"Mark will take good care of her, honey."

"Like Jake took care of you?" he said, sarcasm coating his words.

"Exactly like that," LeAnne defended hotly. "Buzz, you don't know all that happened. But I promise you this: Jake kept me alive. If not for his instincts, I might not be here."

He looked even more stricken. "Don't even say that."

She laid a hand on his arm. "But everything's

okay now. I know it doesn't feel that way, but when this is all over, things will be fine." She smiled brightly. "Better than fine."

"They're relocating her after the trial," he said softly. "Anywhere she wants to go."

LeAnne stared at him. "I'm about to lose you, aren't I?"

"Lord knows I don't want to leave. I love this place."

"Why can't she come here?" she asked.

Buzz shook his head. "I don't think she'll agree to that. She's already too upset about how much trouble she caused."

LeAnne stamped her foot in frustration. "What is *wrong* with all you people? Why is everyone so hell-bent on taking the blame? The blame lies squarely and completely with those awful thugs!"

She held up a hand and began ticking off fingers. "Jake came for an enforced vacation. Mark and Elisa came because it seemed the perfect hideout. Which it would have been if not for the fact that"—she dropped a third finger—"someone they trusted betrayed Jake and Mark. It was *no one's* fault but the bad people!" She stuck a finger in his face. "And I'd heartily appreciate it if you'd stop making Jake feel guilty. He's carrying around enough guilt to sink the *Titanic*."

"That's what's different," Buzz said. "You fell for the guy."

LeAnne's indignant finger dropped to her side. "Well, yes."

Buzz's frown slowly evaporated and his standard grin bloomed. "Aren't we a sorry pair?"

LeAnne smiled back. "I prefer to consider us a lucky pair."

Buzz nodded. "I know I am."

She touched his forearm again. "Buzz, Elisa's welcome here. I mean it. If she's got a choice, I'd love to have her. What does she do?"

"She's an accountant."

"Perfect! You know how much I hate keeping the books!"

Buzz chuckled. "You don't keep the books. You already hire an accountant to do that."

"Yes, but she's proven she's an *honest* accountant. Now how rare is that?"

Buzz laughed again. "You know what? She actually told me she'd love to work with animals."

LeAnne shrugged. "Okay, so we train her as an obedience counselor."

Buzz scratched his forehead, but she had the feeling it was more an attempt to cover his eyes for a moment. Finally his hand dropped. "Have I ever told you you're the best?"

"Not nearly often enough," she said, smiling. "I might insist you get that tattooed on your butt or something."

Buzz opened his mouth, but the distinctive sound of Muffin's yip ripped through the air, and they both turned.

Jake was striding toward them almost at a jog, trying to keep up with Muffin.

LeAnne saw the camera in Jake's other hand, and her heart practically did a jig. He'd been out shooting pictures. She watched, trying not to drool, as he strode toward her with that sexy male swagger she'd come to love. And although he was yelling at Muffin to behave, he had a grin on his face that could charm a snake into handing over its fangs.

Jake finally gave up the good fight and released Muffin from his leash. Muffin took the opportunity to race straight to Buzz, a hopeful gleam in his eyes.

Buzz pulled a small dog bone from his pocket and bent to hand it over. "Take it nice, my man."

Muffin slowly wrapped his lips around one end and tugged.

Jake finally made it to them. "Looking for me?" he asked, the gleam in his eyes more hopeful than Muffin's.

"Yes," LeAnne said, then remembered the envelope. "Buzz was bringing this to you."

Jake nodded and took it. "Would you two like to come in?" he asked, looking straight at LeAnne.

"Yes," LeAnne said, then frowned at Buzz, who instantly said, "Nope, gotta go."

"Too bad," Jake said, still looking at LeAnne. "Maybe some other time."

"Yeah, I know you're real disappointed,"

Buzz commented. He started to turn away, then swung back. "Y'all take care of Elisa, you hear?"

"We're planning on it," Jake said.

"You do that." And with that, he was off.

Jake spared him about a second's glance, then returned his attention to LeAnne. "Come in."

They were barely inside before he took her in his arms. "Damn, I missed you."

"I missed you, too."

"Pretty silly, I guess. I mean it's only been"—he checked his watch—"one hundred and fifty-eight minutes."

"Shut up and kiss me," she demanded.

He was really good at following orders. She liked that about him. She also loved the way he kissed. He poured his entire body and soul into it.

She melted into him, felt his lips move over hers with such passion, such need. And she responded almost desperately.

They might have dropped right there and made love if Muffin hadn't interrupted with a barrage of yapping. They looked over and saw him bouncing around at the glass door to the porch.

Jake scowled at him. "Muffin, you're a real pain sometimes."

LeAnne laughed. "How about you pour us some wine and I'll take care of Muffin."

"Does that mean you can stay awhile?"

"For a while, yes."

"The night?"

She punched him in the arm. "You know, you're the greediest spy I know."

"It's in our nature. Bag a few third-world dictators and suddenly you want more."

She smiled, then grabbed his right arm and held it up between them. "You shot some pictures tonight?"

"Yes. This might come as a surprise to you, but Muffin's a real ham."

The ham in question yapped again.

They both glanced over at the glass door. "Cool it, mutt!" Jake called. "I don't interfere when *you're* trying to flirt."

"Are you trying to flirt?" LeAnne asked.

"Spies don't *try*. Spies automatically succeed. We're irresistible."

"Is that engraved on your badge? 'We pillage, we overthrow, we're irresistible.' "

"Yes."

Muffin barked.

LeAnne reluctantly pulled her gaze from Jake's. "I'd better take care of him." She headed toward Muffin.

"LeAnne, wait."

She looked back. "What?"

He held up the camera. "I have three more shots on this roll."

"And?"

"I'd like to finish up the roll." He grinned and

353

swept his gaze over her in a deliciously lecherous manner.

LeAnne caught his meaning. "I look awful!"

"Lady, you're beautiful. You couldn't look awful after a mud-wrestling competition."

She tucked her hair behind her ears and wished she could take about two hours at a salon. "Oh, Jake, this is silly."

"Please?"

She threw her arms out. "What do you want me to do?"

Jake grabbed her hand and yanked her back to the wall across from the door to the kitchen. "The wallpaper is subdued enough to be a great backdrop. Just stand and smile." Then he backed up into the kitchen a few steps and aimed.

"God, woman, you were made for a camera," he said. "Say 'pretty please.' "

She laughed and he snapped a shot before she could pose.

"Say 'spies have fleas.' "

Grin. *Click.*

"Say 'I'm a tease.' "

"You are definitely a tease."

Click.

He lowered the camera. "Thank you."

Muffin whined.

"May I go now?" she asked, embarrassed, but inordinately pleased he wanted a picture of her.

"He's all yours."

LeAnne walked toward Muffin, who seemed to be too intent on something outside. She hadn't been a spy for long, but long enough to know to be careful. "What is it, sweetheart?"

His hackles weren't raised and his eyes were intently following a moth. So she began to unlock the door to let him out. But just then her eyes landed on a manila file folder sitting on the table. The handwritten name on it stuck out like a neon sign. Her hand flew to her chest and involuntarily she cried out.

Jake heard LeAnne's loud gasp and he stopped pouring, plunking down the wine bottle. He raced around the corner and saw what she was staring at, and his heart twisted in horrible knots.

"It's not what you think," he said quietly.

She looked up at him with such hurt in her eyes, Jake wanted to club himself.

"It's not?" she asked, in a grainy voice he'd never heard from her before. She tossed it open and began flipping through it. "Tax records, court records, government documents, personal mail. What am I supposed to think? This landed on your doorstep by mistake, spy?"

"I asked for that when I thought you were swindling Aunt Sophie."

"You thought I was swindling Sophie," she stated so flatly, he knew he was a goner.

355

"I don't believe it now," he said, but knew that wouldn't mean a thing, considering the look in her eyes and her posture.

"To tell you the truth, I don't give a damn what you believe. Do you know how horrible, how *invasive* it is to know that someone is digging into every private detail of your life? How would *you* feel if you found out you were being spied on?"

"Angry."

"You're damn right about that."

"LeAnne," he said, waving at the file, "that was all public knowledge."

"My dead husband's tax returns are public knowledge?"

"Well, no."

"Get out."

"LeAnne, I was confused."

"Get out now."

"I didn't even look at that file."

"If you aren't off this property within the hour, I'll have you arrested."

"Technically—"

"Don't even try it, spy guy. Get out. Leave us alone."

He stared at her, and couldn't stand the thought that it was over. "Okay, I'll leave," he said quietly. "But just remember this: I love you, and that's not going to change. Never. We've been together and I don't think what happened was one-way. So if you're so sure you want me gone, then it's on your shoulders."

She glanced at the file, then back at him. "I want you gone."

"LeAnne—"

"No! I don't want to hear it! You've invaded every piece of my life that matters, and practically ruined it all. Leave. Get away from me before you ruin *everything*."

He couldn't argue with that. He *had* been responsible for turning her life into a shambles. And he hated himself for it. He'd hoped he'd get a chance to make it up to her, and instead he'd blown any chance they might have had to carve a future together. "We'll be gone within an hour."

She practically crumpled before his eyes, dropping to her knees in front of a very confused Muffin. "Good-bye little guy. I love you."

Jake hadn't known how desperately he'd wanted to hear those words directed at him until he heard them now. His heart felt leaden and bruised.

Muffin licked LeAnne's cheek, then turned accusing eyes on Jake. Just what he needed. Condemnation from the only two creatures in the world he loved.

LeAnne looked up at him, tears streaming down her face unheeded. "If you want to leave Muffin with me, I'll be happy to take him."

"No!" Jake said swiftly, automatically. "He's coming with me!"

The contempt in her eyes could have felled

trees. "Don't worry, I won't tell on you, or contest the will."

"It has nothing to do with the will. Take it all; I don't give a damn. But Muffin's mine."

Something flickered in her eyes, but was gone before he could figure out what it was. She gave Muffin's head a final kiss, then stood up, looking so weary and defeated, Jake would have done anything to make it better. But the disgust in her expression told him he'd lost her for good.

She walked to the door without looking at him again. Jake felt desperation unlike any in his life. "LeAnne?"

She didn't turn around. "What?"

"I wish you well."

Part snort, part sob greeted that pronouncement. She walked out, closing the door quietly.

"I love you," he added, far too late.

The trial of Jacob and Millicent Winston lasted three weeks. Elisa was on the stand for four of those days. No matter how the defense attorneys attempted to discredit her, she held her ground admirably. And as much as Millicent Winston's lawyer attempted to point the finger straight at Millicent's husband, Elisa's testimony blew that defense out of the water. It took the jury thirty minutes to return verdicts of guilty on all counts.

Cameras had not been permitted in the courtroom, but *Court TV* had covered the sensational event the entire time. So when Jimmy "Bunny" Delaney testified as part of his plea agreement, it became public knowledge that the Happy Hounds Health Spa had been one of several places the FBI had used as a safe house for their star witness.

Jake cringed every time he heard that name or the name of the owner. He and Mark had convinced the lead prosecutor that LeAnne's testimony wasn't necessary, so she hadn't been subpoenaed. But by the end of the trial, the entire country knew the names of LeAnne Crosby and Happy Hounds.

Jake could just imagine how thrilled LeAnne was by that. In fact, he didn't really have to imagine. He'd kept in touch with Buzz on a nearly daily basis.

The first time he'd called the man, Buzz had nearly chewed off his head. But after Jake silently accepted all his recriminations, then totally agreed with him, Buzz had given him a small break—just big enough for Jake to assure Buzz that his number one goal was to be certain LeAnne came out of this mess all right.

The news was mostly grim. Buzz reported that LeAnne wasn't eating, wasn't sleeping, wasn't talking. Her business was still reeling from the impact of recent events, and she basically didn't care. Her name was being mentioned in households across the nation, and many personal details about her life were being discussed or speculated upon.

And all thanks to Jake. He wanted to shoot himself.

He felt utterly helpless to make things better for her. That was, until the trial was over, the gag order lifted, and Nancy Grace from *Court TV* contacted him, requesting an interview.

That was when he'd formed a plan. And he'd called Buzz and made certain Buzz would tape the interview when it aired.

He arrived at the TV studio in D.C. at noon on the Wednesday following the end of the trial. They put gunk on his face, messed with his hair, miked him, and had him sitting in front of a monitor and camera by twelve-thirty.

After the show came back from the commercial, he watched Nancy make a rather lengthy introduction, portraying him as one of the "heroes" involved in bringing down the evil Winston empire against monumental odds.

After all that, she said, "Welcome, Agent Donnelly, and thank you for talking with us today."

"You're very welcome. Thank you for asking me."

For the next five minutes she asked him salient questions pertaining to the case. He answered as best he could and waited for the moment he expected—when she turned to the heroism displayed by Elisa Johnson.

Jake nodded his head. "No doubt about it. Elisa displayed monumental courage in agreeing to testify." Nancy began to open her mouth for another question, but he cut her off. "However, Elisa wasn't the only courageous civilian involved in this case."

"Oh?"

"You have to give credit to a couple of people down in southern Virginia, who were dragged into this mess against their will, but stepped up to the challenge when called upon.

"If it weren't for LeAnne Crosby, owner of the Happy Hounds Health Spa, and Buzz Coltraine, her amazing assistant, there might never have been a trial, and Elisa might not be alive. It was their courage in helping keep Elisa safe that helped Lady Justice prevail."

Nancy laughed. "And how clever was that, to hide your witness at a dog resort. Who'd have ever thought to look there?"

"Well, it was actually a fluke. I happened to be vacationing there with my dog. Most fantastic resort I've ever been to, by the way. I highly recommend it."

"Putting in a plug, Agent Donnelly?" Nancy said, grinning.

"They deserve it. The place is truly spectacular. But the point is, my partner made the decision to bring Elisa to me, since he was the only one who knew where I was vacationing. What neither of us could foresee was that we had a traitor in our midst," he said, not even attempting to keep the disgust out of his voice. "Unfortunately, the entire affair has wreaked havoc on innocent citizens' lives, and for that I'm so sorry," he finished, looking directly into the camera and seeing LeAnne's smiling face.

"Let's talk about the next trial," Nancy jumped in, and Jake allowed her to steer him in that direction. The interview lasted only a few minutes longer.

When he returned home that afternoon, Muffin was waiting for him, his big brown eyes expectant. Jake had explained the plan on their walk that morning, and from all indications, Muffin was for it.

Jake shrugged. "I don't know if it will help or not."

Muffin yipped.

"I hope you're right." He scratched behind Muffin's ears. "Okay, let's move it, mutt. We have an appointment with Rip-'em-off."

"Let me get this straight," Rapinov said. "You're telling me you violated the terms of the will."

"That's right. Aunt Sophie stipulated that I had to spend two weeks at Happy Hounds. I violated that stipulation. I was there only a week."

"Are you giving up the dog?"

"No. Muffin stays with me. But I want you to be aware that I've given up all future rights to Aunt Sophie's estate."

"Okay," the man said slowly, looking at Jake as if he deserved to be in a straitjacket.

"Which means, according to the will, all of

her assets not already bequeathed elsewhere automatically revert to LeAnne Crosby upon Muffin's death, correct?"

"Correct."

"And until that happens, which isn't going to be for a long, long time, the trustees will make sure that LeAnne has access to any and all funds necessary to keep the properties functional, correct?"

"Yes."

"And she has free access to all of those properties, correct?"

"Correct."

"Good." Jake stood up. "Come on, Muffin, time to finish our vacation."

LeAnne opened her door unenthusiastically when she heard the knock. Buzz stood there with Elisa, looking determined. LeAnne mustered a smile for the other woman, who looked so ethereally happy, LeAnne envied her.

"I'm glad you came back," she said. "Lord knows we have plenty of room."

"Thank you. It's so good to be here again."

"If things keep going the way they have the last two hours, we won't have room for long, I'm guessing," Buzz said, pushing his way into her bungalow with Elisa in tow.

LeAnne didn't have any idea what he was talking about, and worse, she didn't have the energy or desire to ask.

Buzz had a VCR tape in his hand, and without preamble he went directly to LeAnne's entertainment center.

"What are you doing?" LeAnne asked.

"Showing you why we booked over fifty reservations in the last two hours," he answered, shoving the tape into the player.

"We have?" she asked, not all that interested.

Nothing interested her any longer. Nothing. The world was a flat, black place for her now. She sometimes woke in the morning and just lay in bed, trying to drum up any reason to get out of it. The only one that worked was the fact that her employees counted on her, needed her. If not for them, she'd have probably closed up shop long ago, sold the place, and run as far as she could from the demons haunting her.

It had been worse the last few weeks, when she couldn't pass by a television without seeing news of the Winston trial. It broke her heart every single time. That was Jake's case, Jake's trial, Jake's triumph.

She'd taken to avoiding any place at Happy Hounds that sported a television. But she couldn't avoid newspaper headlines, nor the constant calls from the media requesting an interview. It had gotten out of hand after the guy who'd tried to shoot her had testified.

She felt invaded, soiled, torn apart.

Her life wasn't her own anymore. All because of Jake.

Jake. How she longed to hate him, to feel righteous indignation whenever she thought of him. Instead, her heart and mind betrayed her completely by missing him so much, she cried herself to sleep at night. When she slept.

How was it possible to know that the man had betrayed her in the most personal way possible, and still crave the sight of him, the taste of him, the feel of him? How stupid could she be?

"Pay attention, LeAnne," Buzz commanded, switching on the TV.

"What is this?"

"An interview with Jake."

LeAnne panicked. "No! Don't turn it on! I don't want to see it!"

"Too bad," Buzz said. "You're going to watch it."

She sat down heavily on the couch and put her head in her hands. She didn't think she could possibly stand to see him.

As she listened to the interviewer's introduction she thought she'd cry. The man whom everyone was lauding as a hero was the man who'd torn her heart to shreds.

She wanted to block it all out, tear up the tape, run from the room. Instead, when Buzz barked, "Watch!" she lifted her head and stared at the screen.

The woman interviewing him was a beautiful blonde. When the producers finally split the screen, bringing Jake's handsome face into view, she cried out involuntarily.

His blue eyes sparkled, his lips moved. He

answered the questions thoughtfully and thoroughly, skirting nothing, and LeAnne's heart broke even more. She missed him *so* much.

And despite his TV makeup, she could spot the circles under his eyes, the tightness around his mouth. He was tired and tense, and she wanted to soothe him. God, she was going insane.

"Listen closely," Buzz finally said.

And she did. She listened as Jake called her and Buzz courageous heroes, talked openly and glowingly about Happy Hounds, the place he'd considered a scam not two months ago.

When the interview ended, Buzz clicked off the VCR and then plunked his hands on his hips. "Well?"

LeAnne burst into tears.

"Aw, honey," Buzz said, sitting beside her and pulling her into his big, bearlike embrace. "There, there."

"Why . . . why did you show me this? You h-hate him."

"I have to admit I don't think the guy's good enough for you, but I don't hate him. LeAnne, honey, he's been calling me every day checking up on you."

She glanced up in surprise. "He has?"

Buzz nodded. "Whatever else the slug is, a deserter is not one of them. He is crazy about you, and worried sick."

"He . . . he betrayed me."

"I don't know what happened between you

two, but I'd bet my left arm that he never meant to hurt you. It's killing him, LeAnne."

And stupid woman that she was, she hated the thought that Jake was hurting. After all, she was the wronged party here. She'd put her faith and trust in him, and he'd destroyed it all by having her life investigated as if she were a common thief.

She sat up. When had he had time to research all of that? That had been a thick file, and he hadn't exactly been spending time on a computer before they'd returned. He hadn't brought it back with him from D.C., either. They'd been traveling light, and she would have known if he'd had a file in their duffel bag, or anywhere in his car, for that matter.

So he'd gotten his hands on it here. But how?

She'd seen his handwriting when he'd written the note to the caretakers of the cabin, and it was nothing like the handwriting on the tab of the file. That handwriting had been sloped differently, as if penned by a southpaw.

LeAnne wiped at the tears on her cheeks, then glanced at Elisa, who was looking so distressed, LeAnne felt awful for her.

LeAnne swallowed hard and got her tears under control. "Elisa, you spent a lot of time with Mark. Did you notice if he's right- or left-handed?"

Elisa's smile was wobbly. "He's a lefty all the way. Why do you ask?"

Shaking her head, LeAnne said, "Oh, nothing

major. It just explains something." And what it explained was that Mark had most likely compiled that file, not Jake. Although she would bet he'd done it at Jake's request.

Which didn't let Jake off the hook in the least. Except that Jake had to have made the request long before their trip north. And she couldn't really hate him or blame him for being a little skeptical. After all, she'd been a total stranger, and she'd been named in his adored aunt's will.

In his line of work, he'd be an imbecile not to suspect a fraud.

LeAnne stood up and began pacing. "Did you say we're getting new reservations?"

"A ton. Immediately after that interview aired on *Court TV*."

"Probably mostly out of ghoulish curiosity," LeAnne surmised.

"Who cares? We've had skeptics before. A few days here and they all change their mind," Buzz replied.

That was so true. Come to think of it, even a cynical Jake had seemed won over by the place toward the end. And won over by his dog.

She remembered the fierce way he'd demanded to keep Muffin with him. He could have easily dumped the poor dog on her and walked away, but he hadn't. And not just because he'd wanted to ensure that he would eventually inherit Sophie's property. In fact, he'd offered it all to her. Of course, that could have been an act.

And he'd told her he loved her. A man like Jake wouldn't speak those words lightly. He certainly hadn't said them to get her into bed. She'd jumped in there on her own before he could blink.

And, oh, how she'd craved being loved by him.

Confusion jumbled her mind. She looked over at Buzz, sitting there worrying his lower lip. "What should I do?" she whispered.

Buzz was silent for a moment, glancing at Elisa, then back at her.

"Follow your heart."

Chapter Fifteen

After Buzz and Elisa left, LeAnne paced some more. She knew where following her heart would lead her, but she wasn't quite sure she was prepared to go there.

Would this thing with Jake turn out just like the relationship with Stephen? Would he continually shadow her, constantly checking up on her? She had nothing to hide, but she also didn't want to feel that every single moment of her life was open to scrutiny. Jake had called Buzz daily, checking on her. Although he'd respected her wishes, he'd still insinuated himself in her life, wanting details, logging her movements, her emotions.

She couldn't live with another relationship

like the one into which her marriage to Stephen had disintegrated.

Yet she was miserable without Jake, no doubt about that. At some point her misery had morphed from thoughts of betrayal to thoughts of never having him in her life again. Of never having him in her body again.

She waffled over and over. Fear of making a huge mistake either way was paralyzing her. When her phone rang, she picked it up absently. "LeAnne."

"Dr. Crosby?" an unfamiliar male voice said.

"Yes?"

"This is Alan Rapinov."

The name was vaguely familiar, but she couldn't quite place it. A former guest? She didn't think so. One of the zillions of reporters hounding her?

"Sophia McAfee's estate lawyer," he clarified.

"Oh! Oh, yes, of course, Mr. Rapinov. What can I do for you?"

"I just wanted to touch base and let you know I'm mailing you some papers I'll need you to sign and have notarized."

"For what purpose?"

"We need to finalize the changes in the trust arrangements for Sophia McAfee's estate."

"Excuse me?"

"The new provisions. Transferring control of the estate to you."

"Mr. Rapinov, what in the world are you talking about?"

"You haven't been in touch with Sophia's nephew, I take it?"

"No, I haven't," she said softly. "What's going on?"

"Mr. Donnelly has made arrangements to abdicate management of Sophia's estate and relinquish his claim to any part of the estate held in trust. Under the provisions of the trust, this puts the estate in your care—with the understanding, of course, that you will become the ultimate beneficiary when Muffin passes on."

"He can't do that!"

"He can and he has."

"But . . . he kept Muffin! The estate belongs to them!"

"Yes, he did. But the provisions of the trust are unambiguous. According to Mr. Donnelly, he has violated one of those provisions."

"Which one is that?"

"The one that stipulates he and the dog spend an entire two weeks a year at your resort, ma'am."

"But that's ridiculous! I'm the one who threw him out!"

"He didn't mention that. All he said was that he'd failed to honor the provisions of the trust. Therefore the care of the estate—and its ultimate disposition—revert to you."

"Under no circumstances are you to send me those papers, Mr. Rapinov."

There was a long, stunned pause on the other

end of the line. "Dr. Crosby, do you realize this means you stand to inherit some twenty million in assets?"

"I'm not inheriting a dime. That property belongs to Jake and Muffin."

"But he's handing it over to you!"

"Not in this lifetime, he's not."

Another pause. "I've never seen so many people refuse to inherit so much money. If you're officially relinquishing your claim, then we go on to the third party named."

LeAnne took a deep breath. "Mr. Rapinov, don't make a move until we've cleared this up."

"Mr. Donnelly's wishes were quite clear."

"Do you know that I'm a trained psychotherapist?"

"Yes, ma'am."

"My official analysis of Mr. Donnelly is that he's temporarily insane. Therefore he's not currently in the frame of mind to make such a decision. Do not make another move regarding Sophie's estate until I get the poor, deluded man some help," she said.

LeAnne couldn't believe how slowly the minutes ticked by while she anxiously awaited a return call from Jake's partner, Mark.

She'd tried Jake's home, but had gotten an answering machine. Then she'd tried the FBI office, but was told Agent Donnelly wasn't available. So she'd asked for Mark and was told he was in a meeting. She gave them her name and number and demanded that he call her the moment he was free.

That had been an interminable hour ago, and still no call. How long could meetings last, after all? She reached for the phone again—fully intending to demand they break in on the meeting—when it rang all by itself. She snatched it up.

"LeAnne? It's Mark Colson. I got your message. What's up?"

"Where's Jake?" she asked bluntly.

"He's on vacation. Why?"

"I need to get in touch with him. Can you give me the number where I can reach him?"

"Now, no offense, LeAnne, but if you're calling him to give him more shit, I'm going to have to say no. He's gone through enough with you."

"Gone through enough?" she all but shrieked. "Are you out of your mind?"

"No, but he practically is. And it ain't a pretty sight."

"I saw his interview on *Court TV.* He looked pretty normal to me."

"Five minutes before he left to give that interview, he walked into the office and declared he was taking a leave of absence. Does that sound normal to you?"

Her heart dropped to her toes. "A leave of absence? But he loves his job!"

"Not anymore he doesn't, lady."

"Please, Mark, tell me how to get in touch with him."

"How about I call him and ask if he wants to talk to you?"

"Look, you son of a bitch," she said in a growl, using that word for the first time in her life, "you owe me. You turned my life upside down and inside out. I need to see Jake, to talk to him. Give me his number and location right this very minute, or I'm making my own appearance on *Court TV.* And trust me, you and the FBI won't come out smelling like roses."

"Whoa!" Mark chuckled. "LeAnne, you're cute when you're mad."

"And you're not cute when you're a condescending jerk. Give me his number. Now."

There was a pause. "Promise you're not calling to give him more grief," Mark said quietly. "Please. Honestly, he's in enough pain."

"I'm calling him about something that's important to both of us," she said, skirting the grief issue. She was pretty sure she was going to give the man grief. Just not the kind Mark was worried about.

He paused again. "All right, but if he murders me for this, my blood is on your hands."

"I'll be sure to take full responsibility."

"He's at his aunt's cabin. He mentioned something about seeing it one more time."

LeAnne almost broke out in tears again. But

she blinked and swallowed them back. "Thank you," she managed.

"Have a pen? I'll give you the number."

"No need. I know it." *And besides, I'm no longer planning on calling him.*

LeAnne wasn't able to leave for Pennsylvania until the next day. She'd had too many details to take care of, details she became increasingly and appallingly aware she'd been neglecting for weeks.

With a brief stop in D.C. to pay a call on Mr. Rapinov—demanding keys to the Pennsylvania cabin—the trip took a little over seven hours.

She arrived at the cabin at five in the afternoon. It was a humid but sunny day, and LeAnne smiled as she parked behind the door to the detached garage. They'd spent one night in this place, yet so much had happened during that time, her memories of Sophie's cabin nearly overwhelmed her.

She peeked into the garage, and sure enough Jake's blue station wagon sat parked inside. So he and Muffin were definitely there.

LeAnne debated just storming right on into the cabin, but couldn't actually justify it. After all, she'd renounced ownership now and ever after. So she really had no right to barge into Sophie's home.

She knocked on the door and waited nervously. She'd had plenty of time to rehearse her script, but her head had drained of all coherent thought the moment she'd driven up and realized she was about to confront the man of her dreams. And nightmares.

He didn't answer the knock, so she pounded harder. Still no answer.

LeAnne debated about a minute, then fished the set of keys out of her pocket and let herself in.

"Hello?" she called.

Silence.

She figured they must be out on a walk or something. She should just wait outside. But her nervousness had made her throat dry and scratchy, so she headed to the kitchen to get a glass of water.

As soon as she hit the kitchen, she noticed that the door to the basement was open. Abandoning her search for water, she moved directly to the basement steps.

No sounds carried to her, but she still had the feeling Jake was below. He'd never left the door to the basement open while they'd stayed there, except when he'd sent her down for wine. And the bulb illuminating the steps was turned on.

She descended, again calling out. Still no answer.

LeAnne didn't know why, but she took the steps softly. At the floor of the basement she glanced around. Nothing. She walked toward the wine cellar, feeling the hairs on her arms stand at attention. Something didn't feel right.

She passed the wine cellar and moved to the old darkroom, where she heard the first noise since she'd entered the cabin. A voice. A low, male voice. She prepared to knock, but her fist went still in midair.

". . . now this is the cool part," she heard Jake say. "This tray's the developer."

LeAnne pulled her fist back in horror. What if he had a woman in there? She'd die of embarrassment.

"I'd pick you up and let you watch, but I don't want you getting it in your head to drink this stuff or anything."

She heard a muffled bark.

"Yeah, yeah, I know you're smarter than that. But after that fiasco with the hot salsa, I'm not taking any chances."

A pause.

"Oh, man, this is great. My favorite part of photography. And just in case you're interested, she's real photogenic. No surprise there . . . Damn, she's so beautiful."

LeAnne hugged herself, remembering the pictures he'd taken of her. Was he talking about her? She lifted her fist again, and again stopped when Jake started speaking.

"Okay, now we head to the fixer. This just arrests the development process. We want her just like this. . . . Stop looking at me like I'm pathetic. I'm allowed to want a picture of her."

Tears popped into LeAnne's eyes.

After a while he said, "Okay, final step before the drum. This one's just to wash all the gunk off the picture. Is this great, or what?"

At her feet, LeAnne saw light suddenly leak out from underneath the door. She knocked.

"One second, Mrs. Paxton," Jake called.

"It's not Mrs. Paxton," she replied, her voice shakier than she'd like.

Muffin started barking wildly and the door flew open. Jake was drying his hands on a paper towel. "LeAnne?" he said in a growly whisper. "What's wrong? What are you doing here?"

Muffin nearly knocked her on her rump as he jumped up and drove his front paws into her legs. She gave him head scratches, smiling down at his adorable doggy grin. "I'm glad to see you, too, little boy!"

She glanced up to see Jake staring at her as if she were an apparition. "Hi," she said, her rehearsed script erased from her brain as she stared into his electric blue eyes. A chemical scent that she couldn't identify filled her nostrils—something between a car battery and vinegar.

"Hi," he responded, looking as dumbfounded as she felt. Here was a man she'd never, ever expected to see again in her life. And she was drinking in his features like a beggar in the Mojave.

"I'd say something real clever here," he said, "but I'm fresh out of brains."

"Me, too."

"Is everything all right?"

"No."

He flung the paper towel into a trash can and stepped out of the room, taking her shoulders. "What's wrong?"

"I think I'm in love with you," she blurted.

He gaped at her, then grinned about the sexiest smile she'd ever witnessed. "And that's a real big problem?"

"It sucks."

"Because I'm such a jerk and everything?"

"Yes."

He started to advance on her, but Muffin still stood on his haunches, front paws against her thighs, begging for attention.

"Muffin?" Jake said. "A moment, please?"

Muffin ignored him.

LeAnne scratched the crown of Muffin's head. "There's something in it for you if you let me talk to your dad for a minute."

The dog looked back and forth between them, then hopped down and scuttled up the basement steps.

"Resorting to bribery, Doc?" Jake asked.

"See how low you've brought me?"

He reached out a hand, then let it drop. "What's going on?"

"Can we go upstairs?"

He glanced over his shoulder. "Just let me do one more thing. I don't want to ruin this picture."

381

Nosy, she followed him in to see if the picture was what she thought it was. She wasn't mistaken. It was of her. She watched him pulled the photograph out of the tray and drop it into a large tub of water with a bunch of others already developed.

Jake covered some of the trays with what looked like Plexiglas. Then he reached over and shut off the slow stream of water that had been trickling into the big tub. The pictures in it stopped rolling around, and settled on the bottom.

Jake grabbed another towel and dried his hands and arms thoroughly. "Let's go upstairs."

His hand rested on the base of her back as he guided her up to the kitchen. "A glass of wine?" he offered.

She shook her head, not sure she wouldn't be heading out in her car very shortly. "Better not."

"You think you might love me?" he asked.

"Isn't that awful?"

"The pits."

"It would work a lot better if you reminded me you love me, too." She finally sucked air into her lungs. "You still do, don't you?"

His hand cupped her face. "More than you can possibly imagine."

"Jake?"

"Yes?"

"Something I need to tell you. I admire the hell out of you. You were knocked around as a kid, but you didn't let it keep you down. You became the best you could be."

"That's Aunt Sophie's fault. She was pretty relentless."

"She did a good job."

He smiled, but it wasn't a happy smile. "She'd be riding my ass . . . excuse me . . . my butt right now, for putting you through the hell I did. I'm so sorry."

"I know you are."

"Do you forgive me?"

"I'm still thinking about it. But I'm pretty sure you're forgiven."

He released a breath. "LeAnne, you're not leaving here tonight," he told her. "Wine?"

She would have protested if she weren't so ready to stay. "Yes, please."

While he uncorked the wine they'd opened over a month earlier, he said, "I have to tell you something I don't think you know."

"What's that?"

"Sit down."

She did, and he sat down beside her, taking her hands. "You love me?"

"I do. I think."

His head dropped, then lifted as he looked into her eyes, and LeAnne tensed. "What?"

"You might end up hating me again for what I'm about to say, but if I'm going to ask you to marry me and have my kids and all, I'm doing it with a clean slate."

"You're going to ask me to marry you?"

"Pay attention to the clean slate part, okay?"

LeAnne thought her heart was going to leap out of her chest. How she managed, "Okay," she couldn't imagine. She *really* wanted to get to the "marry me" part.

"I read the file on Latimer. And checked even more. LeAnne, your husband wasn't spying on you; he was trying to protect you."

"What?"

"He hired those PIs to protect you. He never thought you were cheating on him. He became paranoid that you'd be kidnapped because of his research."

"But he admitted—"

"He loved you. He didn't want you living in fear."

She sat there, stunned. All of these years she'd resented Stephen for his belief in her supposed unfaithfulness. And it was all a sham. "Why didn't he just say so? That lie ruined our marriage."

"My guess is he loved you enough to ruin the marriage. Your life was more important. I can relate."

She laid her forehead on the table. "Oh, my God, I've fallen for another Stephen! What is *wrong* with me?"

His fingers slipped into her hair. "The only way I'm another Stephen is that I love you. I don't have his brains. I just have his ability to love a woman. Trust that, LeAnne."

She looked up, and her anger slipped away. "Damn it, I do."

"You're cute when you swear."

She poked him in the solar plexus. "I really, really don't like being patronized."

"Sorry," he said, his grin anything but repentant.

"Why'd you turn over Sophie's estate to me, Jake?" she asked.

His grin disappeared. "I'd taken so much away from you. I just wanted to give something back." He rubbed the back of his neck. "To tell you the truth, I've never cared about inheriting Sophie's money. The only thing that mattered was this place, and even that wasn't as important as somehow making it up to you."

"Well, you probably ought to be aware that it's all right back in your hands again."

He raised his eyebrows. "That can't be. I officially renounced all claim."

She looked away. "Well, I . . . sort of . . . mentioned to the attorney . . . that you're a little . . . out of your mind and therefore not responsible for your actions."

Out of the corner of her eye she saw his jaw drop. "You told Rapinov I'm insane?"

"Temporarily!" she clarified. "I assured him you'd get better."

He stared at her for a moment before bursting out laughing. "Dr. Crosby, you are one amazing woman." And then to her astonishment he dropped to his knees in front of her. "LeAnne, you are singularly the most beautiful woman I've ever met, inside and out. I love you, I respect you, I admire you. And I want, more than anything else in this world, to make you my wife. Please marry me."

"Oh, Jake!" she said, tears popping into her eyes. "I've missed you so much."

His eyes, too, went damp. "Nothing mattered to me anymore. Plain and simple, life sucks without you."

"Life sucks without you, too."

"Marry me."

"Yes."

Muffin yipped.

Epilogue

The day after Jake and LeAnne returned from their honeymoon in Hilton Head, they were still unpacking clothes and washing sand out of them when there was a knock at LeAnne's bungalow. They'd decided to stay there temporarily until they could find property close to Happy Hounds with enough yard to satisfy seven active dogs.

Jake opened the door to find Mrs. Merriweather, with Dolly and Muffin in tow. Upon seeing Jake, Muffin went ballistic, nearly knocking him flat.

Jake was just as happy to see Muffin. He'd never admit it out loud, but he'd missed the mutt like crazy the last two weeks.

The season was officially over at Happy

Hounds, but Mrs. Merriweather had agreed to stay on a little longer to dog-sit, seeing as Buzz and Elisa were on an even more extended honeymoon in Hawaii.

Muffin went crazy again when LeAnne popped her head out of the bedroom door to greet their guest.

"Thank you so much for watching Muffin," Jake told the woman, as LeAnne came up to stand beside him. He couldn't help it. He put his arm around his wife. He couldn't seem to keep his hands to himself.

His wife. Every morning for the last two weeks he'd awakened to look at her and marvel that she was his for eternity. He had to be the luckiest guy on earth.

"It was a pleasure," Mrs. Merriweather said. "I hope you enjoyed your honeymoon."

"It was *wonderful*," LeAnne answered with a smile that could incite a thousand fantasies in Jake. Although his number one fantasy these days was just looking forward to a lifetime with her.

"Well, I can't stay long," Mrs. Merriweather said, digging through her large purse. "But I wanted to make sure to give you two this." She pulled out a VCR tape labeled *Jake and LeAnne*.

Jake frowned at it. "Is that a copy of our wedding?"

Mrs. Merriweather smiled. "No, but I'm looking forward to seeing a copy of that when you get it back. I've never been to a wedding that had a best dog before."

Jake glanced down at Muffin, who was prancing proudly. As well he should. He'd done a great job standing up for Jake.

"Then what's this?" LeAnne asked, as Mrs. Merriweather handed it to her.

"Just watch it when you get a chance. The sooner the better." She turned to go. "Welcome home and congratulations again."

"Thank you so much," LeAnne said.

They closed the door, then looked at each other quizzically. With a shrug Jake said, "Might as well watch it now."

The three of them settled on the couch, Jake a little put out that Muffin insisted on sitting between them. As he clicked the remote, his other hand reached across the back of the couch to rest on LeAnne's shoulder.

The screen was fuzzy for a moment, and then both of them gasped as Aunt Sophie's smiling face appeared. LeAnne's hand lifted to cover his. She squeezed.

Aunt Sophie looked a little pale and much thinner than the last time Jake had seen her, but her blue eyes were still bright and clear and shrewd. "Good. You're watching this," Aunt Sophie said. "That means that my plan finally worked."

She paused and the two of them looked at each other, the amazement in LeAnne's eyes most likely matching his. Aunt Sophie laughed. "Why are you so surprised? You don't think I made up that ridiculous will for any other reason, do you? You two were too stubborn to listen to me while I was with you, so I had to come up with a plan for after I was gone. And see, I was right. If Elaine followed through and you're viewing this tape, then you have found each other. And that's all I ever wanted. For the two people I loved most to be together."

She paused again. "I love you both. God bless."

Long after she disappeared from the screen, they sat there in stunned silence. When Jake turned again to LeAnne, tears were streaming down her cheeks. That was when he realized his face was wet, too.

"I love you, too, Aunt Sophie," he said in a choked whisper to the woman who'd basically raised him. "And thank you."

BODY & SOUL

JENNIFER ARCHER

Overworked, underappreciated housewife and mother Lisa O'Conner gazes at the young driver in the red car next to her. Tory Beecham's manicured nails keep time with the radio and her smile radiates youthful vitality. For a moment, Lisa imagines switching places with the carefree college student. But when Lisa looks in the rearview mirror and sees Tory's hazel eyes peering back at her, she discovers her daydream has become astonishing reality. Fortune has granted Lisa every woman's fantasy. But as the goggle-eyed, would-be young suitors line up at Lisa's door, only one man piques her interest. But he is married—to her, or rather, the woman she used to be. And he seems intent on being faithful. Unsure how to woo her husband, Lisa knows one thing: No matter what else comes of the madcap, mix-matched mayhem, she will be reunited body and soul with her only true love.

___52334-5 $5.50 US/$6.50 CAN

Romeo & Julia
Annie Kimberlin

An Original Sin

Nina Bangs

Fortune MacDonald listens to women's fantasies on a daily basis as she takes their orders for customized men. In a time when the male species is extinct, she is a valued man-maker. So when she awakes to find herself sharing a bed with the most lifelike, virile man she has ever laid eyes or hands on, she lets her gaze inventory his assets. From his long dark hair, to his knife-edged cheekbones, to his broad shoulders, to his jutting—well, all in the name of research, right?—it doesn't take an expert any time at all to realize that he is the genuine article, a bona fide man. And when Leith Campbell takes her in his arms, she knows real passion for the first time . . . but has she found true love?

___52324-8 $5.99 US/$6.99 CAN

Something Wild

Kimberly Raye

Dependent only upon twentieth-century conveniences, Tara Martin seeks to make a name for herself as a top-notch photojournalist. But when a plea from her best friend sends her off into the Smoky Mountains to snap a sasquatch, a twisted ankle leaves her in a precarious position—and when she looks up, she sees the biggest foot she's ever seen. Tara learns that the big foot belongs to an even bigger man—with a colossal heart and a body to die for. And that man, who was raised alone in the wilds of Appalachia, will teach Tara that what she needs is something wild.

___52272-1 $5.50 US/$6.50 CAN

Mr. Hyde's Assets

Sheridon Smythe

Get Ready . . . For the Time of Your Life!

Rugged Austin Hyde's mad-scientist brother has gone and appropriated Austin's "assets" to impregnate a tycoon's widow at his fertility clinic. Worse, rumor has it that the elegant Candice Vanausdale might be making a baby simply to inherit big bucks! Mr. Hyde is fit to be tied—but not tied down by a web of lies. Yet how to untangle "Dr. Jekyll's" deception?

Clearly, Austin has to go undercover. Get close enough to the breathtaking blonde to see for himself what the woman is made of. Hiring on as her handyman seems the perfect solution. Trouble is, the bashful, beleaguered beauty unleashes Austin's every possessive male instinct. Blast! How dare "Dr. Jekyll" domesticate Mr. Hyde?

___52356-6 $5.99 US/$6.99 CAN

Dorchester Publishing Co., Inc.
P.O. Box 6640
Wayne, PA 19087-8640

Please add $1.75 for shipping and handling for the first book and $.50 for each book thereafter. NY, NYC, and PA residents, please add appropriate sales tax. No cash, stamps, or C.O.D.s. All orders shipped within 6 weeks via postal service book rate. Canadian orders require $2.00 extra postage and must be paid in U.S. dollars through a U.S. banking facility.

Name_____
Address_____
City_____State_____Zip_____
I have enclosed $_____ in payment for the checked book(s).
Payment must accompany all orders. ❑ Please send a free catalog.
CHECK OUT OUR WEBSITE! www.dorchesterpub.com

More Than Magic

Kathleen Nance

Darius is as beautiful, as mesmerizing, as dangerous as a man can be. His dark, star-kissed eyes promise exquisite joys, yet it is common knowledge he has no intention of taking a wife. Ever. Sex and sensuality will never ensnare Darius, for he is their master. But magic can. Knowledge of his true name will give a mortal woman power over the arrogant djinni, and an age-old enemy has carefully baited the trap. Alluring yet innocent, Isis Montgomery will snare his attention, and the spell she's been given will bind him to her. But who can control a force that is even more than magic?

___52299-3 $5.99 US/$6.99 CAN

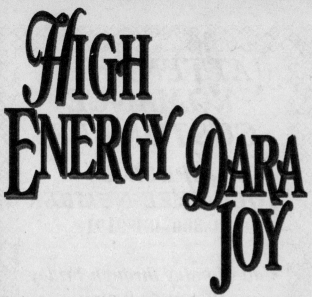

HIGH ENERGY DARA JOY

Zanita Masterson knows nothing about physics, until a reporting job leads her to Tyberius Evans. The rogue scientist is six feet of piercing blue eyes, rock-hard muscles and maverick ideas—with his own masterful equation for sizzling ecstasy and high energy.

___4438-2 $4.99 US/$5.99 CAN

Dorchester Publishing Co., Inc.
P.O. Box 6640
Wayne, PA 19087-8640

Please add $1.75 for shipping and handling for the first book and $.50 for each book thereafter. NY, NYC, and PA residents, please add appropriate sales tax. No cash, stamps, or C.O.D.s. All orders shipped within 6 weeks via postal service book rate. Canadian orders require $2.00 extra postage and must be paid in U.S. dollars through a U.S. banking facility.

Name_____
Address_____
City_____State_____Zip_____
I have enclosed $_____ in payment for the checked book(s).
Payment <u>must</u> accompany all orders. ❑ Please send a free catalog.
        CHECK OUT OUR WEBSITE! www.dorchesterpub.com